Meghan's Dragon

Also by the Author

EarthCent Ambassador Series:

Date Night on Union Station

Alien Night on Union Station

High Priest on Union Station

Spy Night on Union Station

Carnival on Union Station

Wanderers on Union Station

Vacation on Union Station

Guest Night on Union Station

Word Night on Union Station

Party Night on Union Station

Review Night on Union Station

Family Night on Union Station

Book Night on Union Station

Meghan's Dragon

Paradise Pond Press

ISBN 978-1-948691-16-1

Copyright 2016 by E. M. Foner

Northampton, Massachusetts

"Show me a dragon. Show me a dragon."

Meghan paused the mumbled incantation long enough to reach for the stone bottle and take a sip of watery beer for her parched throat. Most mages could get magical results without vocalizing their wishes, but despite years of practicing in secrecy, she still needed to shape and expel the words to get any action.

"Show me a dragon. Show me a dragon."

The bronze relic gripped in Meghan's left hand was her most precious possession, but it was so worn from handling that only the closest examination would reveal the outline of a dragon in flight. Once the emblem had stood out in proud relief from the surrounding metal and could be pressed into hot wax to create a seal. Now, worn around her neck on a leather cord, the medallion served a more important purpose as a lens and a reservoir for magic. Every day she worked with it for hours, using it to focus her search, while at the same time storing up her excess magical energy for what would be the turning point of her young life.

"Show me a dragon. Show me a dragon."

Her mind soared above Dark Earth like a bird of prey, watching for a hint of the pattern that would trigger an all-or-nothing effort. When she had embarked on the quest for a dragon in her fifteenth year of life, each outing had required nearly an hour of preparatory meditation to sharpen her concentration and awaken her senses. After two years of practice, Meghan was able to launch into the extra-dimensional search like slipping on an old dress, which, coincidentally, was the only sort of dress she owned.

"Show me a dragon. Show me a dragon."

The dragon pendant began to glow softly and vibrate in her hand, like a crystal that was tuning a sympathetic source of energy. Horrific scenes of battle and villainy danced before the girl's tightly shut eyes as she allowed every intense emotion rising from Dark Earth to sift through her consciousness. Before too long she'd have to break off and leave for work, but there was just enough time left to investigate the brightest death vision she had ever encountered.

"Send me a dragon. Bring me the dragon!"

For the first time in more astral outings than she could count, everything fell into alignment. With a muffled cry that expressed more pain than triumph, Meghan opened the floodgates and allowed her stored up magical energy to begin coursing from the relic clenched in her left hand, through her slight body, and into her outstretched right arm and hand.

"You must come with me. NOW!"

The sole surviving marine of the Dankner Expedition to the Alpha Centauri colony refused to give up the fight. As battered war drones returned in a steady stream to his defensive position, he worked like an automaton, field stripping the useful parts and rapidly reassembling them into useful weapons. The temperature on the battlefield was becoming intolerable, and Bryan took a quick slug from his canteen before wiping the sweat from his eyes. Cathy Trichet, the beautiful young mission specialist, emerged from the doorway of the command bunker and gazed at him in admiration. In that moment, he realized that the perimeter breach alarm had sounded, and all of the drones froze in place.

"What are you doing?" Cathy asked.

"Huh?" Bryan replied. He looked down at the collection of damaged drones, glanced up at Cathy, and then back to the drones again. During the millisecond he had looked away, the war drones had somehow morphed into heavy, white restaurant dishes.

"The alarm," Cathy said, pointing at the blinking red light on the dishwashing machine. "We can hear it in the dining room every time the door swings open."

"Oh. Sorry, Cathy. Just daydreaming, I guess."

Bryan hit the "Stop" button to silence the alarm and to disengage the drive that conveyed the racks of dirty dishes and glasses along a closed oval track through the stainless steel washing machine. He ducked under the outer conveyer track and stood up in the center of the oval, a position from which he could slide open the machine's access panels. Steaming water dripped from the perforated tubes at the top of the final rinse stage, and he could almost feel the temperature in the small room spiking up.

"Anything serious?" the waitress asked. "They're about to start clearing the Lincoln Room after that retirement bash, but I could tell the other girls to take a break first."

"It's just jammed with a kitchen spoon," Bryan grunted. He yanked out the offending industrial-sized utensil, which was longer than his forearm. "Handle slipped through the rack under the high-pressure wash jets. Man, that's hot," he concluded, tossing it into one of the now-stationary racks so it could go through the machine again. Then he slid the access panel shut, ducked back under the front section of the oval track, and hit the green "Start" button. The train of racks jerked back into motion, and the sound of water jets spraying inside the stainless steel box began again.

"They shouldn't make you work alone," Cathy observed, setting her tray on the counter. "All of the other dishwashers work in pairs, with one guy scraping and loading and the other guy taking off and stacking."

"I've been doing this since I was sixteen, and I'll bet I get through the rush faster working by myself than any of those two-man teams."

"But do they pay you twice as much?" Cathy asked. Then she offered him an ironic smile before heading back through the swinging door to the east wing of the restaurant and banquet facility. The afterglow of her perfect white teeth made Bryan fumble a wine goblet that he was putting into the sectioned glassware rack, though as always, he caught it before it hit the no-slip floor.

The solo dishwasher grabbed a clean rack of coffee cups off the moving belt, put it aside, and replaced it with the newly loaded rack of wine goblets. The next rack on the conveyer held a silverware carrier and he couldn't remember if it was the second time through yet, so he let it go by and moved the coffee cups to the drying area. He hadn't been lying when he told the waitress he could get as much work done by himself as the typical two-man crew.

Towards the end of his shift, he rescued a short-haired girl disguised as a young soldier who turned out to be a princess, and together they manned the only undamaged laser cannon left to defend the castle. Moving faster than he ever had in his life, Bryan worked alone at loading the white, one-shot crystals into the breach of the crew-served weapon. Peering through the open sight mounted on the laser's barrel, the princess targeted and destroyed their nightmarish attackers. The burnt air began to stink of rotten eggs, and as lights began to flash in Bryan's peripheral vision, a man's voice shouted something indecipherable.

"You must come with me!" the princess yelled at him.

Bryan looked up from the nearly empty ammunition crate to see the gunner's chair empty and a ghastly red and yellow cloud billowing toward them like a fireball in a disaster movie. A small white hand, so pure it could have been sculpted from steam, reached down for him from above. He thought he saw the delicate features of the young princess swirling in the mist, her mouth stretched wide as she shouted, "NOW!"

He grabbed the hand a split second before the wall of fire swept through their position, and as she pulled him through the vaporous white curtain, Bryan felt every individual cell in his body burn.

An oil lamp guttered in a nook set into the stone wall, casting a flickering light over the sleeper. A somber middle-aged woman stood over the cot, humming a tuneless song while she moved her hands in a series of intricate passes above Bryan's prone body.

"Is he alright, Hadrixia?" asked the anxious girl standing by the healer's side.

"He's fine, Meghan," the healer said. "They say the passage from Dark Earth takes a toll on those who travel it, though it's been hundreds of years since I've heard of a mage managing a retrieval."

Meghan blushed in the dim light and mumbled something about her skills being nothing out of the ordinary. Bryan moaned in his sleep and rolled onto his back, his mouth falling open as he began to snore.

"His clothing doesn't resemble any uniform I've ever seen, and I can't figure out why he's wearing an apron," Meghan said. "Do you think it's to protect him from the blood of his enemies?"

"Sometimes an apron is just an apron," the older woman chided the girl. "Perhaps he was working in a kitchen when you pulled him through."

"I could see clearly through his eyes," the girl protested. "He was in a desperate battle to protect a princess, and I reached him just as the castle he was defending was destroyed."

"Perhaps," Hadrixia said. "Turn around."

Meghan reacted automatically, turning her back to the older woman, who stepped closer and began to separate the girl's raven black hair into four equal parts.

"I wish you had told me what you were planning," Hadrixia continued in the same gentle tone, as she began to expertly plait the girl's hair into a long braid. "If somebody with sufficient power was watching the passage and traced your magic back here, you would be discovered before you're ready."

"Was I that loud? Would you have noticed if your public visiting-room wasn't next door?"

"You're a very stealthy mage," the older woman assured the girl. "You couldn't have survived all these years in the castle without being detected if you weren't. But as your power grows and you expend more energy in the higher realms of magic, it will become harder and harder to hide your trail."

"I've been searching for him every afternoon before work and every night after I get home for over two years," the girl said. "We both know that I need a dragon if I don't want to spend the rest of my life in hiding."

"You've been patient to this point," Hadrixia admitted. She wrapped a short length of ribbon around the end of the long braid and tied a knot.

A bell began to toll somewhere in the castle, and both women counted silently along with the sounds.

"Fifth watch already," Meghan groaned. "I'm going to be late for work again." She dashed to the door of her small room, but there she came to a sudden halt. "What am I going to do? He won't know where he is when he wakes up, and he'll only be able to speak his Dark Earth language. If he transforms when he regains consciousness, he might not even fit in the room."

"Now you sound like a frightened child who doesn't know that dragons are just alternate forms assumed by powerful people," the healer scolded the girl. Hadrixia saw Meghan's face fall and she relented. "I'll stay with him. I've had some luck in the past teaching foreigners our language while they slept. It's been a while, but hopefully I haven't forgotten how."

"You never forget anything," the girl declared confidently. "I'll be back before the seventh watch," she added before fleeing from the room.

Hadrixia dragged the sole chair over to the cot and sat down next to the young man. She sighed and shook her head ruefully at his undeniable physical presence in her young friend's bed. Did

Meghan think that once her guest woke up he would never need to sleep again? There was barely enough space in the room for the narrow cot, the small corner table with the unmatched chair that she now occupied, and the wooden chest that held the girl's meager possessions.

Bryan made a sound like he was choking on his tongue and then rolled back onto his side. The healer sat very still in the flickering light, humming beneath her breath and concentrating on something that only she could see. A faint yellow aura began to form around her hands, and she slowly extended her left arm out over the sleeping youth's head. Placing her right hand on her own forehead like she was checking herself for a fever, she curled the fingers of her left hand around the empty air as if they were gripping a funnel. A stream of liquid yellow light began to cascade through her fingers and fall into Bryan's ear.

"Has he woken up yet?" Meghan asked breathlessly. She had run all the way home from work with her small daypack bouncing off her back, and then up the stairs to her room in the castle's outer wall. Most of the servants and less successful tradesmen had their lodgings in the wood structures built up against or inside the wall, which was wide enough for easy movement of a small catapult on the wall-walk behind the crenellated battlements. The palace and the keep had their own higher walls in one corner of the castle grounds, which all told housed over a thousand people.

"He's ready to wake, but I put him into a light trance so you could be here to explain what happened," Hadrixia said. "He should be able to speak and understand you, but he's going to be very hungry and may believe that he is dreaming."

"I brought some bread and cheese, and there should be some beer left in the jar," Meghan replied, working one arm out of her daypack and letting it slide off the other. She hesitated for a moment. "I was thinking while I was at work that I may not have prepared as thoroughly for his arrival as I should have."

"Like where he's going to stay?" the older woman asked, raising an eyebrow.

"I guess I thought he would either fly off to the mountains to sleep or claim quarters as a visiting knight, but dressed like he is, they'd probably put him in the stables. I'm going to have to risk passing him off as a long-lost relative, and I'll ask Phinneas to loan him enough equipment to compete in the next tournament."

"There may be a complication with that," Hadrixia said quietly. "I would never look into the mind of another person without permission, but a few impressions leaked through while I was teaching him our language."

Meghan did her best to ignore the sudden hollow feeling in the pit of her stomach. "I know I should have talked to you about choosing a dragon beforehand, but I was afraid you'd tell me to wait until I was older. Do you think he'll refuse to fight for me?"

"He may not be a professional soldier," the older woman hedged.

"Do they have yeoman on Dark Earth?" Meghan asked, exhaling in relief that it wasn't something more serious. "That would make him a small landholder who was called up to fight for his local baron."

"Not exactly," Hadrixia said. "Are you sure you were concentrating on finding a warrior when you were searching this afternoon?"

"Of course," Meghan declared, but an overwhelming dread reduced her voice to a hoarse whisper. She had spent well over half of the magical energy she had stored up over the years to claim her dragon from Dark Earth. "What else do I think about day and night? I've been working towards this my whole life!"

"Isn't there something else you work at?" the older woman hinted.

"You know better than anyone that my only goal is to control my own destiny. I've dedicated every waking hour outside of work to building my skills and—oh, no! Please don't tell me that I was thinking about work," she begged, as the meaning of Hadrixia's last question sank in.

"You've been searching twice a day for two years and you've put yourself under tremendous pressure. It's normal for a young person's mind to wander."

"The other scullery maid got married last week, and they haven't replaced her yet," Meghan practically wailed. "There's always a mountain of pots waiting for me in the kitchen, and I'm beginning to see them in my sleep. But I know that my dragon was fighting a hopeless battle to defend a castle at the moment I pulled him over."

"What do you daydream about while you're at work?" Hadrixia asked softly.

Meghan's legs turned to jelly beneath her and she half sat, half collapsed into a cross-legged position on the floor, where she buried her face in her hands.

"He's a scullery maid?" she sobbed out the question.

"According to the secret lore, he will have as much potential as any other soul retrieved from Dark Earth," the older woman reassured her. "He just isn't a trained warrior. I gather that in his world, most of the dishwashers in large establishments are male. Are you ready for me to wake him now?"

"Do we have to?" Meghan replied glumly.

The first thing Bryan saw when he regained consciousness was the face of a kindly, middle-aged woman who was wearing a brilliant blue hood that for some reason struck him as an official badge of office. The second thing he saw was a skinny teenage girl with a long black braid and a red face and hands who looked like she'd been crying. He wondered what they were both doing in his basement apartment and why the flickering light from the failing compact fluorescent bulb was even weaker than usual.

"I am Hadrixia, and this is Meghan," the older of the two females said.

"Why are you in my room?" Bryan demanded in return. His own voice sounded strange to him, as if he were speaking a foreign language, but the words came fluidly and he understood what he had said.

"It's my room," Meghan retorted. "Your daydreams tricked me into bringing you here."

"What are you talking about?" Bryan sat up rapidly and was rewarded with a spell of dizziness for his efforts.

"Meghan," Hadrixia admonished the girl. "Even if there's been a mistake, you are responsible for his being here and there's no sending him back. I have to make my final rounds now, and as we discussed, I expect to find this young man informed of his situation by the time I return." The healer reached out and took hold of a hand from each of the young people, and then she pronounced, "Happy truths."

Bryan and Meghan both snatched their hands away as if they'd been burned, but Hadrixia merely smiled and left the room without another word. Behind her, the two young strangers regarded each other sullenly. The sight of the rough stones of the outer wall revealed by the feeble light from the oil lamp was enough to confirm for Bryan that this wasn't his room after all. He swung his legs off the bed so he could sit facing the girl, who took the seat vacated by the older woman.

"Well, we're in for it now," Meghan informed him. "If you didn't hear her, she put the whammy on us so we can't lie to each other. What's your name, anyway?"

"Bryan. Bryan Lazard. I didn't catch your whole name."

"You have two names?"

"Bryan is my first name and Lazard is my last name."

"How strange. Are you sure you don't want to add something in the middle?"

"Alexander Hamilton," Bryan admitted. "Bryan Alexander Hamilton Lazard. Do you really just have the one name?"

"Of course," Meghan replied. "If everybody had more than one name, how would anybody know who was talking to whom?"

"Nobody uses them all in—forget it. What did you mean about that woman putting the whammy on us?"

"Are you sure you're strong enough to hear the answer?" Meghan asked, not unkindly. "I thought I was bringing over a war hero to be my dragon, but Hadrixia tells me you're just a, a dishwasher."

"It's a job, not a career," Bryan responded in irritation. "I dropped out of college because I got sick of everybody telling me how to live my life. Ever since I was a kid I always felt like I was being punished for something I didn't do, like school was a prison I'd been sentenced to for a crime I didn't even get to commit. I thought college would be different, but it wasn't."

"I don't know what college is and I have the feeling that school means different things to us as well. In any case, dishwashing isn't a high-status job here."

"I started working at a fancy restaurant and banquet place when I was sixteen, as soon as I was legally old enough to have a job. When I quit college, I needed to make some money in a hurry and my gaming skills didn't turn out to be as marketable as—why am I telling you all of this?" he interrupted himself.

"Happy truths," Meghan replied. "She's a healer, and part of her magic is being able to help people communicate. Hadrixia says that an honest discussion has cured more ills than every plant in the herbalist's shop. Her magic won't force you to answer a question if you're not willing, but it won't allow us to lie to each other until the next sunrise."

"You want me to believe that lady put a spell on us?"

11

"It's not a spell. It's magic. It just works."

"There's no such thing as magic," Bryan grunted dismissively. "Hey! If you believe in what you just said, that means I can't be lying to you about magic not existing." He crossed his arms and looked at her triumphantly.

"It's true that there's no magic on Dark Earth where you come from, because your ancestors traded it away long before either of us were born. You got to keep the contraptions and we got to keep the magic."

"So you're saying we're not on Earth?" Even as Bryan asked, part of his mind wondered why he wasn't getting angry or freaked out. Was that part of the spell the supposed healer had put on them as well?

"We're on Earth, the real Earth. You're the one from the defective copy," Meghan replied, her small, pointed chin jutting out pugnaciously. "You have inventions that let one man do the work of ten, right?"

"Along with lamps you can actually see by and iceboxes to keep food from going bad," Bryan answered her, glancing around the room's primitive furnishings. "Speaking of iceboxes, you wouldn't have anything to eat around here, would you? I'm starving."

"I brought you some bread and cheese from the kitchen." Meghan quickly produced a broken loaf and a large wedge of yellow cheese from the daypack she had dropped earlier. "And there's small beer in the stone bottle."

Bryan hesitated for a moment at the dusty condition of the food, but then he decided he was too hungry to care. He bit directly into the narrow part of the cheese wedge, and then put it down so he could tear a piece of bread off the loaf with his hands as he chewed what tasted like mild cheddar.

"Did you say something about a small bottle of beer?" he asked a minute later through a mouth full of cheesy bread.

"Not a small bottle, small beer. The kind you don't get drunk on. They make it for the servants because drinking the castle water without boiling it first can be tricky, if you know what I mean." Meghan pulled the cork and extended it to him.

"And you're a servant?" Bryan asked, reaching for the stone bottle.

"I'm a mage!" Meghan flared up.

"So why do you live in a little room and drink servant's beer?" Bryan paused to wash down his first course with the warm, weak beer. He took an even bigger bite of the cheese the second time around.

"I'm in hiding," the girl replied before she could stop herself. "I can make water safe to drink without a fire, of course, but not bringing home my allotment of beer would arouse suspicions." A look of intense frustration rose on her face. "Oh, why did Hadrixia have to put the whammy on us? You can't tell anybody what I just said or we'll have to leave, and I've never been anywhere else. Wouldn't that be ironic if the warrior I summoned to be my dragon ended up getting me expelled from the only home I've ever known."

"Mmph." Bryan nodded in agreement. He chewed for a moment and then chased down the second course with another swallow of beer. "Who are you hiding from?"

"Pretty much everybody," Meghan admitted. "Look, you can't go back home and I can't just keep you in my room for the rest of our lives. We're going to have to work out an arrangement so we can help each other until you transform."

"Why can't you send me back?" Bryan demanded. He tried to recall if he'd ever dreamt about magic and really bad beer before, but he couldn't come up with a precedent.

"It doesn't work that way," Meghan replied. "You'll go back when you die, if that's any consolation."

"Except my family and friends will have given me up for dead long before that."

"You go back at the instant you left," Meghan said, but she didn't elaborate. "Can I get you anything else to eat? I've never had a dragon before, so I wasn't sure what you'd like. I can sneak into the kitchens anytime."

13

"I could eat a horse, but what did you mean about having a dragon?"

"You. You're a dragon, or you will be," Meghan said confidently. "What you just said proves it. Who else but a dragon could think about eating a horse?"

"It's just an expression. I'm as human as you are," Bryan protested. "Before your healer friend's happiness spell wears off and I start freaking out, I want to understand what's going to happen to me here. I've got no money, nowhere to live, and I'm beginning to wonder if I'm really alive."

"Oh, you're alive alright," Meghan reassured him. "Are you feeling sleepy again yet?"

"Sleepy and hungry," Bryan confessed, leaning back against the wall.

"According to the scrolls, it's going to take a few days to get adjusted. I'll get you some more food, and then I'll see if Hadrixia will let me sleep on her examination table tonight. Don't you leave the room under any circumstance, and keep the bar on the door when I'm not here."

"What if I have to go?" Bryan asked.

"Don't go. Stay. Don't you listen?"

"I mean, you know, go-go."

"Oh, there's a chamber pot under the bed. Put it outside the door after you use it. Washing dishes isn't the worst job in the castle."

Meghan gave the secret knock they had agreed on, and Bryan let her into her room. "It's all set," she told him immediately. "I explained that you're my third cousin twice removed from a

14

village outside of Castle Trollsdatter, and you start work with me in the kitchen tomorrow."

"What if somebody has been to Castle Trollsdatter and wants to talk to me about it?" Bryan asked.

"That's impossible. I made up the name this morning. I told them that you're a magical cripple like me, which they'll believe since it runs in families and because a man would never take a, uh, dishwashing job otherwise. But everybody is still going to expect you to at least understand what magic is, so I'm going to give you a crash course."

"Why would they expect me to understand magic?"

"Because it's all around us. I'm sorry I haven't had a chance to take you outside yet, but you were always busy eating or sleeping when I wasn't in work. Hadrixia warned me that if I don't show you some basic stuff before we go out, you'll jump out of your skin the first time you see somebody light a fire."

"I've seen people light fires," Bryan said, affecting a long-suffering look. Then she set her pinkie on fire and he jumped out of his skin. "What!"

"This is the basic fire-starter magic every child learns by the age of ten," Meghan continued, turning her hand this way and that to admire the tightly bound flames. "Some people never get much past being able to hold a finger under something combustible until it catches fire. Others..." She made a fist and her whole hand burst into flame, then she opened her fingers and a ball of fire shot off to splash harmlessly against the stone wall.

As soon as he recovered from shock, Bryan demanded, "What do you need a dragon for if you can do that yourself? And exactly how did you do that?"

"I thought you dropped out of school because you knew everything."

"I dropped out of school because I wasn't learning anything," Bryan retorted. "There's a difference. So how did you make your pinky burst into flame and why didn't it burn you?"

"Rule one. Magic is. Nobody makes magical fire, we just welcome it. And fire that you invite can't burn you."

"I don't get it. How do you invite fire?"

"We learn magic the same way that small children learn a language. You show a baby a spoon and you say, 'spoon.' You give the baby the spoon and you say, 'spoon.' The baby says, 'spoon,' and then she throws the spoon on the floor and laughs at you. The point is, the baby learns what a spoon is without being told that it's a handle attached to a small bowl that you use to eat soup."

Bryan looked at her blankly.

"Maybe I could have picked a better example. It's more like how you teach a baby what the moon is. You say, 'moon,' and you point at it. The baby never touches the moon, never uses it for anything, doesn't understand that it goes around the Earth, but she still knows the moon when she sees it."

"And what does that have to do with magic?" Bryan asked in frustration.

"With magic, once you recognize how something happens, you can encourage it to happen for you. Fire is easy to learn because of the way flames seem to leap and appear out of nowhere when you watch a fire burn. If you have any magical ability at all, you just repeat that moment in your mind, that feeling, and the fire appears for you."

"So how did you bring me from my world?" Bryan pressed her. "Do people come popping out of fires here so you know how to call for them?"

"I started with honeybees," Meghan explained. "Nobody knows why, but honeybees from your world are always appearing here lately. You can be staring at a flower and suddenly, pop, there's a honeybee from Dark Earth sucking at the nectar. By the time I was twelve, I could bring them myself, though it used to make me dizzy. Most grown mages never develop that ability, and it took a lot of practice with Hadrixia to learn how to keep it hidden. I've been pretending for the last seven years that my magic burned out when I started to mature."

"So your parents were powerful mages?"

16

"I don't know," Meghan admitted. Her face went from open to closed as if somebody had thrown a switch, and Bryan backed off on that line of questioning.

"So let me make sure I have this straight. You're saying that magical events occur naturally on this world, and if you observe something magical happening enough times, you learn how to repeat it by imagining how it looked?"

"And felt, and smelled, and tasted, and sounded."

"And I didn't know about this because there is no magic on Dark Earth?"

"That's right. Your ancient mages traded Dark Earth's magic to our ancient mages in return for a world where everything worked according to a fixed set of rules. So you can create machines that fly in the air and grids of wire that somehow capture lighting, while our most advanced contraptions are windmills and catapults."

"Flying machines are airplanes, and tame lightning is electricity," Bryan told her. "But why can't you have them here?"

"They just don't work. Could your flying machines stay in the sky if little pieces reshaped themselves at random, or if the rules that kept them aloft didn't work the same from one cloud to the next?"

"But I've seen birds flying outside of your window," Bryan objected.

"It's an arrow slit, and living things all have their own magic so they can naturally adjust to changes. It's only machines that don't work here. The more complicated they are, the quicker they will go wrong."

"And you brought me here like I was some kind of giant honeybee?"

"It only started with honeybees. When I was just a girl and I saw them popping into existence in the orchard, I realized that I could catch a glimpse of where they came from as well. After Hadrixia taught me to read and got me a morning job cleaning the baron's library, I learned from a scroll that I wasn't really seeing Dark Earth, but each honeybee's memory of it as they came through the passage. Eventually I discovered how to open myself to other impressions from Dark Earth and that's how I searched for you. It felt like I was flying over your world and being drawn to scenes of war, but now I realize that I was also seeing dreams, and in your case, daydreams," she concluded in an accusatory tone.

"I didn't ask you to eavesdrop on my daydreams," Bryan reminded her. "And I still don't get why it was so important for you to bring me here that you spent years searching and saving up magic to do it."

"Because I want to be free," Meghan replied quietly. "Because I didn't want to be forced into a marriage with some man who doesn't care anything about me and just wants to steal my magic."

"You said that before but you didn't explain it. How can a man steal your magic? If you keep hiding things from me, I'll never be able to help either of us."

"It's not the sort of thing that a girl should have to explain to a boy," she told him, turning away as she began to blush. "I assume you know that married people sleep together to make babies."

"You brought up bees and I brought up birds, and now you're trying to put them together?" It was a lame attempt at a joke, but Bryan was hoping to ease the sudden tension between them. He'd never seen anybody so embarrassed before, and he was starting to feel uncomfortable in sympathy.

"I'm talking about something serious here," Meghan insisted, keeping her face averted. "When a man and a woman get married and, you know, their magic equalizes between them. That's why rich and highborn men and women always marry somebody with stronger magic. Most of the top mages never start families because they aren't willing to give up that much power. After a person physically joins with another, their magic remains coupled until one of them dies, and then half of it is lost."

"But what about dating and, uh, hooking up before you get married?" Bryan asked. "Do you mean to say that everybody here waits for marriage and then stays together like swans?"

Meghan turned back to look at him, her face still hot, but now she was curious as well.

"Do people where you come from do THAT before they're married?" she asked incredulously.

"Pretty much everybody," he replied, though now it was his turn to redden, and he hurried on. "So you're pretending not to have any magic so that the men will leave you alone, like a beautiful girl cutting off her hair and wearing baggy clothes?"

"I don't have any family to protect me," Meghan told him sadly.

"But if you're such a strong mage, why can't you protect yourself?"

"I think I could protect myself against some magical attacks, but nobody has ever tried so I can't be sure," she replied. "Against an older mage who has been practicing magic for hundreds of years or more I wouldn't stand a chance. But your magic will be different, and nobody would think of attacking a person who had a dragon on their side without a serious reason."

"Show me the fire trick again," Bryan said. "I'm not much for theoretical discussions, but if I see something enough times, it usually sinks in."

"That's exactly how magic works," Meghan said enthusiastically, causing her hand to burst into flames. "I knew you'd come around."

It wasn't until Bryan met Meghan at the foot of the stairs to the courtyard that he realized he was a full head taller than the girl. The ceiling in her small room was so low that he couldn't stand up without crouching, and he had spent all of his time sleeping in bed or sitting in any case.

19

"It's like a movie set," Bryan whispered to Meghan, bending to get his mouth close to her ear.

"I didn't understand one of your words, so it's probably not something that exists here," Meghan whispered back. "Please try not to say anything we wouldn't want overheard while we're outside. You never know who might be listening, even if they're a distance away."

"You mean that some people can use magic to listen at long distances?"

"Of course, my simple-minded cousin," she replied in a normal tone of voice. "We of Castle Refuge are highly advanced, so I'm sure you'll see many things here that you never dreamed of back home."

Bryan took her cue to act the part of a country bumpkin and pointed at a woman who was staring intently at a pair of men's pants.

"What's she doing?"

"The cloth fixer? Surely you have cloth fixers where you came from, uh, outside of Castle Trollsdatter."

"She's sitting there holding up that guy's trousers and staring at them while he stands there in his underwear looking foolish. How is that fixing anything?"

"Your clothes haven't been fixed?" Meghan asked. "Hmm, I guess that explains the smell. She's fixing his pants so they can't get dirty or wear out, though the fixing fails if the cloth is torn with something sharp enough to cut all the way through the fibers."

"That isn't poss—" he let his objection trail off at her sharp warning look. "But how do the clothes makers stay in business if everything lasts forever?"

"Oh, you really are a bumpkin," Meghan said with a genuine smile. "People will pay much more for something that suits them if they know they can get it fixed so it will last as long as they want. And it's expensive to fix clothes because the fixer has to trace every individual fiber through the weave."

"Can you do it?" Bryan whispered.

Her sudden look of irritation tinged with worry reminded him that he wasn't supposed to ask potentially dangerous questions while they were outside.

"If I wasn't magicless, like you, I could fix cloth," she told him pointedly. "But they say that even powerful mages need to follow every thread, so it takes time and patience. Fixer Sandra has less magical aptitude than most people, but she practices the one thing all day, every day, so she can do it faster than anybody else in the castle."

They passed by several other small tradesmen whose stock of goods was limited to what they could haul in a handcart. The whole setup reminded Bryan of the background scenes from a swords-and-sorcery-style video game he used to play, but the sounds and smells were something else altogether. He followed his guide through a small passage to an inner courtyard, where a group of boys was watching a number of young men practice with quarter staffs and wooden swords. The boys had chosen favorites and shouted encouragement to them like fans at baseball game.

"Get after him, Stavy. Come on, now!"

"He's a bum, Dorman. Wipe the floor with him."

An older man with a severe limp moved between the sparring pairs, correcting the young men when they failed to execute the proper forms. Bryan winced when one of the would-be warriors whose padded head protection had slid down over his eyes mistakenly slashed at the instructor's neck with the wooden broadsword, but the old man stopped the strike with the back of his hand without even looking. It was the sword that shivered into splinters on contact.

Bryan couldn't stop himself from uttering "How?" before he remembered his instructions and clamped his mouth shut.

"Phinneas is the castle's war master," Meghan said. Something in her voice hinted that she had a soft spot for the aging warrior. "His magic for fighting is very strong, and he's been to war so many times that he doesn't even count them anymore. That limp is the result of a battlefield healer doing a rush job to get him on his feet again. By the time he got back to the castle, it was all Hadrixia could do to save his leg."

"Who are you fighting against?" Bryan asked.

"We of Castle Refuge are always at war over something or another," she replied sadly. "The last one was because Cynthia, our baron's daughter, tricked a dressmaker at King's Castle into believing that she was the daughter of Baron Thundercrack and stole a dress the Thundercracks had special ordered months before the Harvest Ball. Cynthia is very good at glamour and impersonation."

"You fought a war over a ball gown?" Bryan asked in astonishment.

Meghan shrugged. "Warriors have to fight over something, don't they?"

"Why?" A sharp elbow in the ribs informed him that it was a stupid question. "I mean, we don't have so many wars around Castle Trollsdatter."

"Then what does everybody do?" a gravelly voice demanded.

"Phinneas," Meghan squealed, and flung her arms around the war master's neck. Up close, Bryan saw that he was at least in his early sixties, maybe even older if magic could slow the aging process. "How is your leg feeling these days? We worried when you weren't back after the second week."

"The War of the Dress did grind on longer than we expected," Phinneas replied sardonically. "The Thundercracks asked for a temporary truce in order to attack the Castle Edgestorm in support of the Firehearts, with whom they have some treaty obligation. Our baron didn't see the point of packing up and coming all the way home just to set out again, so we went along to observe. It was good training for the young men, seeing a siege set up."

"Don't sieges usually go on for months?" Bryan couldn't help asking.

"I see your young friend isn't a complete military ignoramus after all," Phinneas said to Meghan. He turned his attention to Bryan. "Normally, waiting out a siege on the sidelines wouldn't be high on my to-do list, but our baron received news by carrier pigeon that his cousins, the Barleyhops, planned to move against Fireheart Castle. After two weeks of siege, the Firehearts got word of the Barleyhop attack and had to rush home to raise the siege on their own castle, so the Thundercracks finally made the time to pick up our battle where we left off. Good thing, too, since we were running out of supplies."

"I didn't hear any mourning cries when you returned last night so it must have gone well," Meghan said.

"Bit of a letdown," the old war master replied. "The Edgestorms hadn't been happy about the Thundercracks joining the siege against them in the first place, so when the Thundercracks finally broke it off to fight us, the castle's defenders sallied out and attacked them from the rear. Turned into something of a rout." He paused to draw a dagger from his belt and flipped it at Bryan. The surprised dishwasher blinked, but he still managed to get a hand up and catch it by the butt.

"Knew you'd be quick just by looking at you," Phinneas continued, speaking directly to Bryan. "I haven't trained soldiers for five decades without learning how to spot the likely candidates. Will you be participating in the tower climb?"

"He doesn't have any magic," the girl said quickly. "He's starting with me in the kitchen tomorrow."

"Ah, that's a shame," Phinneas said, turning to the girl. "Well, I have to get back to these young idiots before somebody gets a splinter in the eye. Tell Hadrixia I'll come to see her later."

"Bye," Meghan replied, dragging Bryan back through the passage to the main courtyard.

"I thought you were supposed to be a friendless orphan," Bryan said. He was annoyed that she had answered for him about the tower climb, whatever that was. If Phinneas was willing to accept him for training, fighting with wooden swords couldn't be any worse than washing dishes without a machine.

"When Phinneas returned home five years ago with his leg all black and rotting, Hadrixia stayed with him day and night for a week. I was the only one she let in to bring them food, and I

23

watched him while she slept. After that, he was confined to bed for nearly a month, and I stayed with him when Hadrixia started doing rounds again. I think she used me on purpose, so that Phinneas would look kindly upon me."

"Trying to match make you with that old man?" Bryan asked half-seriously.

"He's the second most important man in the castle after the baron, and he could have left to become the king's war master if he wasn't loyal to our baron's family," Meghan replied with dignity. "And he has granddaughters older than I am."

A swarm of children engaged in some sort of game suddenly enveloped the pair, danced around them for a moment, and then streamed away like receding floodwaters. That's when it hit Bryan that there were more children than adults in the courtyard, and that even the toddlers seemed to be teetering about without supervision.

"Where did all the kids come from?" he asked.

"I thought we covered that earlier," Meghan replied, glancing up at him in amusement.

"No, I'm serious. I've never seen so many little kids in one place, other than a schoolyard, and nobody seems to be paying attention to them."

"Do they send children that young to school at Castle Trollsdatter?" Meghan asked with an edge in her tone, adding a reproachful look. "Around here, the small children are too busy looking after their younger brothers and sisters, and they usually start working with their parents as soon as they can do something useful. The smarter boys might be apprenticed to a better trade if their parents can afford it, but only the rich and highborn kids go to school at King's castle, and that doesn't start until they're older."

"That's not what I meant," Bryan said. He was about to tell her that families where he came from usually had just one or two children, but he didn't want to get stuck explaining what made that possible and decided to let it pass. "Where's the kitchen you keep complaining about?"

24

"We're still using the summer kitchen, which is the area over there by the wall of the keep," Meghan told him. "The winter kitchen is in the keep itself, with the bakery. When you aren't washing pots and pans in the scullery, the cooks may have you running pie fillings to the bakers. The full pots were too big for me to carry by myself, so for the last week the baker's assistant has come for them."

"What's a scullery?" Bryan asked. He felt like he should know what the word meant, but somehow he couldn't make the connection.

"It's the room built onto the kitchen for the dishwashers," Meghan replied. "Didn't you have a scullery at Castle Trollsdatter?"

"I guess we did," Bryan replied, thinking about the steam filled room and the oval-tracked dishwashing machine. "How do we get paid around here?"

"Coppers, or if you tell them not to pay you every week, you may get a silver."

"No gold?" Bryan asked in disappointment, unsure what had even prompted the question.

"There's my dragon," Meghan replied happily. "You could work in the scullery for a year and not earn enough for even a small gold ring."

"You use rings rather than coins?"

"We have both, but people prefer the rings because you can put a cord through them and wear them around your neck. Don't worry. Stick with me and I'll get you a whole pile of gold and jewels for your dragon's hoard."

"I've got a surprise for you today," Bryan announced. He took a break from scouring the giant copper pot and looked over at Meghan for her reaction. Compared to what he had imagined medieval cookery might entail, this castle's kitchen was surprisingly clean. The soap wasn't the best, but they used boiling water to keep the grease off of the counter surfaces and the stone floor, and strong lye produced locally from ashes kept the drain channels clean. The food was simple and hearty, though Meghan explained that he had arrived at the start of the harvest, which was the best season for eating.

"So, what is it?" the girl asked, not taking her eyes off of the carving knife she was whetting on a well-worn stone. She never imagined when she had pulled Bryan over from Dark Earth a week earlier that she would be welcoming his help in the scullery. It turned out that working in the kitchen was the easiest way to keep him fed, not to mention earning some money so he could save for his own room. She was getting tired of sleeping on Hadrixia's examination table.

"It's a surprise," he replied smugly. "You'll have to wait and see."

Meghan stopped sharpening the knife and looked around the scullery to make sure they were alone.

"Don't get cocky," she warned him. "Thanks to Hadrixia you can speak the language like a native, but everything you say and do makes it clear to anybody who's paying attention that you aren't from around here. Just keep your head down and give me time to figure out why you aren't transforming."

"First of all, I'm at least two years older than you, so I don't see why you keep trying to tell me what to do," Bryan replied calmly. "Second of all, I don't understand why you think I would want to turn into a giant winged lizard."

"Dragons are not winged lizards. You just take on that form when you fight or fly, I think. According to the scrolls you'll become a powerful mage, and wise too, though I wouldn't know it from talking to you," she concluded.

"Just wait until the morning shift is over," he told her with an infuriating smile.

"Pot call," Peter said, sticking his head into the scullery. "Going to give me a hand with the fillings?"

"I'm there," Bryan responded, happy to take a break from scrubbing. "But how come the bakers don't just cut up the ingredients in the bakery?"

Meghan shot him a look.

"The cooks here would never allow it," the baker's assistant explained. "Meat and vegetables have to come from the kitchen. We get to buy our own fruits, flour, eggs, even lard. But my first week as an assistant, the bakers sent me to buy chicken and carrots for pies, just as a joke. The kitchen assistants found out and they hung me upside down in the stables over a mound of manure."

"Why?" Bryan asked.

Meghan rolled her eyes and groaned.

"Why do the cooks and the bakers protect their privileges?" Peter asked in surprise. "How could we all get along living in the same walls if bakers started cooking and boot makers started baking? You wouldn't want anybody else coming in here and scrubbing pots, would you?"

"Be my guest," Bryan said, stepping back from the copper tub on a wooden stand that served as the soaking sink.

"Stop it," Meghan commanded, and gave him a push towards the exit. "I don't know how you did things at Castle Trollsdatter but it must have been a disaster. Go with Peter, and then hurry back and help me with the wooden plates for the lower table. I wish they'd go back to using bread trenchers, but the bakers claimed they took too much time."

As Bryan followed Peter out of the scullery, she heard him ask the other young man, "What's a trencher, dude?"

"You better not be doing anything stupid," Meghan muttered under her breath after Bryan lost her. She couldn't figure out how he had even known she was following him, much less how he'd turned the corner between the practice yard and the courtyard and suddenly disappeared. She looked around again, shaking her head in disbelief and causing one of the cooks who had left work right after them to stop and address her gruffly.

"Lose something, girl?"

"No, Cook," she replied meekly, looking at the ground. She had been playing the role of the magicless waif for so long that all the bowing and scraping came by instinct.

"That new boy working with you seems a likely sort," the cook continued. "I'm going to try him out as my assistant next week, so you better start looking for another scullery maid if you don't want to do the work alone."

"Your assistant?" Meghan spluttered, forgetting her carefully constructed image. "I've been slaving in the kitchen since I was ten years old and he just started a few days ago!"

"Exactly," the cook replied. "If you had the slightest bit of potential, somebody would have noticed by now." He paused and peered at her suspiciously. "Are you feeling alright?"

"Yes, Cook."

Meghan kept her head down as she hurried back to her room, hoping that Bryan would be there waiting with her surprise. She was going to have her dragon's hide for making her forget the character she was playing in front of the cook, even if it was just for a few seconds. Meghan groaned inwardly at the thought of all the magical savings she had squandered on a dishwasher who had never wielded a weapon in combat. It didn't help that he boasted about being an unbeatable warrior in multi-player Internet games, whatever they were.

Her room was empty, but she decided to wait and spend the time recharging her pendant rather than chasing around the castle and potentially missing his return. She dropped the bar into its slots so nobody could burst in on her and began concentrating on storing up magical energy. Just when she was starting to make progress, somebody began pounding on her door and calling her name. Meghan leapt up to unbar the door.

Miri, the chandler's daughter, burst into her room. "Meghan!" she shouted, her orange-flecked eyes as wide as cantaloupes. "You have to come right now. Your cousin is climbing the tower."

"That idiot," Meghan hissed from between clenched teeth. She chased after Miri, down the stairs in the hollow wall, and through the twisting passages back towards the courtyard of the castle keep. "It takes years of practice to climb the tower. He wanted to surprise me by breaking his neck?"

"He's already halfway up," Miri informed her. "My brother was trying today also, but he slipped back down before he got very high. That's when he sent me to get you."

"Peter?" Meghan asked. Of course it was Peter, she told herself. Miri's other brothers didn't work in the kitchen, and in just three days, Bryan and Peter had become thick as thieves. Her dragon even had the other young man calling everybody in the castle "dude."

The two girls burst into the courtyard of the inner keep, and sure enough, Meghan could see Bryan more than halfway to the top of the tower. There were exactly three hundred stairs winding around the interior of the round structure, which soared above the castle's walls and the tallest trees that had been spared in the clearing of the surrounding fields. Seeing him rapidly ascending the curved wall high above their heads made Meghan sick to her stomach. Even worse, Bryan was taking the path that was only used by the young men who had the magical strength to freeze the guardian gryphon.

"Dude!" Peter yelled, his hands cupped around his mouth. "Dude! You're going the wrong way. You have to get to the other side of the arrow slits."

"What?" Bryan's faint reply reached the growing crowd.

"Dude! You have to go to the other side," Peter yelled, pointing frantically. "There's a magical gryphon above you. Dude! You're going to die!"

"I can't die. I can only go home," Bryan's faint reply reached the ground.

"What did he say?" Miri asked Meghan, tugging at the older girl's sleeve. "Why isn't he changing direction?"

"He doesn't understand," Meghan cried, half to herself. She cupped her hands around her mouth and muttered, "Voice tunnel," before shouting, "Your body will go back but you're already dead there."

The climber stopped as if he had been frozen in amber, and Meghan glanced around to see if anybody else had overheard. She hadn't used the voice tunnel trick for years, but nobody was staring at her, so it must have worked.

"Dude! You have to get to the right of the arrow slits," Peter yelled again. "You need magic to get past the gryphon."

"What?" Bryan called weakly. To the observers on the ground, he wasn't much larger than a squirrel sitting on a low limb, but they saw his head tilt back as he scanned the wall above for threats. He hadn't planned on falling to his death, but in the back of his mind he believed that it would mean waking up from this dream. Now he wasn't so sure.

"Dude! It's going to get you," Peter yelled unnecessarily.

Bryan tried to move horizontally, but an old arrowhead he hadn't seen lodged in a crack cut open his big toe. He'd thought that tackling the tower without his rock-climbing shoes would be a piece of cake since there weren't any overhangs, but the other young men of the castle spent most of their lives barefoot, and the skin on the bottoms of their feet was like leather. The pain was barely noticeable, but the cut began bleeding freely, creating a deadly slipping hazard.

"Come down!"

For the second time he heard Meghan's voice as if she was standing right behind him. He was momentarily furious with her for letting him think that dying here would get him home again, but that quickly gave way to the desire to get out of his current predicament. His fingers had already begun to cramp from holding the same position too long, and the clickety-click of the stone gryphon's claws reminded him that he had to get moving. Three points of contact, he reminded himself.

"He's coming down," Peter said, pointing out the obvious. "The gryphon won't go below the lower arrow slit, right?"

"It's moving faster than he is, though," a man commented, as if he was discussing the comparative merits of knights at a joust. "I make it fifty-fifty."

"Even money?" another man asked. "Are you taking bets?"

Before the would-be bookmaker could answer, Bryan's bloody toe cost him another foothold, but this time the slip came while he was moving his left hand. The center of his body arced outwards with the sudden shift in weight, suspended only by the fingers of his right hand and a tenuous toehold of his left foot. Then the magical gryphon extended its long, stone tongue, and flicked away his fingers.

Miri screamed as the climber's body separated from the wall and began to drop. Bryan made a futile grab at the passing courses with both hands, but he was already falling too fast to have regained his grip even if his fingers had found the edge of an undressed stone. The crowd let out a collective gasp.

"Slow," Meghan muttered under her breath, gripping the dragon pendant around her neck. "Slow. Slow. SLOW!"

Bryan's acceleration towards the ground seemed to go into reverse, and he twisted in the air like an acrobat to get his feet pointed down. He landed with his knees slightly bent and then went into a roll, but nobody was even watching him by that point. They were all staring at Meghan.

"It was the scullery maid," somebody said.

"It couldn't be her," one of the cooks objected. "She doesn't have any magic at all."

"I once saw a war mage catch a soldier who fell off a battlement, but that was Bronzehead, and everybody knows how strong he is," a guardsman contributed.

Meghan looked around at the surrounding faces and saw a mixture of greed and calculation. In an instant, she had gone from being an insignificant scullery maid to an unprotected prize. She turned and fled for her room.

"Are you alright, dude?" Peter asked Bryan. He helped the dishwasher to his feet and brushed the dirt off his back.

"I'm fine," Bryan replied, though his toe was burning where the cut had filled with dust and grit. He limped over to one of the water troughs by the stables to wash it out, the baker's assistant staying by his side. "What happened?"

"Your cousin yelled, 'Slow!' and just like that, you stopped falling so fast," Peter explained. "The weird thing is that everybody knows she doesn't have any magic, or at least, we thought she didn't. Dude. Do you know if she's seeing anybody? I always thought she was kind of cute."

"I am so dead," Bryan said out loud.

"You should have told me," Phinneas grumbled. "My grandson Harold is only seven years older than you, and if I had known, I would have made him wait to get married until you were ready."

"I'm sorry," Meghan said, looking genuinely contrite as she refilled the soldier's silver wine cup.

As soon as she heard the news, Hadrixia had insisted on hosting a farewell dinner in the small chamber where she usually saw patients. Since the guest list was limited to Phinneas, Bryan, and Meghan, it hadn't required any special preparations, other than throwing a cloth over the examination table and rounding up some chairs. Phinneas brought a jug of Castle Edgestorm red, and Hadrixia contributed some fresh fruit to the standard evening ration from the castle's kitchen. Nobody bothered sending a messenger to find out why the dishwashers hadn't showed up for work.

"Where are you going to go?" the old war master continued gruffly.

"I don't understand why we have to leave," Bryan said, feeling terrible that he had precipitated the very crisis he knew the girl had wanted to avoid.

"Don't feel badly, Bryan," Hadrixia told him. "We know you were climbing the tower to be accepted into the guards for military training, and I'm sure you would have made it if your friend had done a better job explaining the route to you. It's quite an accomplishment to climb as high as you did without your own magic."

"Everybody thinks she helped him," Phinneas said. "I mean, everybody else thinks that. In answer to your question, boy, she can't stay in the castle because the baron will be back within a few days and he'll want her for one of his sons. If I were in his shoes, I'd probably send out the guard to bring you back."

"But not you," Hadrixia said sternly.

"Not me," Phinneas agreed. "But there will be many willing to earn a bounty. If the word gets out, and it probably will, every nobleman in the country will be after her, including the king."

"I won't give up half of my magic to a stranger, or all of anything else for that matter," Meghan declared. "We'll head east and I'll be able to practice in the open until my block clears."

"What block?" Bryan asked.

"You didn't tell him?" Hadrixia gave Meghan a piercing look.

The girl shook her head. "I couldn't for some reason. You explain it to him, Hadrixia."

"Meghan doesn't remember her parents or anything that happened before the age of ten because of a magical block. I can't remove it, but I've seen similar blocks, and I believe it will dissolve itself when she reaches her full potential or accomplishes some special task," the healer said.

"If she lives that long without a real dragon to protect her," Bryan said glumly.

"You'll do, boy," Phinneas reassured him. "You have fast hands and a brave heart. To climb the tower without knowing any magic, I've never heard of such a thing."

"That's because almost everybody living here knows at least some magic," Meghan reminded the old soldier.

"It was just an accident that you were forced to reveal your abilities," Hadrixia said to the girl. "I suggest that after you leave, you go back to concealing your true potential until you are in a better position to protect yourself."

"That suits me," Bryan agreed immediately, since playing dumb about magic didn't require any effort on his part.

"I have a suggestion, but don't tell me if you choose to try it, so I'll be able to answer honestly if the baron asks if I know where you've gone," Phinneas said, adding a sly wink. "We crossed paths with Rowan's players on our way back from Castle Edgestorm and they were just starting their eastern harvest festival circuit. I know their stage master, an old soldier by the name of Simon who may believe he owes me a favor. If the two of you could catch up with them there should be work for you, a measure of protection, and a chance for young Bryan to get some training in the sword."

"It's something to consider," Meghan said noncommittally, reaching out at the same time to cover Bryan's mouth with her hand.

"And I have another suggestion," Hadrixia said. "I'll be back in a minute."

34

The healer rose and went into her bedroom, where she approached one of the larger stones in the wall. She made a motion like untying a knot with her fingers, and a hollow space suddenly appeared in the previously solid-looking rock. The space contained a few bits of jewelry that were largely of sentimental value, a number of scrolls, and her earnings from healings. Hadrixia removed all of the copper coins plus half of the silver, and placed them in a small leather change purse. Then she carefully chose two different-sized gold rings from the string of three dozen or so that represented her savings since coming to the castle. Performing the untying motions in reverse restored the stone to its previous state, and she returned to her guests.

"Here you go," Hadrixia said, handing the change purse to Meghan. "It's just a bunch of coppers and a few silvers. And try these on," she added, casually handing each of the young people a gold ring.

"We can't take gold!" Meghan exclaimed. "Besides, I have a little money saved."

"Nonsense," the healer replied. "It's fair payment for all of the years you've helped me, and you shouldn't think of these rings as money in any case. You don't have any experience traveling and Bryan has barely been on our world for a week. The best chance the two of you have of keeping safe out there is pretending to be married."

Meghan opened her mouth to protest and then snapped it shut again. She had already acknowledged how unprepared she was when she pulled Bryan through from Dark Earth, and now it struck her how little she really knew about life outside of the castle and its immediate neighborhood. She'd never slept outside of the castle's walls, and everything she knew about the world was from the stories of travelers and the scrolls she was able to scan while dusting the baron's library each morning.

"I'll keep mine," Bryan declared, slipping it onto his ring finger. For some reason his voice deepened, and there was an edge of a threat in his words. He gazed greedily at the ring he now wore, and his green eyes seemed to sparkle with the candlelight reflected off of the narrow band of gold. Then the moment passed, and he shook his head as if he needed to clear his thoughts.

"Maybe our young friend knew what she was doing after all," Phinneas commented, helping himself to a refill. "If you should become her dragon, boy, remember that too much love of gold can get you killed. Don't forget the story of how Gwyneth met her end because she refused to leave her hoard when an earthquake shook her mountain lair to pieces. And she was the most powerful dragon in New Land."

"I'm not going to become a dragon," Bryan said angrily, pushing his chair back from the small table and rising. "I'm sorry I fell off the tower and forced Meghan to save me, but I didn't ask for any of this. Why did you wait until I was two-thirds of the way up to tell me that I'm dead back on Dark Earth? Did you have to kill me to bring me here?"

He towered over the seated girl, who was frozen in shock by his sudden change of attitude. Phinneas rose from his own chair and moved to put himself between the young people, but Hadrixia grabbed his arm.

"Wait!" the healer ordered the old soldier. "Meghan didn't kill you to bring you here, Bryan. She saved your life. I told her to give you a chance to settle in before explaining that part to you, but I see now that was a mistake."

Bryan shifted his intense stare from the old soldier, to the healer, to the young mage who looked like she had been slapped in the face. Part of him wanted to apologize, but an unfamiliar feeling of distrust welled up from somewhere, and he couldn't decide on what to say or do.

"I hoped to make this offer later, but since you're leaving tonight and we don't know when you'll be back, I can try to help you recover your memory of your final moments on Dark Earth," Hadrixia continued rapidly. "There's no guarantee it will work, but I can't send you off together if you don't trust each other with your lives."

36

"I trust…" Bryan began, but then he cut himself off. He wanted to know more, and despite having finished eating just minutes before, there was a strange emptiness in him. He felt starved for knowledge, for power, and he didn't know why he suddenly felt so suspicious of everyone. "If you can help me remember my death, let's do it."

"Please sit down again," Hadrixia said. "I have to put my hands on your head, and your height makes it awkward for me."

Bryan settled slowly back into his chair, keeping an eye on the old soldier the whole time as if he expected a trick. His vision seemed to be changing, and he noticed that the slightest movements of his companions immediately drew his attention, just like when he got into the zone playing first-person shooter games. The healer came and stood in front of him.

"Don't be afraid now," she said. "With your permission, I'm going to join you in remembering so I can guide you past whatever it is that's keeping you from seeing what really happened. Are you ready?"

Bryan nodded, and taking a deep breath, he closed his eyes. He didn't know where the feeling of paranoia was coming from, but if Meghan had wanted to kill him, she could have simply let him fall to his death a few hours earlier and skipped the elaborate charade. Even the gold ring he felt ready to defend with his life was a gift from the healer which he'd received only minutes before. He wondered if he was going crazy.

"Remember," Hadrixia intoned in a low voice that seemed to penetrate to the depths of his being. "Remember with me."

………

Bryan struggled to load a fresh crystal into the breach of the laser cannon. The disguised princess, whose features bore a suspicious resemblance to Meghan's, occupied the gunner's chair and swept the sights across the tree line, scanning for targets. Monstrous attackers came at them out of the woods, and the air stank of sulfur.

"See with your eyes, hear with your ears," a woman's voice said inside his head.

Bryan's eyes snapped open, and suddenly he was standing in front of the dishwashing machine, loading the final bus pan of dishes into an empty rack. The radio was playing, which meant it was long past closing time, and the waitstaff and cooks were all gone. The only people left in the place at this hour were Bryan and the night manager, and the air really did stink like rotten eggs. There was a weird flickering at the edges of the dishwasher's vision, and his eyes felt oddly numb, like somebody had put in anesthetic drops.

"Not done yet?" the manager slurred as he entered through the swinging door from the dining room. He was drunk, as he always was by one in the morning, and he squinted tightly against the smoke from his own cigarette. Bryan didn't even acknowledge the question as he worked scraping and loading the dishes. He still needed to take out the garbage, break down the machine, and wash the floor with the hot water sprayer. The manager hadn't expected an answer, and he continued through to the kitchen on his final inspection.

"Do you smell gas?" the manager called back through the doorway.

A white hand reached out of nowhere above Bryan's head. He heard Meghan's voice shout, "You must come with me. NOW!"

Bryan reached for the hand as a fireball billowed through the kitchen door. He saw a copy of his body peel away from him and fly over the oval track to impact the stainless steel dishwashing machine, his head making a respectable dent in the access panel. The white hand drew him impossibly through the roof, and he looked down at the rapidly shrinking banquet facility to see flames vomiting from the windows. Then everything went dark.

"It blew up," he mumbled, looking at his companions. "They were having problems with a leaky gas fitting on the new stove, but the prep cook wrapped it in tape so they could use it until the installer came back. I guess the tape didn't hold."

"You have to untie the pack," Meghan whispered. "I can't reach that high."

"I still don't see why we couldn't leave through the main gate," Bryan grumbled in reply. He reached up and untied the travel pack from the slender rope. "It's humiliating to be lowered from the wall by a rope in the dark like we're running away or something."

"We ARE running away," Meghan whispered back in exasperation. "What's come over you lately?"

"Here," Bryan said, thrusting the pack into her hands. "If we're going to leave then we should go already."

Meghan shook her head in disbelief and shrugged her way into the pack. Then she waved a final goodbye at the flicker of light high above, not that Hadrixia or Phinneas would be able to see her. She was using magic to enhance her own vision in the moonless and cloudy night, and even so, she could barely make out Bryan's tall form as he strode off in the direction of the road.

"Wait," she hissed at him. "You're going to fall in a ditch and break your neck. I'll go first."

He halted long enough for her to catch up, and then to her surprise, he grabbed her hand and started off again.

"I can see fine," Bryan told her, keeping his voice low. "I used to run at night after work. As long as the moon and the stars are out, I can manage."

"It's a new moon and the stars are clouded over," Meghan whispered back. She raised her free hand. "Please, stop for just a minute. How many fingers am I holding up?"

"Three," he replied immediately, and inexplicably found himself licking his lips. "Three fingers and one gold ring."

Meghan stared at where she knew her hand to be, but even with her enhanced vision, she had to strain make out the individual fingers.

"You're changing," she whispered with a feeling of awe. "Dragons have perfect night vision."

"I ate a lot of carrots on Dark Earth before I got burned to a crisp," he replied curtly. "Let's go already. From what Phinneas said, if we don't catch the players at Castle Foregone we probably never will. There are too many different mountain passes they can take from there."

The two young people walked on silently in the dark, and Meghan found herself struggling to keep up with his long stride. In less than the time it takes an hour candle to burn down, she found herself tiring. As much as she hated dipping into the store of magic in her dragon pendant, she grasped it with her free hand and muttered, "Strength."

"Why did you say that?" Bryan asked in a normal tone of voice. To the girl's ears, it sounded almost like he was shouting, but of course, there was nobody out on the road to hear. Only soldiers and nobles traveled in the dark, and not without a mage or torchbearers to light the way, so a surprise encounter was unlikely.

"I was talking to myself," Meghan replied. "I'm not used to walking this speed with a full pack, and I've been up since early this morning."

"I'm sorry," Bryan said, coming to an abrupt halt. "Not just for walking fast, but for making you flee and for accusing you of killing me. And I feel like an idiot carrying a sword that I don't know how to use wrapped up in a bedroll where I couldn't get it free if I needed it."

The fact that she couldn't make out his features let her imagine that a look of sincerity had accompanied his apology. "Could we just rest for a few minutes?"

Bryan looked around in all directions and said, "There's nothing to sit on." He sounded confident about the contents of their surroundings, despite the fact that she could barely identify the road by its slightly lighter shades of black.

"The road is fine," Meghan replied, slipping out of her pack and sitting down cross-legged in the narrow strip of grass that ran between the dirt tracks carved out by wagon wheels.

Bryan shrugged off his own pack, but rather than sitting, he went through a series of stretching exercises, and then asked, "Why wouldn't Phinneas let me wear it across my back so I could grab the hilt if I needed to quick-draw?" He drew an imaginary sword over his shoulder and slashed downward in a single movement, a move he had seen in countless movies and video games.

"Nobody wears swords across their backs," she replied. "The tip would stick out past your side and you'd keep knocking things over or running into people. Most warriors who use long swords carry them on their shoulders like a spear or an axe when they march. Aren't you tired at all?"

"Not really," Bryan admitted, lunging and bouncing to stretch his Achilles. "I guess all the extra sleep I got sort of charged my battery, the way you say that bronze medallion works for you."

"Did you have a, uh, battery on Dark Earth?"

"Actually, sleeping too much used to make me tired. I guess things are different here."

"I wish I had done more to prepare for this," the young mage said with a sigh. "I spent most of my free time practicing magic to build my ability, and after Hadrixia taught me to read scrolls and got me the extra work cleaning the baron's library, I only read about magic and history. I know very little of the world beyond the castle lands, and I was sure you'd already have all the basic dragon skills. I didn't realize you'd have to start at the beginning, as if you just hatched out of an egg."

"I wish you'd stop referring to me as a dragon." Bryan grunted as he squeezed a knee in towards his chest. "Hey. I don't remember ever getting a knee this high before without losing my balance. And anyway, what's so great about having your own dragon? From what everybody says, they just fly around raiding herds and stealing treasure to bring home and sleep on."

"That's all superstition and stories parents tell their children to make them behave. Well, it is true dragons end up with fortunes in gold and jewels, but that's because they're so powerful and live a long time. I need you because nobody in their right mind would pick a fight with a dragon, so once you show your true colors, I'll be able to practice magic openly and build my strength. Then when the block breaks down and I recover my memory, I'll be able to fulfill my destiny."

"What's the special task you need to perform that Hadrixia mentioned?"

"I don't know," Meghan confessed. "There may not even be one. It could be that the block will disappear when I'm strong enough."

"What makes you so sure that you'll know what to do when the block is gone?"

"I just know," Meghan said stubbornly. "The same way I knew I needed a dragon."

"You don't need a dragon to take you east," Bryan argued. "We'll just catch up with this band of players and travel there in style."

"I always thought I'd be riding when the time came," Meghan said with a sigh.

"I've never been on a horse, but I'll bet I can learn," Bryan said. "We'll find some gentle ones."

"I meant you."

"Meant me what?"

"You know, ride. I was going to ride you."

Bryan broke off the stretching routine to stare at Meghan. It really didn't seem that dark to him, and he could make out an embarrassed smile on her small face.

"Ride me?"

"I've never actually seen anybody riding a dragon in person, but it's a popular woodprint subject for artists," Meghan blurted. "Sometimes they show the rider sitting between the dragon's wings, and other times the rider is on the dragon's neck behind the head. I was going to ask you what was more comfortable — for you, I mean."

"How can you believe anything so silly?" Bryan demanded. "Look at me. How am I going to turn into a dragon big enough to carry you on my back? I may have dropped out of freshman physics, but I understand enough of the laws of thermodynamics to know you can't push energy and matter around like that."

"None of that means anything here," she replied calmly. "Would your laws of thermo-whatsits have allowed me to catch you when you fell off the tower? Would your Dark Earth laws even allow me to make a simple flame?"

Meghan lit up her hand, in part to demonstrate the fallacy of his argument, and in part so she could see his face. To her surprise, he looked curious rather than argumentative, as if he had forgotten the whole dragon subject and moved on to something else.

"Do that again," Bryan said. "The fire trick."

The young mage shook her head at his inability to stay focused on the discussion, but she put out the flames with a muttered word and then rekindled them.

"Again," Bryan said. "I think I saw it that time."

Meghan understood what he was getting at now, and she grew excited as she extinguished and rekindled her magical flame half a dozen times. Her traveling companion watched with unnatural concentration.

"I think I've got it," he said, after she brought the fire from her fingers a seventh time. His face glowed with joy at the discovery of a whole new way of seeing things. "I'm going to try it now."

"Be careful," Meghan cautioned him, but before the words had finished coming from her mouth, he had already kindled the largest fireball she had ever seen. It burst from his palm and shot off into the sky in a single action, expanding as it went until it faded into the dark.

"Did you see that?" he asked excitedly.

"Me and everybody else within a day's walk who happened to be looking up," she replied, jumping to her feet. "Don't do that again without warning me. We have to get moving in case there was somebody nearby."

"I want to practice," he complained. "Besides, who would bother us if I can make fireballs like that?"

"We don't know how much energy it's costing you," she said. "You have to learn how to control magic on a small scale before you can do large things. Do you feel sleepy, or hungry?"

"Hungry," he replied, and it came out as a rumble, as if his stomach was speaking for him.

It seemed to Bryan that they had just gone to sleep when he awoke to Meghan shaking his shoulder. It was light out, but still early morning. He was stiff from sleeping on the cold ground with only the thin bedroll for a mattress, but hunger drove the sleep from his eyes and he sat bolt upright.

"Is something wrong?"

"Just that we need to keep moving if we're going to catch the players," Meghan said. "I'm still half asleep myself, but we'll nap in the midday heat."

"I'm starving." Bryan pulled his pack over and began sorting through the contents. "What happened to the cold roast chicken?"

"You ate it," Meghan replied, rummaging through her own, smaller pack.

"And the apples?"

"Gone."

"The jerked beef?"

"You didn't even stop walking for that."

"Wasn't there a meat pie?"

44

"You had it for dessert."

"You mean all we have left is bread and cheese?"

"All you have left is bread and cheese. I'm still digesting our farewell dinner so I haven't touched my provisions yet."

"Oh." Bryan eyed the girl slyly. "You still look pretty worn down from last night. I could carry your pack for you."

"Do you really think I'm that dumb? Besides, everything we brought wouldn't hold you to until lunch. Whether you're on your way to becoming a dragon or not, we've discovered that you have a gift for making fire. I warned you that all that magic would make you hungry."

Bryan tore his remaining loaf of bread roughly in half, unwrapped the cheese from its cloth, and made a crude but effective sandwich.

"Are you going to eat that whole thing right now?" Meghan asked. The bread and cheese ration for each of them had been intended to last for five days. "At least add some roughage. Those dandelions growing next to you may be a little bitter, but it's better than plugging yourself up."

"I don't want to waste the water to wash them. My waterskin is almost empty and it smells pretty dry around here."

"Why would you wash dandelion greens?" Meghan asked.

"Who knows what could be on them," Bryan said. "Didn't they wash the vegetables in the palace kitchen?"

"Yes, but that's because the farmers deliver them in the same handcarts they use to take away the night soil," Meghan pointed out. "Would you worry about washing an apple you picked from a tree?"

"Sure, to get the pesticides off."

"What was that long word?"

"It's like poisons for killing the insects that would eat the crops otherwise," Bryan explained. "You probably don't have them here."

"You purposely put poison on your food?"

45

"It's—never mind." Bryan picked a handful of dandelions and stuffed them into the sandwich. Then he had a wonderful thought and caused his hands to burst into flame, quickly dialed down the heat, and toasted his breakfast. "Grilled cheese. Want some?"

"I think I'll just eat a couple of hard-boiled eggs and an apple," Meghan said. "We should be able to buy provisions today, and between the money Hadrixia gave us and my own savings, we won't go hungry any time soon, even with your appetite. Here," she continued, tossing him the leather change purse Hadrixia had pressed on her. "In case we get separated or something it doesn't make sense for me to carry all of our money."

Bryan let the change purse land between his crossed legs, since both of his hands were occupied in keeping the monster sandwich held together while he rended it with his teeth. Meghan peeled her eggs, and the two finished their breakfasts in silence, which was enforced by a constantly filled mouth on Bryan's part. Incredibly, he polished off the loaf-sized sandwich before the girl finished her apple.

"The dandelions were a good idea," he said, speculatively eyeing the patch. "Maybe I'll just pick a couple handfuls to bring along."

"Don't bother," Meghan told him. "Too many aren't good for you, and they grow so commonly that the farmers complain about them. Do you need to visit the woods before we leave? I went before I woke you up."

Bryan looked puzzled for a moment, and then he rose to his feet.

"Yeah, that's a good idea." He took about ten steps into the woods, looked back, and saw the girl rolling up the blankets. He took another twenty steps.

"Remember," she called a warning to him. "Leaves of three, let it be."

The first cluster of human habitations they came across barely qualified as a hamlet. There were six crudely built log cabins, arranged in a rough circle, a palisade connecting each house with its neighbor to create a closed space. A ramshackle tower stood in the center of the protected area, reaching twice the height of the highest cabin roof, with a small platform that might allow two archers to draw a bowstring without knocking each other off.

What the settlement lacked for in amenities, it made up for in children, and all thirty or so of them mobbed the first guests of the day.

"Are you from the castle?" a little girl asked.

"Do you have any candy?" a chubby boy wanted to know.

"My mother sells vegetables and salt meat," an older girl informed them.

"And mine!"

"And mine!"

Meghan smiled at all of the little faces which reminded her of home. "We're just traveling through, but we do need to buy provisions," she replied.

"We haven't had breakfast yet," Bryan said hopefully. When Meghan looked at him in disbelief, he added, "That was just a wake-up snack."

"Travelers pay two coppers a bowl," the oldest boy in the crowd told them. At eleven or twelve years of age, he already had the callused hands and square shoulders of a young farmhand. "You must have camped out on the road to be here so early. The house with the chimney has the kitchen."

"Thank you," Meghan replied. "I'm afraid we didn't bring any candy. Is there a place nearby where you can buy some to share?" She brought out her own change purse and shook a couple of coppers onto her palm. Bryan scowled, but he didn't say anything as all of the children began to talk at once. It was impossible to follow their discussion of the relative merits of sweets makers in the surrounding area, but they quickly settled on the oldest girl as their spokesperson.

"Farmer Greswald in the meadows sells maple candy for three coppers a measure," she said shyly.

"Three coppers it is," Meghan said, extending them to the girl. "Oh, and we set out before the rest of our party because neither of us likes to ride, but if horsemen come asking for us, you can tell them we were headed for Castle Strongbow."

"Castle Strongbow," the children repeated in a chorus. Then the girl with the coppers started off on her way to Greswald's farm, and the other children went back to their chores or games. The two travelers entered the cabin with the chimney.

"Pretty smart," Bryan said, "For a minute there, I thought you were giving away treasure for no reason."

"Treasure?" Meghan asked, as they removed their packs and took seats at the long table built of rough planks. "Three coppers is exactly enough to buy a bowl and a half of whatever they eat for breakfast around here, and I have a feeling that you're at least a two-bowl man."

An older woman approached from the smoky fireplace where she had been stirring the contents of a large pot with a long wooden paddle. Her clothes were made of some rough homespun stuff, but they showed that peculiar cleanness that Bryan had come to associate with magically treated fibers.

"Two for breakfast?" she asked in a friendly voice. "We don't get many this early. You must have been caught by the dark between settlements and camped out on the road."

"Yes, ma'am," Bryan said, anxious to move things along and find out what was cooking.

"Are you trying to get a free bowl?" The woman regarded the pair suspiciously. "I'm a simple goodwife and that's more than good enough for me."

"He didn't mean anything by it," Meghan said hastily. "My co—husband isn't from around here," she added, hoping the woman didn't notice her verbal slip. Meghan had gotten so used to calling Bryan her cousin in dozens of introductions to curious castle dwellers that it had become second nature.

"Co-husband?" the woman repeated, nodding her head in approval. "I didn't know you castle folks went in for the old traditions. I have five co-husbands myself, and eight co-wives. Men will run off to war and get themselves killed." She paused and muttered what might have been a prayer for the departed or a curse against kings. "Well, it's two coppers a bowl, but seeing how you're our kind of people, I'll throw in a pinch of salt for free."

"Thank you, goodwife," Bryan answered for Meghan. The girl was at a loss for words on finding she had graduated from playacting a wife to being taken as a participant in a plural marriage without ever having received a proposal.

The woman went back to her pot and used the paddle to fill two wooden bowls with oatmeal. Giving the young couple a broad wink, she reached into a small clay container and added a pinch of salt to each serving. Bryan's mouth began to water as he rooted through his pack for his eating spoon.

The oatmeal was tasty, but Meghan had eaten two eggs and an apple a few hours earlier, and her stomach began to protest after a half a serving. She looked up to see how Bryan was progressing and found that he was staring at her bowl in rapt attention.

"Here," she said, sliding it across the table. "At the rate this is going, you're going to be twice my size by the time we catch up with the players."

"How much does a horse outweigh a person?" he asked playfully during a pause between heaping spoonfuls. "If I'm ever going to carry you, I have to bulk up."

Meghan rose to question the woman about the location of their water well, and Bryan powered through the remains of her second breakfast. On finding that the well was on the opposite side of the hamlet from the communal outhouse, she asked for and was granted permission to fill their water skins. Bryan had polished off two more bowls by the time she returned. After paying the woman eight coppers for the oatmeal and receiving one back as a quantity discount, she purchased provisions for the road, and they left the hamlet.

"So were all those people back in the settlement magicless?" Bryan asked as soon as they reached a discreet distance from the stockade.

"No. What makes you say that?"

"She said it's a communal marriage, and I just assumed…"

"Oh. I guess I've heard it's the way that people in some rural communities manage things, to keep one person from dominating a group. They all end up sharing what magic they have as equals. Nobody in the castles follows the old ways."

"They'd fit right in where I came from," Bryan commented. "Everything here is different than I would have expected, you know?"

"No, actually. What would you have expected?"

"Like, everybody living up to their ankles in manure, and guys riding through on horses and cutting people down with swords. A lot of crying and wailing, people with horrible diseases. You know, a lot darker."

"Darker than Dark Earth? That doesn't make any sense."

"Well, we have modern medicine and everybody goes to school, not to mention indoor plumbing. You guys are living in the Dark Ages, after all."

"Not in your Dark Ages, we aren't. Do you think we're some crippled version of your world that's stuck in the past because we don't have your fancy toys?"

"But you already said that the barons are at war all the time and the whole place is ruled by some king who everybody hates. What happens when the soldiers steal the crops, burn down the houses and take the women?"

"Do soldiers do those things on Dark Earth? Here they fight each other. The barons buy food from the farmers to feed the armies and the soldiers wouldn't fight otherwise. Who burns houses and takes women? If any soldier tried that, the other soldiers would kill him. There are rules about those things, just like there were rules in the kitchen."

"But if they have the swords and the spears, who can stop them from doing what they want?"

"Why should they want to do those things? They're soldiers, their job is fighting other soldiers. And if they tried, there are a lot more farmers than there are soldiers, and plenty of them have fighting experience from their own time in the army. Would you want to get in a fight with a farmer who's sharpened his strengthening magic pulling up tree stumps?"

Bryan though it over for a minute. "Maybe not."

By the time the sun was directly overhead, Bryan was hungry again. It didn't help that he was playing with fire almost continuously now, putting it out only when other travelers came into view. There was just something about producing flames that felt so right to him, but the girl kept pushing him to try something else.

"Look," Meghan said. "It's great you can do something magical now because it means I'll be able to use magic without putting to lie that we're man and wife. But everybody I've ever met can do fire, and unless you're training to be a war mage, bigger isn't better. If you'd just put in the effort I'm sure I could teach you something more useful."

"Like what?" Bryan asked grudgingly. He flicked a ball of flames into the sky, and then cast another one up to intercept the first before it dispersed. "Can you show me how to make food?"

"You can't just make food out of thin air," she told him. "You can only encourage things that might have happened anyway."

"You keep saying that, but what about the farmers giving themselves strength, or Hadrixia's healings?"

"Those are things that already exist," Meghan replied patiently. "Farmers and laborers use the memory of strength to add to their ability. There's a magical cost, of course, and even the strongest mages have a limit to their capacity. Hadrixia uses her magic to help people heal themselves. It's as if she serves as their—what did you call it? Magical battery."

"But how?"

"It's—I can't explain everything I've spent years studying in one sentence."

"Then start with the 'Happy truths' thing. What did Hadrixia learn from nature that would let her do that?"

"You've never seen a happy person?" Meghan asked incredulously. "No wonder we call it Dark Earth. And can't you tell whether somebody is lying to you or being sincere? If you start paying attention you'll see how things are actually put together, including emotions, and before you know it you'll be able to reproduce them. But to affect a person directly, like healing, you need physical contact."

"So you could teach me to make myself stronger?"

"If you have the capacity, yes. But I'd rather you started with some more practical things which you can show off when we're around other people because that will free me to use more magic myself. Remember, we're supposed to be in perfect balance."

"I'll make you a deal," Bryan offered. "I'll try to learn whatever you want to teach me until we get to the next place selling food if you pay for lunch."

"But I gave you all of the money Hadrixia gifted us," Meghan replied in surprise.

"Well, somebody has to be a saver or we could find ourselves broke."

"I'm beginning to think I summoned the only dragon in the world whose only talents are eating and hoarding," Meghan muttered.

"And flames," Bryan said cheerfully, tossing another fireball into the sky.

"Alright, alright. If you're so focused on dragon talents, how about we work on levitating?"

"You mean flying?" he asked, obviously intrigued by the idea.

"No. Flying will have to wait until you learn to take on a dragon's form. Levitating comes in handy for all sorts of things, like my slowing you down when you fell from the tower."

"But how can you show something like that for me to see it?" Bryan demanded. He immediately felt bad about being so strident when he knew the girl was trying to help him, but something at the back of his brain kept telling him he should assert control over his surroundings.

Meghan stopped and reached down to pick up a pebble. Next she displayed it to him between her thumb and forefinger to show there was nothing special about it.

"Now watch closely," she instructed him. Then the girl tossed it in the air in the direction they were traveling and walked forward to catch it, mouthing commands under her breath. The pebble seemed to take forever to fall, almost coming to a halt before she got her hand under it. Meghan turned to her companion with a small smile of pride, but his eyes were following a little ball of fire he'd quietly flung off.

"Hey! If you don't pay attention I'm not buying lunch."

"I tried, but all I could think was, 'Oh, a flying pebble.' Who cares?"

"I have an idea," she said. "Give me your ring."

"What?" he growled, sticking his ring hand in his pocket to hide it. "Use your own ring."

"I can't believe you," she said in frustration, working her fictitious wedding ring off over her knuckle. "Now watch."

Meghan tossed the ring in the air, higher than the light pebble had gone, and muttered to slow its descent. Bryan watched with a look of intensity that was almost frightening. If somebody had stuck a log in the road, he would have tripped over it.

"Do it again," he ordered when the ring came to rest in Meghan's hand.

She tossed the ring forward again, and this time she got the arc just right, so that with a little magical levitation, it came down in her hand as they walked forward at their usual pace.

"I think I'm getting it," Bryan said. "Again."

This time she flipped the ring upwards by flicking her thumb off of her index finger, like children throw marbles. It rotated rapidly, glittering like a small golden ball in the sun. Then a crow came flashing down, caught the ring in its beak, and began flapping away.

"Don't!" Meghan cried, but a blast of fire from Bryan's hand had already caught the crow, and it crashed down in a ball of flame. "I could have called it back or followed it to its nest," the girl said sorrowfully.

"My way works better," Bryan retorted, striding into the tall meadow grass and making sure the crow was dead with a stomp of his boot. "How are you going to survive out here if you cry over killing a crow?"

She swallowed dryly when he returned with the ring and placed it in her hand. It was barely warm.

"Again," he demanded.

This time, Meghan was careful to check the sky for birds before throwing the ring.

After polishing off a whole chicken by himself, along with three baked potatoes, a family-sized plate of green beans, and a pitcher of hard apple cider, Bryan felt satiated for the first time since he discovered the joys of fire making. Even though he had made good progress with levitation before they reached the inn, the fact that his magic instructor was paying for the lunch made the meal even tastier.

Meghan barely made it through a serving of hearty soup, despite the fact that she thought she had never been so hungry when they sat down. Bryan's progress at magic in less than a day was truly astounding, and she suspected he might have equaled her own ability in levitation if she hadn't broken off the lessons every time other people appeared on the road. Her fear was that a stranger might make a playful grab for the gold ring, triggering a deadly reaction from her student.

During the years she had spent searching for a dragon, Meghan had always imagined a loyal companion who could transform into a creature with a mouth full of frightening teeth and stand between her and danger. She was starting to realize that the legends and popular woodblock prints of girls riding dragons in flight may not have told the whole story. Bryan clearly had a mind of his own and would act according to his own wishes, and that was beginning to scare her. Meghan wondered if her time would have been better spent training a large dog.

"Are you not talking to me because of the bird thing?" Bryan demanded. He sensed a change in Meghan, a drawing away, and he decided that he didn't like it.

"Yes. I mean, no. I mean, I don't know." Meghan exhaled sharply and mentally berated herself for sounding like a child. "Crows eat crops, though they eat the insects that damage crops as well, so the farmers around the castle mainly leave them alone. It was how you killed it without a thought, like brushing away a fly."

"Sorry," Bryan said, but the simultaneous shrug made it clear that he was only sorry she was unhappy, not that he had roasted the crow. "I've been listening in for a while on those guys at the table in the corner and they talked about taking a shortcut to Castle Foregone. One of them said it cuts a day off of the trip, plus there aren't many people."

Meghan put a finger to her lips and shushed him, looking towards the corner at the same time to see if the well-armed trio had overheard Bryan's recitation of their private conversation.

"You can hear what those guys are saying?" she whispered.

"Sure. The one they call Dagger is telling the other two about the time—uh, I don't think you want to know," Bryan concluded awkwardly.

"They're bandits," she hissed at him. "No, don't look over there. I'm not interested in a shortcut that has men like them traveling it, and you realize that leaving the road means no inns or settlements to buy food."

"Forget that!" Bryan exclaimed. "Hey, since you're buying lunch, how about asking if they'll sell us a couple of chickens to go?"

"You're impossible," Meghan retorted, though his obsession with food was sort of endearing. "Uh, oh. I think those bandits are looking at us now. It was a mistake getting your clothes fixed for you. We should have just bought you something new."

"What's wrong with blue jeans and a white T-shirt?"

"Nobody else wears anything similar if you haven't noticed. It may lead some people to assume you're from a rich family, since they're the only ones who can afford to spend money on clothes for the sake of looking different. Oh, crumbs. They're heading over here, so let me do the talking."

Three tough-looking men with iron spurs strapped to their boots approached the young couple's table. Two of them rested axes on their shoulders, and the third carried a short sword by the scabbard in his left hand.

"My friends and I noticed that the two of you kept looking our way," drawled the bandit with the sword. An ugly scar ran from the corner of his mouth up to his left eye, as if he had tried eating something on the tip of a knife while drunk and missed badly. "The only explanation we could come up with for your interest is that you wanted to treat us to lunch."

"Dream on," Bryan growled, ignoring Meghan's frantic gestures and rising to his feet. He was a fist taller than the scarred leader, and somehow he seemed to loom over all three of the older men, even with the table between them. He lazily stretched his hands above his head, causing his vertebrae to crack loudly, and a subtle red glow danced around his fingertips.

"Watch it, Dagger. That one's packing heavy magic," said the man to the leader's right. He spat ostentatiously on the floor.

"They're kids," Dagger snorted, moving his free hand deliberately to the hilt of his sword.

"He'll burn you before you draw," the sideman stated flatly, backing towards the door to be out of the line of fire. "You know my talent is measuring what people have inside, but even you should be able to see it in his eyes."

Meghan risked a glance away from the bandits and saw immediately what the man was talking about. Little flames sparked in her companion's green eyes, as if they were just waiting for an excuse to get free and burn something. She shuddered involuntarily, and then forced herself to speak.

"Please, just leave," she said, reaching for the talisman hanging around her neck. Meghan wasn't sure what she would do if the highwayman drew his sword, but she knew if she didn't come up with something, Bryan might accidentally send the whole place up in flames.

Dagger didn't like what he saw in the younger man's eyes any more than Meghan did, and he turned suddenly and strode out the door. Bryan waited until the three men were outside before he sat down with a lazy grin.

"I told you to let me handle it," Meghan reproached him, though she found herself strangely drawn to his aggressive attitude at the same time.

"How many fights have you been in?" he asked her offhandedly.

"What?"

"You heard me. How many fights have you been in?"

"None," she said. "And I want to keep it that way."

"I took my share of bullying," Bryan told her, ignoring the latter part of her response. "Every couple of years in school I'd have to fight some guy to keep from getting picked on. I'm not saying that I ever intimidated anybody, but I know how to stand up. And whatever you think, I had those guys beat."

"You would have killed them and burned down the inn!"

"Yes to the first, maybe to the second." Bryan reached across the table and took one of Meghan's hands in his, and she noticed for the first time that she was trembling. "Are you sure you're up for this adventure? I'll admit I don't have a clue where we're going or what's going to happen to us, but I've played enough fantasy games to imagine I have a better grip on what we're headed into than you do. Your friend Phinneas didn't get his scars eating prickly fruits, and he wasn't training those guys with wooden swords to be chefs."

"Aren't you afraid of anything?" Meghan asked softly.

"I used to be afraid of almost everything. Then I died and you brought me here. Now I'm, I don't know, but I'll be damned if I'm going to let anybody push me around or take my treasure."

He released her hand and sat back, looking rather pleased with himself.

"I'll talk to the cook and see if I can get a chicken to go," Meghan said.

By the time they stopped for supper, Bryan could bring the falling gold ring to a dead stop in the air. He could also make it come to him, though he found himself more and more reluctant to hand it back to Meghan each time he touched it. There was just something about gold.

"We're making good time, and it would be nice to sleep in a bed tonight," Meghan hinted after their picnic meal was finished. "It will be dark in a couple of hours, so maybe we should stop at the next inn or settlement to ask."

"Bad strategy," Bryan replied, wiping his hands on his T-shirt. He couldn't get over the fact that the grease came off of his fingers, but rather than staining the cloth, it balled up and fell to the ground like tiny beads of water rolling off a waterproofed poncho. He wondered if there was a magical landfill somewhere overflowing with the stuff people wiped off on their shirts and pants.

"How is sleeping in a bed a bad strategy?"

"If somebody from your castle is trying to chase us down on horseback, they're sure to stop at every place we could take shelter. You already have us diving in the bushes every time I hear horses coming."

"But nobody will ride at night."

"They might if they want you badly enough," Bryan said. "Besides, the last inn we passed had their prices posted on the hanging slate, and it was five coppers to share a bed."

"Share?" Meghan couldn't believe she had momentarily forgotten all of the stories about sharing beds with strangers on the road. Only the wealthy could afford rooms and beds to themselves. "Maybe you're right."

"That's ten coppers for the two of us," he continued, not noticing her discomfort with the concept of sleeping with strangers. "Ten coppers would buy five bowls of porridge, or two loaves of bread, or one roasted chicken. How many coppers are there in a silver again?"

"Ten in the small silver, twenty five in the big silver, though if you're buying from one of the tradesmen in the castle, they usually weigh them to catch the shaved coins. Out in the countryside, people will just refuse a coin if it looks light."

"All I'm saying is that inns are dangerous and a waste of money. It's not even that cold out at night."

"It will be by the next full moon," Meghan told him. "Don't forget we added an extra month at the spring equinox so it's actually later in the season than Ninth."

"What's Ninth?"

"You don't count the months of the year where you come from? How can the farmers know when to plant seeds or the soldiers know when to go to war?"

"We have names for the months, and our soldiers fight year-round. What kind of a dumb name for a month is Ninth?"

"It's a smart name for the month after Eighth and before Tenth," she retorted. "All I'm saying is that there was a double Fourth this year, so everything is later than it seems."

"Hey, you stole my expression!"

"What?"

"All I'm saying. I'm the only person here who uses that."

"Oh brother," Meghan muttered. "You're the weirdest cross between a grown man and a little boy I've ever met."

"Anyway, if you have to add months, that means you're using a lunar calendar, and it will still go off track whatever you do."

"For your information, I studied calendars with Hadrixia and they all go off track. In addition to the extra months, we add a day every couple hundred years. It has to do with how fast the sun is going around the Earth."

"What!" Bryan stared at the girl in disbelief. "You think that the sun goes around the Earth? Do you also think that if we walk far enough we can fall off the edge because the Earth is flat?"

"Who thinks the Earth is flat? That's just stupid. But I can see with my own eyes that the sun goes around us every day."

"I forgot you've never been to school," Bryan said. "Earth spins on its axis as it goes around the sun. That's where days come from."

"So why doesn't the moon spin when it goes around us?" she asked triumphantly. "You can always see the same face on it when it's full."

"Let's get going," Bryan said, suddenly tiring of the argument. If she wanted to believe that the sun went around the Earth, what difference did it make? "We agreed on not blowing any money sleeping at inns. Right?"

An owl hooted its displeasure as the humans set up camp below the towering, old-growth trees. The diameter of the fallen red oak was higher than Meghan's shoulders, and it shielded their tents effectively from the view of any passersby on the road. The forest floor was rich with fallen chestnuts, acorns, and hickory nuts, and the tenants of the hollowed-out red oak—chipmunks, mice, squirrels, and even the occasional baby raccoon—were viewed by the great horned owl as fast food.

"I can't get over how big these trees are," Bryan said for at least the third time since they had moved beyond the settled river valley area. "Haven't you people ever heard of lumber companies?"

"The wood from just one of these trees would be enough to build a half a dozen houses," Meghan told him. "Hadrixia once took me to watch the sawyers cutting up the trunk of an old tree that came down the river after a storm. It took them all week, and when they were done, there was enough wood to keep the carpenters busy building all winter."

"We used to have forests like this on Dark Earth, but other than a few parks, they've long since been cut down. Even when the trees grow back, it's not the same because the natural rhythm has changed."

"There are barely enough people in New Land to occasionally clear a new field, much less cut down a whole forest. I don't think our landmasses can be any different than those on Dark Earth just six thousand years after your world was exiled to its own place. If you recognize all of the trees and animals, you must have come from somewhere around here."

"Maybe within a month's walking on decent trails. Hey, that's not what I meant to say. Is there some reason Hadrixia didn't teach me units of measure? Every time I want to explain a distance, it comes out like I'm talking about taking a trip."

"That is how we measure long distances," Meghan replied. "Soldiers use marching or riding days, and I've heard that people who go to sea have a completely different system. When would you ever need to talk about distances without wanting to know how long it takes to get there?"

"Well, say I wanted to cut down one of these trees and float it to whatever castle controls the mouth of the river. I might ask you how far it is to the castle so I could divide that by the distance my tree can float in a day and figure how long it would take to get there."

"But if we were people who cut down trees and floated them on rivers, we'd know that. You'd ask me how far it is to some castle and I'd tell you how many tree-floating days it is."

"You mean that everybody in the different trades uses different measures to talk to each other?"

"Of course," Meghan replied. "That's part of learning a trade. Do you need to know how many fingers your waist is so you can order a dress?" She burst out laughing at the mental picture of Bryan in skirts.

"But how can you build anything to plans or make new parts for stuff if everybody in one castle measures boards in lengths of Uncle Joe's forearm, and everybody—no, half the people in another castle measure boards in lengths of Aunt Sally's leg?"

"Now you're being silly on purpose. Why would people in one castle need to know how people in another castle measure boards?"

"It's like, you're pre-industrial," Bryan exploded in frustration. "How about map making? How can you tell how far apart the land masses are if you don't have a scale?"

"You mean like the distance between New Land and Old Land? Even with a mage onboard a ship to ensure a steady wind, there are too many variables to give the distance with any precision. A storm could come along and delay passage for days or even blow the ship entirely off course. And supposedly there are rivers in the oceans that affect the journey as well."

"Currents," Bryan supplied the better word. "But you're proving my point exactly. If everybody knew that from point A on the coast of New Land to point B on the coast of Old Land was a hundred days walking—I hate this language."

"Why would anybody want to know how long it takes to walk across an ocean?" Meghan asked, not understanding the source of Bryan's frustration. "I suppose a mage with the right talents could do it, but it doesn't seem like very useful information."

"I give up," Bryan said. "Do you have any of that pie left?"

"I recognize those horsemen," Meghan whispered. "They're personal guards of our baron and they wouldn't be here unless he sent them looking for me."

"Why don't I zap 'em."

"Stop," the girl hissed, pulling Bryan down again as he began to rise. They were hiding in a patch of tall grass not far from the road, a spot they had reached by running down the small stream they were crossing when Meghan's magically enhanced hearing had told her horses were coming. Bryan had heard the horses before her, but he hadn't said anything.

"Is this your idea of a quest? Running from everybody who wants to stop you?"

"They've passed now." Meghan sighed in relief and stood. "I recognized the men but I don't know them. Maybe they have wives and children at home and they're good husbands and fathers. Besides, men don't have feathers to burn, and even if you could kill them, it's not the right thing to do."

"It is in every game I ever played," Bryan retorted grumpily.

"This isn't a game," the girl responded, stamping her hiking boot in the grass. "How can you be so eager to kill when you've never been a soldier except in your dreams?"

The young man shrugged as the horses disappeared from view. "I don't know. Just seems to be the logical thing to do. And I'll tell you one thing for sure. If you keep grabbing me every time I want to fight, one of these days you're going to get us both killed. From what you've told me, unlike my previous life on Dark Earth, there's no second chance around here."

"But we didn't get killed, and we barely got our feet wet. Do you want to break for lunch?" she added, knowing that food was the most effective way of improving Bryan's mood. She glanced over with a small smile, looking forward to seeing his face change at the suggestion of eating, but he was staring at something high in the sky.

"That hawk is eyeballing us," Bryan stated flatly.

"Are you sure?" Meghan asked, all of her faculties coming to attention. "Near," she muttered under her breath as she stared up at the circling black dot. "Nearer. I can't make out the eyes. Maybe it's hunting something else we can't see."

"It's looking right at us," Bryan insisted. "I could always tell when somebody was staring at me."

"But it's not a somebody, it's a hawk. Unless—I should have thought of this. Can you kill it from here?"

"You want me to toast the bird?" Bryan asked in surprise. "I don't know. It's awfully high and my fireballs seem to fall apart with distance."

"I can't tell without being closer but I think it's being controlled. It's not the kind of magic our people use, but the natives of New Land have different abilities. Supposedly a shaman can occupy an animal with his spirit and see through its eyes. But why would a shaman be interested in us?"

"Gold for your bounty," Bryan said. "Anyway, if he's going to stay that high, the only way I'd get him with a fireball is if I made it big enough for everybody around to see."

"Let's not worry about it," Meghan decided. "Maybe it's just a regular hawk, and even if it is controlled by a shaman, maybe he's just curious."

"What's with that clown?" Bryan whispered as they entered a roadside inn.

He didn't need to point out to Meghan the object of his query, who was dressed in a spectacularly tasteless suit of clothes. Each of the man's limbs was encased in a different-colored fabric, and his vest was a patchwork of striped and polka-dotted scraps. Seemingly oblivious of the attention he was receiving from adults and children alike, the man looked perfectly at ease as he sat alone at the common table, devouring his dinner like a trencherman.

"He's a harlequin," Meghan replied excitedly. "If he's not a member of Rowan's players, he likely knows something about them. Let's join him."

"You're not going to offer to pay for his meal, are you?" Bryan asked suspiciously.

"You seem to worry a great deal about how I spend my savings," the girl retorted as she dragged him towards the common table. "Have you even spent a single copper of the money Hadrixia gave us?"

"That looks like prime rib he's eating," Bryan said, ignoring Meghan's question. "You promised if I spent the afternoon practicing that new thing you'd buy me whatever I wanted for dinner."

"That new thing I showed you is basic magical energy storage and it could save your life one day," she whispered. "Now let me do the talking."

Meghan put on her brightest smile and sat down at the table directly across from the harlequin, patting the spot on the bench next to her for Bryan. The stranger looked up, swallowed whatever was in his mouth, and opened the conversation.

"I see you're not afraid of a little color, unlike our country friends."

"Oh, no. I'm a great admirer of performers," Meghan said. "My husband and I are on our way to join up with Rowan's players, if he'll have us."

"Is that a fact?" The man looked skeptically at the young couple. "You don't seem the theatrical types, if you don't mind my saying."

"We're both new to the business, but we're willing to work our way up from the bottom," Meghan said.

"What have you been doing until now?" the harlequin inquired.

"We were both in food service," Bryan said. "Speaking of service, how do I get what you're having?"

"You could fight me for it," the man suggested mildly. "I've already lost once today. If I hadn't taken the precaution of hiding my last silver in my mouth when I heard the bandits coming, I might have been entertaining these good people for a scrap of bread, rather than dining on the Ploughman's Special."

"You were robbed?" Meghan asked. "Was it three men, one of them with a scar running from his eye to his mouth?"

"Friends of yours?"

"They thought so, but I convinced them otherwise," Bryan interjected, drawing a sharp look from Meghan. "About that food…"

"I see you have limited experience as a traveler," the man said. "My name is Laitz, and I'm on my way back to Rowan's troupe myself, so perhaps we can travel together. As to your meal— Waitress!"

The harlequin didn't seem to speak this last word any louder, but his voice cut through the noisy conversations in the tavern like a foghorn. A young woman whose hands testified to her spending the day in the fields before coming to work in the inn materialized at the table, and the background noise returned to its usual level.

"What'll ya have?" she demanded.

"Ploughman's Special," Bryan replied immediately. "And a pitcher of beer."

"Ploughman's Special," the waitress bellowed in the general direction of the kitchen. "And for the little lady?"

"I'll have a half a chicken with a potato and whatever greens you're serving," Meghan replied, trying her best to sound like an experienced traveler.

"We're outta chicken," the waitress replied.

"Do you have any rabbit?"

"Outta rabbit."

"Meat pie?"

"Outta pie."

"What do you have?" Bryan interrupted.

"Ploughman's Special. You're late and it was a busy night. Got cheese if you want. Maybe some vegetable soup."

"Another Ploughman's Special," Bryan ordered. He turned to Meghan. "I'll finish it if you can't."

"Thank you," she replied sarcastically, as the waitress bellowed the order and disappeared.

"It's quite good, really," Laitz said. "Worth every bit of eight coppers, though I anticipate some hungry days before catching up with Rowan."

"So these guys took your purse but they left your clothes?" Bryan asked curiously. Now that he knew that food was on the way, he was happy to engage in conversation.

"The bandits took everything, including the clothes off my back, but the one who went through my bag pointed out that my professional suit would be difficult to sell and wasn't anything he would be caught dead in. The other two agreed, and they seemed to derive a great deal of amusement from leaving it with me. I have to admit that it draws a very different reaction on the road than what I'm used to on the stage."

"How long have you been with Rowan's players?" Meghan asked.

"I traveled with them for almost five years, but six months ago, I made the mistake of taking a castle job as the duke's jester when the troupe completed its engagement there. It seemed like a wise career move at the time, steady pay and limited travel. I soon discovered that Rowan was right and that you can't entertain the same people seven days a week."

"Why not?" Meghan asked.

"Material gets stale," Laitz explained. "If you do two shows a day for a few days and then move on, nobody gets tired of your repertoire. Try staying the same place for a few weeks and they'll be pelting you with rotten fruit. After a fortnight in the castle, I found myself making up jokes on the spot to try to get a laugh out of them. It wasn't long before I made the mistake of doing an impersonation of some of the duke's idiosyncrasies. That earned me three months in the dungeon."

The waitress returned and placed a pitcher of beer and two leather cups on the table before moving on without a word.

"I've never seen Rowan's players," Bryan said, filling both cups from the pitcher. "What sort of performances do you do?"

"Our main event is always a play, either a comedy or a tragedy," Laitz said, eyeing his own empty cup. "Depending on the setup, we often did small skits all around the castle during the day, in order to drum up interest. At festivals, we frequently performed battle reenactments, sometimes playing against a different troupe. Haven't you ever thrown coppers on the stage for a well-acted death?"

"Whenever I got the chance. Is that the pay? Whatever coins people feel like throwing on the stage?"

"Rowan covers all of our basic road expenses, plus a fraction of the take, which depends on your role and seniority," Laitz began to explain, but just then, the waitress returned bearing two Ploughman's Specials, and Bryan stopped paying attention.

"We make better progress in the dark because we don't have to get off the road every time we hear horses," Meghan explained to Laitz.

"Were you bitten by a horse as a child?" the harlequin inquired. "They don't eat people, you know, unlike chasms one might wander into after dark. When we left the tavern I assumed we were just heading down the road a bit for some peace and quiet before choosing a campsite."

"Don't worry," Bryan said, "I'll tell you if there's a hole in the road before you fall in. So what's your magic?"

"Bryan!" Meghan remonstrated. "It's very rude to ask somebody about their magic like that. I'm sorry, Laitz. He's from a village outside Castle Trollsdatter, and they don't have very good manners there."

"Trollsdatter? Sounds made-up to me," Laitz commented. "And I'm not offended by your husband's question. I appreciate a little honesty after that last gig. My magic is creating illusions."

"Really?" Meghan asked in excitement. "I've read about that, but it's so rare."

"So is reading," Laitz replied, causing the young woman to clamp a hand over her mouth. "Look. It's obvious that the two of you aren't the typical castle servants running away to join the players and see the world. That's your business, and I'm not going to pry, but I'm a good ten years older than you both and I've been traveling since I could walk, so maybe I can help."

"What does it mean to create an illusion?" Bryan asked.

"I'd show you right now, but it doesn't work in the dark."

Bryan struck a bright white fireball and grinned at his companions.

"You could have warned us first," Meghan complained. "My eyes were adjusted for the dark and now I can't see a thing."

"That's almost as nice as the orbs Rowan's lighting man creates for our night performances," Laitz said. "Can you keep it steady for a couple of hours?"

"I think so, I haven't tried," Bryan replied.

"You won't go hungry if you can. There's always work in theatre for a good lighting man. Bring down the brightness a couple of levels. A little more. Can you focus the light in one direction rather than shining like a ball? That's good." Laitz closed his eyes for a moment, his look of intense concentration contrasting with his garish costume. "What do you want to see?"

"A dragon," Meghan and Bryan answered simultaneously.

The corners of the illusionist's mouth twitched up, but he maintained his composure and began gathering the night air towards himself with repeated movements of his arms. At the same time, he wiggled his fingers in a calculated manner that made it look like each hand was playing a stringed instrument. A series of flickering shafts of light seemed to grow out of nothing before him.

A dark blob formed in the center of the projection as Laitz continued to groom the air with his hands. The shape slowly transformed into a cross, which then began to flesh out as a head on a long neck, giant wings, and a very long tail. The dark color lightened into a grayish hue, and the dragon's mouth slowly opened, displaying a ghostly collection of dagger-like teeth. Then a sudden gust of wind blew the illusion away.

"I hate working outside," the illusionist groused, but he looked rather pleased with himself. "All the same, the number-one rule of show business is to always leave them wanting more."

"How did you do that?" Bryan demanded. "I thought I saw something familiar at the beginning, but then you just lost me."

"Bryan!" Meghan reprimanded him again. "What did I tell you about asking professionals about their magical trade secrets?"

"I don't mind," Laitz said. "Your husband has a quick eye for a country bumpkin from outside of Castle Trollsdatter. I tried training most of the players in Rowan's troupe as assistants over the years, but none of them had the aptitude."

"I saw something too," Meghan said, since the illusionist was open to discussing his craft. "It reminded me of how the light coming through an arrow slit sometimes looks almost solid, as if it's made up of little particles of light."

"It's dust that you're seeing," Laitz explained. "There are some basic tricks related to the location of the light source and preparation of the performance space, but the toughest part to learn is manipulating the dust for shapes and colors. There was a single light shaft in my dungeon and nothing else to do, so I'm better now than I ever was. Unless Rowan has picked up a top-notch illusionist in my absence, I'm sure he'll welcome me back."

"Can you do any shape, or just things you've seen?" Bryan asked, extinguishing his night lighting.

"Any shape, but it's easier if you know what you're looking for before you start," Laitz replied with a laugh. "Dragons are always the first thing the audience asks for, and if the wind hadn't come along, I could have shown its wings beating. For performances, I seed the illusion space with colored dust while I'm making my arm passes, rather than gathering in whatever particles happen to be floating around in the air."

"Teach us," Bryan suggested. "We can be your assistants."

"Can you both do basic levitation?"

"Yes," Meghan replied. "I've never tried manipulating dust because there didn't seem to be any reason."

"I hate bringing this up, but all I have left to my name is the two coppers in change from the small silver I spent on dinner."

"Training for food," Meghan suggested. "It's a good deal for all of us."

"You made the offer, you buy the food," Bryan grumbled.

"We should make the castle by suppertime," Laitz observed, squinting into the distance. "Considering that it rained every night, I think we've made excellent time over the last few days. Your progress with illusions has been nothing short of astounding, both of you. If Rowan is still there, I'm sure he'll take us all on."

Meghan grimaced at the compliment because she knew that Bryan had surpassed her in the informal training, even though he had been practicing magic for less than two weeks. She was fully convinced that he was her intended dragon and his rapid progress with magic just proved the point. On the other hand, his quick temper coupled with his refusal to let a single copper out of his purse was getting to be a bit depressing.

"Then we should hurry up so we can catch him before dinner and let him foot the bill." Bryan assumed that the others would find this logic unassailable, and lengthened his stride accordingly.

"Don't get too far ahead," Meghan called after him, maintaining her usual pace. Laitz hung back with the girl as Bryan opened the gap in what was rapidly becoming a battle of wills.

"I prefer walking when the road runs through the forest," Laitz said, making idle conversation to cover his discomfort over the young people's latest spat. He couldn't make heads or tails of their relationship. They claimed to be married and wore wedding bands, but they slept in their own bedrolls and showed no signs of intimacy that the harlequin could detect. When it rained at night, and they rigged tents from the waterproof sheets that normally lined their packs and served as back-padding, Meghan insisted that Laitz share with her husband and took the smaller tent herself.

"You don't like the fields?" Meghan asked. "I'd never spent a night in the woods before we set out on this journey and I have to admit that it's a bit spooky."

"Your husband seems quite capable of taking care of you both. Something tells me that those bandits who cleaned me out wouldn't have been so lucky with the two of you."

"He's pretty scary at times," Meghan admitted. "I've never seen anybody learn so fast, and he's not afraid of anything, other than going hungry. I didn't really know him that well before we got married," she added hastily.

"There's no shame in arranged marriages. In Old Land practically all of the matches are made by parents and guardians. It's only here in New Land that young people believe in seeking their own mates, and that's probably in imitation of the natives."

"I thought the tribe's shaman made all the matches."

"The shaman performs the rites, but the participants choose each other. I spent a whole year with the natives when I was younger, a journey from summer camp to winter camp and back again. It's where my love of the woods comes from. The natives cultivate some crops, of course, but they don't build permanent houses and live next to their fields year-round. But listen to me telling you something you must already know."

"No, I didn't, actually. The natives who visited our castle were usually men, so I didn't have any contact with them. I do have a pair of moccasins in my pack that still fit even though I bought them from a native woman four years ago. She told me that the deerskin would stretch as my feet grew with just a little encouragement, but I didn't really believe her at first. Their magic is too different from ours to understand."

"I don't think that's true at all," Laitz said. "Their approach to magic is different, but their skills are very similar. I learned my illusions from a shaman who thought it was astounding I could make fire. They consider it women's work, and to see a bunch of grown men rubbing sticks together to start a fire when they're away from the camp on a raid is wonderfully amusing. On the other hand, I've seen a brave shoot down a goose with an arrow that should have fallen back to the ground at a tenth of the range. Our people and their people have very different gifts for war, and that's why we mainly leave each other alone."

"He's stopped," Meghan said. "I guess he finally figured out that keeping his wife in view is more important than saving the cost of a meal."

"If you say so," Laitz replied agreeably. "He has something of the look of the natives about him, mainly around the eyes and the nose. They have excellent vision, you know. Does he talk about his family background?"

"He lost all of his family at once and he prefers not to speak about it," the girl replied, realizing that this was an opportunity to save Bryan from embarrassing questions. "If you could say something to the others when we arrive, it would make life easier."

"I'm happy to be of service, especially as you've been keeping me fed the last four days."

"Are you two coming or what?" Bryan yelled irritably. He was holding his pack in one hand, and Meghan realized that the reason he had come to a halt was that he was out of food and knew that she had leftovers. They'd eaten lunch at a farmhouse, but with their destination so near, there didn't seem to be a point to buying more food for the road.

"There's no need to hurry, Bryan," Meghan called back. "If they were leaving today, they're already gone. Nobody starts a journey after lunch."

"Yeah, speaking of lunch, that bread must have been full of air because I'm hungry again. Got anything left in your pack you want to get rid of before it spoils?"

"Don't you believe in holding anything back for emergencies?" Meghan asked.

"If you spend all of your time preparing for the future it won't ever arrive," Bryan said.

"Did you just make that up?" Laitz inquired. "It's rather good, like a line from a play."

"It just seems to make sense," the young man replied matter-of-factly. "It seems to me that I spent my whole life waiting for something before I, uh, came here and married Meghan. Now I feel like all the hesitation has been burnt out of me and I just want to get on with the job."

"And eat," Meghan added, surveying the diminished contents of her pack. "There's some dried beef that's been in here since we left. I don't know how good it is."

"It'll be fine," her dragon replied.

"So clowning around for lords and ladies wasn't everything you imagined, Laitz," Rowan said to the illusionist.

The troupe's manager was an enormous man with shoulders as broad as a bull's. Even while seated, his eyes were almost level with Meghan's when the trio approached the table. Laitz shuffled his feet and tried to look properly chastised, but knuckling under didn't come naturally to him.

"I paid my dues, Rowan," Laitz replied calmly, managing a crooked smile. "I think you'll find that the three months I spent in a dungeon perfecting my illusions will work to your benefit. If you can talk my young companions into staying and acting as my assistants, you'll see a show that couldn't be equaled in Old Land."

"Is that so?" Rowan said, reaching for a turkey drumstick. "And you've toured Old Land recently so you know what you're talking about?"

"Not recently, but you'll remember I shipped with a merchant vessel before I started working for you, so I've seen more of the world than most."

"Hey, are you going to invite us to sit down, or what?" Bryan interrupted the awkward reunion. "We've been on the road for almost a week trying to catch up with you. My wife's friend, Phinneas, told us to ask for a man named Simon."

"I'm Simon," an older man on the other side of the table announced. He rose from his place and came around to where the newcomers were standing near Rowan's seat. When he extended his hand to shake with Bryan, the younger man noted that the former soldier was missing the pinkie and ring fingers from his right hand.

"Is this going to be one of those ex-soldier things?" Rowan asked his stage master, after swallowing a mouthful of turkey. He sounded more resigned than annoyed, and Meghan got the impression that the player troupe functioned like a large family.

"I owe Phinneas my life," Simon replied. "If you don't want to give these two a trial run, well, they can just stay on as my guests."

"Now, I never said that, Simon," Rowan protested mildly, wiping his hands on his pants and rising to his feet. He was a true giant, towering over Bryan by a half a head, and he might have weighed nearly as much as the three travelers put together. "If Laitz is willing to have you as assistants, your magic must be…interesting, and if Simon is willing to work you into the fight scenes, you'll have no problems earning your keep. Just remember that we don't tolerate prima donnas in this troupe, as your clown friend can tell you."

"You won't regret this, Rowan." Laitz clasped hands with his new and former boss.

"I'm Meghan," the girl said. "Thank you for giving us a chance." Her hand and wrist felt like they'd been wrapped in a warm slab of meat and disappeared entirely in the giant's gentle handshake.

"I gather from the rings that the two of you are married," Rowan said to Bryan. His eyes locked with the young man's as they shook hands, and it quickly became apparent that he was taking the opportunity to test the new troupe member's strength.

Bryan grunted as the man tightened his grip, but he accepted the challenge and returned the pressure for all he was worth. Four years of rock climbing and holding heavy plates and pans with one hand while scraping with the other had built up his finger strength, and he'd been feeling stronger and stronger every day since Meghan pulled him over from Dark Earth. The veins began to pop out on his forehead as the contest went on, but just when he felt like the bones in his hand were about to crush together, Rowan relaxed his grip.

"I can see you won't drop your sword when you cross blades on the stage," the player's leader said, nodding in approval. "You don't have the calluses of a swordsman though, or of a farmer, for that matter."

"I have a sword that Phinneas gave me, but I've never trained with one," Bryan admitted. "Laitz said something about you paying for the meals of all the troupe members?"

"Find some open spaces and eat all you can," Rowan told them. "You got here just in time. Tomorrow morning we start east after breakfast for the harvest fair circuit, so I hope you like fresh air. We'll begin in the north and work our way south, keeping ahead of the winter."

The troupe owned a dozen draft horses, enormous animals that could have borne Rowan's weight without complaint if he'd chosen to ride, but they were hitched in pairs to wagons, one of which was dedicated to carrying horse feed to supplement roadside grazing. Including the newcomers, there were thirty players in the troupe, but children and a dozen non-performing spouses more than tripled that number. The men all wore swords on the road, and many of the women displayed belt daggers. Highwaymen gave them a wide berth.

The children were on and off the wagons all day, and it was a wonder to Bryan that they were never crushed under the wheels. Simon gave Bryan sword lessons at every opportunity, starting with teaching the young man the basic forms he could practice alone, and quickly introducing a little sparring with dull practice blades and leather armor for their upper bodies.

"How come you're not teaching me stage fighting first and real fighting later?" Bryan asked after one of the training sessions. "I want to show Rowan that I'm worth my pay."

"Don't worry about that," Simon replied. "The big bear has taken a liking to you, and feeding a couple of extra mouths doesn't add much to the overhead, even when one of them eats like you do. I'm teaching you real fighting first because that's what Phinneas would want, and it's dangerous to do it the other way around. I can teach any swordsman worth his salt how to stage fight, but teaching an actor to be a swordsman isn't so easy."

"I'm worried that I'm going to break your ribs sparring even though you're just toying with me," Bryan admitted. "You always wait for the last second to block my thrusts and slashes. Is that a stage thing I'll need to learn?"

Simon chuckled grimly. "I'm not waiting to the last second, boy. You're too damn quick. You move faster than I did when I was forty years younger, and if you knew what you were doing you'd be dangerous. Right now, in a fight against decent swordsman, you'd only be dangerous to yourself."

"How long will it take me to learn?"

"Most boys destined for soldiers start sparring with wooden swords as children and begin serious training when their beards begin to come in. With your speed and enough practice, you might hold your own against an average fighter in a few months, but it takes years to become a real swordsman."

"Then why does it feel like I'm about to cut you in half every time I attack?"

"I'm old, slow, and missing half a hand. But don't hold back because you're worried about getting past my defenses or it will permanently mess up your timing. My wife is a pretty good healer, so as long as you keep that chunk of steel away from my face she'll be able to fix any damage you do. This leather armor is better than it looks unless you take a thrust from something with a sharp point."

"So what happened to your fingers?" Bryan asked with the insensitivity of youth.

"Somebody cut them off," Simon answered bluntly. "I had a special hilt made for my favorite sword with leather straps to help my grip, but Phinneas told me I was just begging for death. After he saved my bacon on the field, I decided he was right and got into show business, which was the smartest move I ever made. Look at me now with a wife and grandchildren."

"Why didn't you have the fingers sewn back on?"

"Sewn?" the old soldier asked. "Gods, boy. You really must be from the backwaters of civilization if they sew fingers onto people. Any folk healer like my wife could have handled the job easy and I'd have been holding a sword again in a week. Well, maybe two weeks."

"So why didn't you take the fingers to a battlefield healer?"

"Couldn't find them," Simon said sourly. "It had been raining for days and the field was all muddy, so one of us must have stepped on my fingers and buried them in the muck. I stopped the bleeding myself, of course. Anybody without enough magic to do that would be insane to take up soldiering, but I've hated Fourth Month with all the rain ever since."

Meghan held the squirming baby boy while his mother, Bethany, was taking care of her business in the woods.

"So when do you expect the blessed event?" the seamstress in charge of costumes asked Meghan.

"I knew it," the baby's mother said, returning to reclaim her infant. "You're so good with my Davie."

Before Meghan could digest what the women were saying and protest, the seamstress continued. "There are lots of good roles for a young woman with your face once you fill out. Can't expect the men to throw coppers if you don't show them a bit of cleavage."

"But I'm not pregnant," Meghan finally managed to object. "We've barely been married two weeks."

"Oh, I'm sorry," Bethany said, putting Davie to her shoulder to burp the fussy baby. "I'm sure you'll have good news for us any day. I guess we all just assumed that Bryan got you in trouble and you ran away from home with him."

"You could try a bit of padding," the seamstress suggested kindly. "With the right dress, it can make all of the difference. They used to throw silver at my daughter's feet when she played Hilda in *The Princess and the Mage*."

"That's the part for her," Bethany agreed. "It works best with a childish face. How old was your daughter when she played it, Brianna?"

"Fourteen at most. Oh, I'm sorry, Meghan. I don't mean to imply that you're a slow bloomer."

"I'm seventeen," Meghan gritted out, kicking the dirt. "I'll be eighteen in less than two months."

"I heard that you're going to be assisting Laitz with his illusions," Bethany said, breaking the embarrassed silence that fell over the group of women. "We all tried out for it before he left the troupe to become a court jester, but none of us could see the patterns he was talking about."

"I guess I was just lucky," Meghan replied, happy to talk about something other than her lack of matronly assets. "I lived all my life in a room with an arrow slit, so I'm used to seeing how the light interacts with things in the air."

"That must be it," the first woman agreed. "None of us are castle folk, though we don't hold it against you."

"Do you have anything in mind for a second job?" Bethany asked. "Rowan insists that everybody try acting and the sooner the better, because you never know if you have the knack for it until you get up in front of an audience. But this is a family business, and he'll give you credit for babysitting if you aren't up to performing."

A vision of herself emptying enchanted diapers for all of the babies in the troupe led Meghan to blurt out the first thing that came to mind.

"I was thinking of doing a magic show. You know, for children?" she concluded lamely, searching for approval in the women's blank faces.

Meghan wondered where that dumb idea had come from, and then she remembered that Bryan had been talking about it when they practiced magic on the road. He claimed that on Dark Earth there were people who pretended to be able to do magic in order to entertain children at birthday parties. It didn't sound as outlandish as his claims that there were famous magicians who could fill a theatre by sawing a woman in half or locking her in a box and making her disappear.

"A magic show for children," a deep voice remarked, and Meghan looked around to see that Rowan had been walking past the wagon just as she spoke. "Where's the entertainment value in that?"

"Uh, it's funny," Meghan replied desperately. "The magic never works out right. See, like I reach into a hat to pull out a rabbit and instead I get a rattlesnake." She almost bit her tongue off to punish it the moment the words left her mouth.

"Snake handling, I like it. Let me know when you have the act ready to go and we'll give it a try. In the meantime, start learning the lines for Elstan. It's always a big draw at the harvest festivals."

Bethany patted Meghan's hand and the others looked on sympathetically as the troupe leader continued on his way.

"What's wrong with playing Elstan?" Bryan asked. "I think it's great you're getting a part."

"Elstan is a boy. He's a prince in Old Land who dresses as a girl to escape a siege and bring help, but he's captured by a captain in the attacking forces who falls in love with him thinking he's a brave girl. It's a tragedy."

"Sounds more like a comedy. I bet you have fun with it."

"But he's a BOY!" she repeated emphatically.

"Playing a girl," Bryan reminded her. "And as long as your baron has a reward out to bring you back, it's a great disguise."

"But Rowan thinks I look like a boy," she reiterated, stamping her foot and wondering if Bryan had always been this dense. "How do you think that makes me feel?"

"Well, why did you volunteer to do a snake handling show if you're afraid of snakes?" Bryan countered. Prior to dying on Dark Earth, his experience with the opposite sex had been limited by his lack of social skills, but he remembered some of the guys on his virtual gaming team complaining about the illogical actions of their girlfriends. The only thing he had gathered from her description of the afternoon was that she was sensitive about her measurements.

"You're not helping," Meghan hissed between clenched teeth. "I need to come up with an act that will make Rowan forget about snakes and get me out of playing Elstan. It's your fault that I'm in this mess. Tell me what you remember about the magic shows you watched on Dark Earth."

"Well, the magicians were usually men. The women were assistants, and they always wore black nylons and skimpy tops, so you could see their, uh…" he trailed off, intentionally looking away from Meghan.

"Don't you start in on me about my lack of so-called assets, I've had enough of that for one day," she snapped at him. "And what was that first thing you said the women wore? I didn't get the word."

"Nylons," Bryan repeated, but her blank look showed that it wasn't a word covered by Hadrixia's translation magic. "Uh, panty hose."

"You mean skin-tight pants? Only men wear hose."

"On Dark Earth, only women wear hose, and they're kind of see-through."

"Now I know you're making it up. Why would a woman wear see-through pants?"

"I don't know," Bryan replied in frustration. "Ask a woman. Now that I think of it, I did see a female magician once on a late-night show, but all I remember is that she was nearly naked."

"That's just great. I can go out there in my underwear and then everybody can tell me how much I look like a boy."

"Forget about the costume for now and focus on the show," Bryan said. "What sort of magic do people here laugh at?"

"Nobody laughs at magic. That would be like laughing at, I don't know, a dragon."

"So choose between playing a boy and snake wrestling."

"Wait a minute," Meghan said, brought up short by her limited options. "How would the audience know that the magician was supposed to pull a rabbit and not a snake out of the hat in the first place?"

"The funny magicians talk all of the time, and they never look at what they're doing," Bryan explained. "You'd say something like, 'I am now going to pull a rabbit out of my hat,' but instead, you'd pull out a snake and not even notice. Imagine you were looking at the audience and telling some story about how you've had the same rabbit for years and how he saved your life by nibbling on your ear to wake you when the room was on fire. While you're talking, you pull enough of the snake out of the hat for people to see a rabbit-sized lump in its belly." Bryan stopped and laughed at the scenario he'd described.

"That's not funny. How can anybody laugh about a poor loyal bunny getting swallowed by a snake?"

"People aren't laughing at the bunny. They're laughing at the magician."

"So you're saying, it's really me they'll be laughing at and not my magic?"

"Right. You said yourself that magic isn't funny."

"I wonder if I'll have to cut my hair to play Elstan," Meghan said mournfully.

"Why don't we stop at any of these villages?" Bryan asked Simon as they walked along behind the props wagon that doubled as the stage master's home.

"Delay would cost us more than the profit. By the time we set up, put on two shows and break down, you're talking about losing at least two full days. Half of the audience in these villages is kids who get in for free, and the adults with coins to spare save them for visiting the festivals. Besides, the villages get plenty of bards and minstrels, and it wouldn't do to poach on their living."

"Rowan said that we'd move south ahead of the snow, but it looks to me like most of the fields we're seeing have already been harvested. If we arrive at the festival tonight and play for a week, we'll never get to the next one in time at the rate we're moving."

"The northernmost festival is the only one that really starts right after the harvest," Simon explained. "New Land doesn't have the population to support enough players and merchants for everybody to hold festivals all at once. By the time we get to the southernmost dukedom in the kingdom, it's two months since they brought in the corn. We do a week on the road and a week at each festival, so with the difference in latitude, we get to all five of them. Some of the farmers blow all their money at the local castles before the festival reaches the south, but most of them wait."

"So the harvest festivals aren't really about farming, they're about business and entertainment."

"There's always plenty of trade in livestock," Simon corrected him. "Farmers also exchange seeds, sell the animals they don't want to feed over the winter, and buy oxen and draft horses they'll need for the spring planting. The only thing you don't see much of at harvest festivals is selling the harvest because that's all done at the local castle markets."

"Were you born on a farm?" Bryan asked.

"Born and raised. But I had three brothers ahead of me to take over the farm when my father was ready to call it quits, and I had bigger things in mind for myself in any case. I took the king's silver and went for a soldier the day I turned sixteen."

"I thought the soldiers all belonged to the local barons."

Simon turned his head to look at Bryan. "Are you sure Castle Trollsdatter is part of the kingdom?"

"We're way up north," Bryan said, improvising an answer he hoped the man would accept. "Beyond the Five Lakes nations."

"Ah, so you're actually under the authority of the Old Land king," Simon said, nodding. "I heard there were a few baronies up there with independent charters that never joined the new kingdom. The barons down here all swear fealty to the five dukes, and the dukes owe their loyalty to the New Land king. Each castle maintains its quota of soldiers for local defense and sends regular allotments to their duke. The dukes provide men for the king."

"If they're all on the same side, why do the barons fight each other?"

"They're only on the same side if the king declares war against the natives, and that hasn't happened in my lifetime. Otherwise, the barons fight the other barons, and once in a while, the dukes fight the other dukes. It keeps everybody in practice and makes spaces for the new recruits."

"Why don't the dukes set up their own kingdoms?" Bryan asked.

"It's been tried, but the king and the other dukes put a quick end to it. You'd have to get two or three of the dukes to agree to a new king to make a contest of it, and for the ones who are going to remain dukes, what's the point?"

"How many battles have you been in, Simon?" Bryan asked.

"Oh, maybe forty, if you include the small ones. You have to figure on at least two a year, and I was twenty years in the service before Phinneas convinced me to quit."

"And how many of the young men who joined at the same time as you stayed in longer?"

Simon shook his head. "You should have asked how many of the young men who didn't quit after a year or two survived. I lasted longer than any of the boys I joined with who tried to make a career of fighting."

"Even with all of the healers? I'm sorry if I sound stupid, but we just didn't have many battles at Castle Trollsdatter. There wasn't anybody to fight, other than, uh, native raids."

"Healer can't put a man's head back on his shoulders, fix an arrow through the eye or a spear through the heart," Simon explained. "Healer can't uncook a man's flesh after he's been roasted by a war mage's fireball, or repair his chest after a catapult projectile crushes it in. Healers are best at broken bones and stab wounds that don't kill you on the spot. A really good healer can handle belly wounds and reverse the flesh rot if you get help in time."

"You said you stopped your own bleeding when you lost your fingers. Can all soldiers do that?"

"A man would be crazy to go for a soldier if he couldn't do that much, but stopping the bleeding from a lost finger isn't the same as healing a deep wound. When things get bad, there are never enough healers to go around, and since the serious cases take more time and magical energy than the easy wounds, the healers concentrate on the men they can get back into the battle line."

"So how does a man like Phinneas last so long?"

"He's practically a war mage," Simon replied. "I've seen him stop an arrow a hand's-breadth from his face, and his counter-fire technique is as good as it gets. If he had a little more natural capacity he'd be a mage, but he makes up for it with his soldiering skills. You know the king wanted him for war master."

"I heard he turned the king down because he's loyal to the baron."

"Is that what they're saying?" Simon laughed and clapped his hands several times. "Phinneas doesn't care one bit for the baron or his family, but he positively despises the king."

"You should practice strengthening magic," Meghan told Bryan as they pitched the two-man tent from the troupe's seemingly endless supply of camping gear. Everybody except for Laitz had assumed a lover's spat was at fault when the two slept in their separate pack-tents their first night on the road with the players. After Rowan jokingly awarded them with the "honeymoon" tent, they both understood that pretending to be married required pretending to sleep together.

"Why? Simon says I've already got more endurance than anybody he's trained."

"However strong eating twice as much as the other men is making you, you never know when you'll need more. Along with good blood clotting, strengthening magic is an absolute requirement for soldiers."

"I can't see myself being strong, so how can I learn it?"

"Just pick up a flour barrel and pay attention to how your muscles feel as you lift it. Repeat it a few times and say, 'strengthen' or 'strong' as you do it to help fix the feeling in your memory. Once you get good at it, saying the word and drawing on your magic will add that much power to whatever you're doing for as long as your capacity holds out."

"I don't say anything when I bring out my fire or levitate the ring," Bryan protested. "And I haven't seen other people muttering to themselves when they do magic, except for you."

"Well maybe you're just smarter than I am," Meghan retorted angrily, turning her back and ducking into the freshly erected tent.

"I didn't mean it that way. I was just saying." Bryan stepped back from the tent and tried to look busy as a few of the troupe's women walked by with buckets of water on their way back from the stream.

"Isn't that cute," one woman said to the others in a stage whisper. "They start fights before bed just so they can make up."

Bryan waited until the women were out of sight before cautiously lifting the tent flap. "Simon was explaining to me today about how the kingdom worked and I didn't understand any of it. Do you know who any of these dukes are?"

"Are you going to sit and pay attention if I explain, or are you going to be looking for an excuse to escape, like I'm a spider who's trapped you in a web?"

"I want you to teach me," Bryan said, trying his best to sound sincere.

"Five dukes," Meghan said, holding up her left hand with the fingers spread out. Then she began counting the dukes off like a to-do list, folding fingers as she went. "Their castles are all close to the coast, except for the northern duke, the Red Duke, whose castle is on a hill or a mountain overlooking a river. The Green Duke has a castle overlooking the ocean, where there's a river mouth and a port. The Blue Duke is a few days further south, just across from King's Island, which has rivers on both sides emptying into the sea."

"They're all named for colors?" Bryan interrupted.

"They have names, but their armies wear different armbands and that's how everybody keeps them straight. The Black Duke's castle is on a river that runs into a large bay. The White Duke's castle is on a really large ocean bay, or at least that's how it looks on the map in the baron's library."

"I wish I had seen that map," Bryan said. "Everything is starting to make sense. I don't know about the Red Duke's castle, maybe it's at the Connecticut river on Dark Earth, but I'll bet the other four locations are the same as major port cities we have. I wonder why Boston didn't make the list."

"I think the native name for the next major river to the east might be something like you said," Meghan mused. "But why would Dark Earth's people build cities around ocean ports if they have contraptions that fly through the air?"

"That's all recent, the cities have been there since horse and wagon days."

"You mean your mages gave up magic six thousand years ago but it took them almost all that time to learn new ways of doing things?"

"Most of what I see here might have fit right into my world a few hundred years ago," Bryan admitted. "I guess there was a lot of resistance to change."

Bryan let his sword fall and pointed at the sky.

"I've seen that hawk before. It was watching us on the road before we joined up with you."

"Gods, boy. I can barely see a moving dot under the cloud and I'm half inclined to think that it's a speck of dust in my eye. And you can recognize the blasted bird?"

"Same one," Bryan affirmed. "Wait, it's going into a shallow dive now."

"At us?" the old soldier asked, squinting at the sky.

"It's heading somewhere up ahead of our wagon train. I'll go tell Rowan."

After a moment's thought, Simon said, "It's probably just Storm Bringer then," but Bryan had already put his words into action and was running past the startled members of the troupe on his way to the lead wagon.

The young man's haste had less to do with the reappearance of the hawk during their morning travel rest than with the fact that he was beginning to dread his practices with the stage master. In just five days of training, he had grazed the grizzled veteran numerous times, and inflicted several deep bruises with the dull sword that required magical healing. His teacher was pleased that Bryan was improving so quickly, but it was the trainee's inhuman speed that accounted for most of the progress.

When Bryan braked to a halt in front of Rowan, the leader of the players immediately demanded, "Did you kill him?"

"What? Simon? No, he's fine," the student swordsman replied when the meaning of Rowan's words sank in.

"I watched you practicing earlier and I think that's enough of that. Tell Simon he can continue teaching you the forms, but he'll be no use to anybody with his ribs staved in, so from now on you'll take your practice with me."

"I'll tell him, but that's not why I ran up here," Bryan said, relieved to find that he wouldn't become the accidental murderer of a man with grandchildren. "I saw a hawk following us, and it suddenly went into a dive towards just ahead there."

"They often circle above us and watch for prey that we startle into fleeing," Rowan told him. "What makes you think it was following us?"

"I can just tell," Bryan insisted. "I saw the same hawk last week, and Meghan said it was probably controlled by a shaman."

Rowan studied the sky and nodded in approval. "Then that will be Storm Bringer. He must have finished with the harvest early this year, so he's come to meet us on the road rather than at the first festival. I'll bet he's waiting just over the next hill."

"You have a shaman who's a farmer working for you?"

"He's not a farmer, boy. If he was born to our people, he'd be one of the most powerful weather mages in New Land, maybe Old Land as well. The natives do things differently though, and they don't specialize as much as we do."

"So he predicts the weather? I wondered how you got by at festivals without a giant tent."

"Weather predictions? Performing inside a giant tent?" Rowan burst out laughing so hard that several of the troupe's members who had gathered around the front wagon during the travel break stopped talking so they could hear what was so funny. "Did you fight your wars under tents at Castle Trollsdatter when your weather mages predicted rain?"

The line brought a laugh from the men near enough to hear, all of whom Bryan had come to realize were ex-soldiers. He had yet to see the troupe perform, but Meghan had told him that a couple of the men played all of the principal male roles, and the rest only participated in action scenes or in non-speaking parts. It was common to see the women and the older children teaching each other lines from the troupe's standard plays as they walked along, but the men mainly talked about the castles and armies, sometimes changing the subject when Bryan approached.

"If he's not a farmer, why did you say he must have finished the harvest early?" Bryan asked.

"He holds off the rain clouds so the farmers can get the crops in and dry their hay. We travel a week for each week we play, and the festivals don't change their dates for the weather, which makes Storm Bringer the most valuable individual in the troupe. I remember one year that people packed our shows just to get out of the rain."

Bryan wanted to ask for details about the shaman's weather-control capabilities, but he saw Meghan walking up to find out what was going on and clamped his mouth shut.

"Your husband was just explaining to me how the people where he comes from pay somebody to tell them what weather is coming," Rowan told the girl, struggling to keep a straight face.

"He must have been trying out material for my magic act," Meghan explained hastily. "Wouldn't it be funny if I told the children I could predict when the weather would be sunny, and then a little cloud came and rained just on me?"

"Just in case that doesn't work out, have you memorized the part for Elstan yet?" Rowan inquired.

"I could play it in my sleep," Meghan replied sourly.

"Why don't you run through it with me while we walk?" Rowan raised and dropped his arm, and the wagons began moving forward again. "I'll do all the other parts, but you pay attention too, boy. The play works best when there's real chemistry between the leads, so I want you to start learning the captain's lines."

A giant boulder left behind by a retreating glacier forced a sharp curve in the road, and Storm Bringer seemingly materialized out of the woods a wagon's length ahead of the column. A hawk was perched on a leather shoulder protector built for the purpose, but the shaman was otherwise dressed in the manner of the natives, in deerskin breeches and moccasins. He wore a necklace of shells and bones across his bare chest, but a castle-style pack lay at his feet.

"Our paths cross again," Rowan called to the shaman. The encounter brought a merciful end to his interpretation of the captain's protestation of love to Meghan, who was playing Elstan's part of a boy disguised as a girl. "You made good time to catch us this far inland."

"Weather didn't cooperate," Storm Bringer replied with a shrug. "Tough to sell your people protection from the rain when there wasn't a cloud on the horizon."

"Why didn't you make some rain and then sell them your services?" Laitz asked. The illusionist had come forward in search of his assistants and fallen in alongside Bryan to see how Meghan performed her lines.

"I don't squander my magic that way," the shaman replied scornfully. "Have you made any progress with your dragons?"

"I'm getting there," Laitz said. "With these two youngsters to assist me, I think I might manage a dragon duel."

"Any news from the south?" Rowan asked Storm Bringer, who took his place walking alongside the leader of the troupe.

"The usual wars and sieges. The castles are cold in the winter, they stink in the summer, and they're crowded year-round. Your barons and dukes tell your people they need castles and armies for protection from us, but the only threats you face are from the soldiers of the other castles."

"You'll get no argument from me," Rowan replied easily. "Let me introduce you to the two newest members of our troupe. The short one is Meghan and the tall one is Bryan."

"We saw your hawk last week," Bryan said, staring accusingly at Storm Bringer.

"It might have been a different bird," Meghan interjected, stepping forward and offering an apologetic curtsey.

"I sent her ahead last week to scout for Rowan," the shaman explained, looking amused rather than intimidated by the naked distrust radiating from the young man. "She shared a vision of two people ducking into a field to avoid some horsemen, and I wondered if they could be the same youngsters who are being sought by everyone. I encountered a patrol of king's men on my way here and the officer told me that a young mage pretending to be a magicless girl had brought down the Castle Refuge tower with just a word."

Meghan's eyes went wide and she stepped back uncertainly, but Rowan and Laitz seemed unsurprised by the news.

"You know the king, always after something he shouldn't be," Rowan replied without breaking stride.

"Come with me and we'll smoke a pipe," Laitz added, taking a friendly grip on the elbow of the shaman, with whom he was obviously well acquainted. "We're interrupting an important artistic rehearsal."

"Try the short one as Elstan," Storm Bringer suggested over his shoulder.

"Rowan is giving your husband a workout, so we'd better start without him," Laitz told Meghan. "Anyway, I suspect he's had more time for practicing illusions than you since he's already mastered the wing beats."

"He doesn't practice at all unless you bribe him with food," Meghan complained. "He's just a fast learner."

The illusionist raised an eyebrow but didn't comment. Both of the young people had progressed much farther than he had hoped, but in different ways. Meghan was proving to be an excellent observer who could imitate Laitz's technique down to the finest level of detail, while Bryan seemed to be endowed with an excess of magical energy that allowed him to overcome every obstacle through brute force. It was the teacher's experience that in magic, as well as in life, brute force trumped technique nine times out of ten.

"I want you to work with colors today," Laitz continued, handing the girl two small pouches. "Use the bands to strap these to the undersides of your wrists. You'll wear long sleeves when we perform, and by turning your hands up like this," the illusionist paused and demonstrated, "while waving your arms, you'll release particles of colored dust. I designed the bags to let out a fixed amount with each pass."

Meghan secured the pouches in place and her instructor showed how bending back the hand at the wrist puffed out a small amount of colored dust. The new complication took all of her concentration, and soon she had managed a brilliant green dragon, which awkwardly exercised its wings without making any forward progress.

"Excellent," Laitz said approvingly. "Now release some powder from the other pouch and let's see what you can do with it."

As Meghan shook out some of the red dust, the slight disturbance of the air caused by the movement of her arms sent a ripple through her carefully constructed illusion.

"Don't worry about that," her instructor hastened to tell her. "To an audience seated more than a few paces away it just makes the illusions seem more lifelike."

"How do I keep the dust from becoming visible before I need it?" she asked. Her dragon looked like it was blushing as she moved one color of dust through the other.

"Normally I'd let the red out first and build the green around it before bringing up the light," Laitz explained. "That's good, let it out in a concentrated stream."

Meghan's dragon opened its reptilian mouth and a stream of fire shot out. She was so amazed by the sight that she lost her concentration and the whole illusion collapsed into a muddy mess.

"Is the dust expensive?" she asked Laitz. "Can I try again?"

"I make the dust from anything that can be mashed into a fine powder," the illusionist said. "Once you start experimenting with preparing colors yourself, you'll find it becomes addicting. Just make sure you grind a little up and sniff it before you get carried away making a whole batch."

"You worry about the smell?"

"Nothing ruins an illusion faster than a sneeze," Laitz informed her.

"That was some workout," Hardol told Bryan, clapping the sweaty young man on the back. "I'm usually the one stuck keeping Rowan in practice but you're welcome to the job. You're certainly up to it."

"I thought my sword would break," Bryan admitted. "Look at all the notches he put in the edge. Can I get this fixed, or will I need a new blade every time I duel him?"

Hardol laughed and clapped Bryan on the back again. "You're funny. A few of us are tapping a keg on the second wagon and we've been waiting to have a word with you."

Bryan willingly followed the older man from the impromptu practice area next to the road back towards the wagons. It was the first time Hardol had spoken to him, and he wasn't going to blow the opportunity to finally get to know some of the former soldiers who had ignored him to this point, even if it meant missing his regular evening session with Meghan and Laitz.

"Did he wreck your sword every time you dueled him?" Bryan asked his new friend.

"My blade is enchanted, same as Rowan's, though you have to use your own magic to keep the edge. You really are new to the fighting business."

"Enchanted, I should have thought of that," Bryan said. "So were all of you soldiers like Simon?"

"Not like Simon. The rest of us got out while we still had all of our fingers," Hardol replied, but the jest carried an undertone of sadness. "Soldiers in this land are like grist for the mill. You might avoid getting ground up for a while, but if you stay in too long, it always ends the same way. Simon served for more years than any of us, despite the fact he's not that strong, magically speaking."

"You must be thrilled that the new kid is giving you a chance to rest up, Hardol." The man who spoke handed each of the newcomers a brimming tankard, then resumed his seat on the wagon's tongue. "If I'm not mistaken, Rowan may actually have broken a sweat towards the end there."

"I thought he was going to chop me in half," Bryan confessed. "With Simon, I was always worried about accidentally hurting him because I didn't know what I was doing. With Rowan, I felt like I was fighting for my life."

"He doesn't play around," one of the other men commented, which struck Bryan as a bit odd, given that they were a troupe of professional players. "Is it true that you and your wife are on the run from the king?"

Bryan almost choked on his ale, but Meghan had prepared him for the question and he replied, "Not that I know of. I've never seen the king, or even a duke for that matter. My wife is the one who knows about that stuff."

"But you acknowledge the king as your sovereign," Hardol pressed, fixing the young man with his eyes. The four other men near the freshly tapped keg fell silent, and Bryan realized they were all waiting for his answer.

"I don't remember voting for him," Bryan replied cautiously. Apparently it was the right answer because the men all laughed and repeated his words like he'd invented the punch line to a new joke. Somebody took his tankard and tossed it to the tap man to be refilled, and the others crowded around to introduce themselves.

"I'm Grey," a heavily scarred man only a few years older than Bryan told him. "We knew Phinneas wouldn't send us a king's man, but we have to be careful."

"Jomar," announced a small man with a mouth full of crooked teeth and a bandolier of throwing knives across his chest. Bryan had seen him casually bring down small game for the communal pot with his knives.

"Theodric," a large man introduced himself, returning Bryan's refilled tankard at the same time. "The five of us are the group leaders, but if things get rough, just stick to Rowan for the time being. We'll figure out where to put you after the festivals."

Bryan nodded. He didn't have a clue what it was all about, but he read their body language well enough to realize they had decided to accept him into something, at least provisionally.

"Chester," the last man said, grasping Bryan's hand. He was the handsomest of the players, around thirty years old, with piercing blue eyes and a long black ponytail that reminded Bryan of a Hollywood pirate. Meghan had told him that Chester played the lead male role in practically every play the troupe put on. "Now that I've seen you fight I'm nervous about playing the captain to your wife's Elstan. Are you sure you don't want to give it a shot?"

Meghan was not a happy camper when Bryan finally crawled into their tent reeking like a brewery. "You skipped our practice to get drunk? How can you smell so bad after I got your clothes fixed for you? Didn't you hop in the stream after your training with Rowan?"

"It wasn't training," he groaned, turning around on his hands and knees and beginning to crawl back out of the tent. "It was that giant beating me down with a sword until I thought my arms would fall off."

"Where are you going now?" the girl demanded.

"To wash, and then to get something to eat. I'm starving."

"I stopped at the cook wagon when they were closing down and picked up a pot of leftovers. I'll warm it up while you jump in the stream."

"Couldn't you just look at me and mutter 'clean' or something?"

"Just go," she told him, adding a playful push on his backside with her foot, but her voice had softened since she realized he was more exhausted than inebriated. Meghan crawled out of the tent after him and decided to reheat the food the simple way, using her own magical fire. By the time Bryan returned from the stream, she had the stew pot bubbling and placed it on the ground to cool a bit.

"Do you know anything about enchanting swords?" Bryan asked, sounding much more awake after his late-night dip in the cold water. "Rowan put so many notches in my blade that it looks like a giant bread knife."

"Let me see it." Meghan accepted the scabbard from Bryan and pulled out a length of the blade to examine it. Like all of the men in the troupe, he kept the sword with him day and night now that they were on the road. "I can see why Phinneas gave you this sword. It's really a practice weapon and it's made to yield without breaking, but you wouldn't want to go into battle with it because it won't hold an edge. I can fix it for now, but we'll need to get you a real sword as soon as possible."

"What about the enchantment?" Bryan persisted. He tried to reach around her for the stew pot but she slapped his hand away.

"It's too hot," she chided him. "Most enchanted swords are just another form of magical fixing. I've never worked on one myself, but I could manage some basic protection that would be better than nothing. You want a blade that stays sharp, of course, but it's also about not getting broken by other enchanted swords. And I'll have to teach you how to maintain the strength of the enchantment with your own magic while you fight."

"Great. Something new to keep me distracted while I'm trying to avoid getting sliced in half," Bryan grumped. "Are some swords better than others?"

"Yes. There are famous weapons that serve as reservoirs and lenses for awesome amounts of magical energy, but they're usually wed to a particular family, with successive generations building up the enchantment."

Bryan lowered his voice and peered around in the dark. He couldn't make out colors, but with his vastly improved vision, it was like being out at dusk or dawn, rather than the middle of the night.

"There's something going on with these guys," he informed Meghan. "I don't know how they are at acting, but they're all too good for their jobs. It's like working in a tavern where the waiters are assassins."

"Huh?" The girl took a spoon of the stew, blew on it energetically, and managed to swallow it without burning her throat. "It's ready if you don't eat too fast."

"If I'm going to breathe fire one day, a little hot stew isn't going to hurt me," Bryan retorted, reaching for the pot. "What's it like with the women? Are they as tough as the men?"

"They aren't like castle folk," Meghan replied thoughtfully. "I've been spending so much time with Laitz that I haven't gotten a chance to know them that well, expect for Bethany, and she mainly talks about her baby. I've caught them a few times changing the subject when I approach, but we are new here, and it will take time to win their trust."

"After I finished getting beaten down with a sword, Hardol took me to meet four other men, who I guess are Rowan's lieutenants or something. I've never been in a military so I don't really get that stuff, but one of them told me that we should stick close to Rowan if things get rough."

"What things?"

"Well, the shaman said that the king has patrols out looking for a young couple, and everybody suspects that it's us," Bryan managed to reply through a mouthful of stew. "Can you fix my sword while I'm eating and we'll talk about this later?"

"They are the most gifted young people I've ever encountered," the shaman answered Rowan's question quietly. Then he lapsed into silence for a dozen heartbeats while the two men stared up at the stars. "The young man is like quicksilver, he changes even as I look at him, and the girl has a wall around her that my vision can't penetrate."

"Phinneas wouldn't have sent them if he didn't trust them with his life," Rowan said. "I put the boy through his paces with the sword. He barely knows the basic forms, yet his speed and strength would give him a chance against an average swordsman. He almost killed poor Simon within days of first holding a blade."

"His magic is something I've never felt before," Storm Bringer said. "It is not the energy of your people or my people, nor is it a mixture of the two. It's more like what I sense from a mountain lion or a bear."

"And the girl is strong enough to block your vision," Rowan prompted the shaman.

"I don't believe she's doing it consciously, though her magic must be strong to maintain the barrier against me. Somebody else must have put the block in place many years ago. We do the same thing with young children whose magical strength grows faster than their understanding, to prevent them from becoming a danger to those around them. The block must be placed by a close relative, usually a parent, and either it slowly dissolves with maturity or disappears when the child achieves some goal."

"And you're sure it's the king looking for them now?"

"The first few days it was just the people from her castle out for the reward money, to make her a prize for one of the baron's sons," Storm Bringer related matter-of-factly. "Then somebody got their messenger pigeons mixed up, and all of a sudden the king became involved. My agents don't know the precise instructions of the king's men, but the reward is fifty gold rings, so you're going to find out pretty quickly if all of your people are loyal."

"Fifty," Rowan groaned. "There's men and women who would sell their own children for that much. The king wouldn't offer enough to buy a productive farm on the off chance that the girl was as powerful as some rumors make her out to be. He's a greedy man but not a fool."

"I agree. If we can find out why he wants her so badly maybe we can use it against him. If we don't act this winter the opportunity may be lost for another year." The two men sat in silence for a while, and then Storm Bringer added, "I think I'll break with tradition this year and offer to help Laitz with his illusions."

"That's a good idea, get closer to them," the big man nodded. Then he barked a short laugh. "But not too close or he may swallow you whole. That one makes me look like a picky eater."

"Why do we need a stage?" Bryan asked. "If the audience sits on the slope so they're looking down at the play, what's the point of raising it up again?"

"First of all, not all of the festivals have a natural amphitheatre space," Hardol told Bryan, grunting as the balance of the timber he held shifted when the younger man hoisted his own end off the ground. "Second, some plays need the trapdoors, and the stage holds the frames in place for the curtain and backdrops."

"It's got to take at least a day to build a stage," Bryan argued, adjusting his hold on the heavy timber to make it easier to walk. "I know that Meghan went with Laitz and some of the others to perform in the market area and try to drum up a crowd for tonight. Won't the farmers be home in bed by the time we're ready?"

"We'll have it all put together well before supper," Hardol said. "Rowan hired a shipwright to build the stage so the joints all fit perfectly. You see the lines cut into your end?"

"Three of them," Bryan affirmed.

"The dirt crew leveled the corner sleepers and put the posts in place while we were unloading the wagon and laying out the timbers. Line up your mortise with the tenon at the back corner as I do with mine."

"My what with the what?"

"The rectangular hole you have your fingers in is a mortise. Take your fingers out of it and slide it down over the piece sticking up there, the tenon."

"Why didn't you say that in the first place," Bryan mumbled, moving his hands and lowering the timber onto the belt-high post. "Hey, if we're building it up off the ground like this, won't everybody be able to see underneath?"

"We hang skirts all around. Save your critique until it's finished."

Theodric and Bryan returned to the stack of timbers for the next structural member, passing three other two-man teams carrying their own beams on the short trip. In less time than Bryan could have imagined, he found himself climbing the pegs on one of the vertical members at the front of the stage, trailing the rope that would help him haul up the narrow top-beam. Before they finished hanging the lightweight curtain, the group of boys who were installing the planking on the stage completed their task.

"I guess you've done this before," Bryan said to Hardol. He couldn't help admiring the solidity of the structure and the speed with which it had come together without any tools, other than the mallets used to drive in the pegs that held the floorboards in place. "I can't believe it will come apart as quickly as it went together, though."

"It takes a little longer," the older man acknowledged. "The peg holes go all the way through so the boys have to drive them out from the bottom, but there are only two per board, so it doesn't take long. The fit is what makes it work. That shipwright Rowan hired specialized in building small boats that could be broken down and stored in the hold of a bigger boat for use in shallow water. Imagine the skill it takes to build boat kits that don't leak."

"Will you be performing tonight?" Bryan asked, as he headed back with Hardol to move the now empty wagon to their camp area.

"I couldn't act my way out of a sack," the ex-soldier admitted. "Half of us work crowd control at festivals. There are always men in the audience who drink more than they can handle, and then the costumes the women wear set them off. Have you seen Juliana and Nesta dressed as elf princesses?"

"The tall, blonde girls with the...?" Bryan made a lifting motion in front of his chest.

"Don't let Rowan see you do that," Hardol cautioned. "They're his daughters. Fortunately, they inherited all of their looks and acting talent from their mother. I've even seen noblemen throw gold on the stage, not that the girls would ever look to see where it came from."

"Noblemen throw gold on the stage?" Bryan repeated is disbelief. "Hey, if you need a volunteer to crawl under there and, uh, work the trapdoors or something, I'm your man."

"It's a dragon, Mommy!" screamed the little boy, bringing the fairgoers within earshot to a sudden halt.

Meghan couldn't help smiling at the child's excitement. She temporarily forgot her own embarrassment at being dressed as a boy in a doublet and short breeches with high boots, though she was thankful that the peaked cap allowed her to hide her hair rather than cutting it off. Laitz nudged her and winked, leading Meghan to expel a thread of red dust from the dragon's mouth.

The crowd's reaction was stunned silence, followed by a roar, and they pushed forward to get as close as possible to the three-sided booth that Laitz had erected from slender poles and blankets. The opening faced away from the sun, but a strategically placed slit in the back allowed a beam of sunshine through to backlight the illusions.

"Tonight, during intermission, the great illusionist Laitz and his assistants will present the first-ever performance of a dragon duel to be seen in New Land," Jomar shouted over the crowd. Meghan had always thought that Phinneas must be the loudest man on Earth when he used magic to enhance his voice and issue commands, but the small man with the throwing knives had the war master beat by a factor of two.

"What's the play?" somebody called from the crowd.

"We open after sunset with *The Stolen Twin*," Jomar thundered, and his voice must have carried for a hundred paces in either direction. "Tomorrow the early show will be *Elstan*, followed by a reenactment of the *The Duke's Uprising*, for which we will be joined by Brom's players, and then a second presentation of *The Stolen Twin*. All week, exclusively with Rowan's players. Laitz, The King of Illusions."

At a nod from her mentor, Meghan swept her dragon out of existence, and Laitz stepped forward, theatrically waving his arms about. A confused mass of half-formed shapes began to materialize in the beam of light filtering through the back of the booth. All of a sudden, the illusion snapped into focus for the audience as if a veil had been drawn from over their eyes, and they saw an impossibly detailed scene of a crowd of people.

"Look, it's us," a woman cried, gripping her husband's arm in excitement and pointing at a couple of figures in the illusion. Other members of the audience gasped and stared, while Meghan looked on in awe of Laitz's control. Then the scene wavered a few times before dissolving, and the illusionist let his hands fall and took a bow.

"Rowan's players. See us tonight at the West Amphitheatre," Jomar thundered. "Now move along and let somebody else get a look."

"How were you able to reproduce the crowd so quickly and in such detail?" Meghan whispered to Laitz. The people reluctantly began to disperse, helped along by scowls and shoves from Jomar.

"I didn't," the illusionist replied with a grin. "It's just a scene I've practiced over and over again so I can build it quickly from memory, like a song you know by heart. The figures are small enough that nobody can make out the faces. I just use dark dots for the eyes and mouths and match a color here and there. Somebody in the audience always believes they see themselves, and then everybody else goes along."

"Stop staring at Juliana," Meghan hissed at her supposed husband, who along with all of the males and not a few females in the crowd, was staring at Rowan's daughter in her scanty elf costume.

"I'm not staring at Juliana," Bryan retorted indignantly. "She's not even on the stage."

"Then stop ogling Nesta," Meghan insisted. She added a punch in the shoulder to prove she was serious, but their difference in height made it awkward and she ended up hitting his bicep. Then curiosity got the better of her, and she asked, "How can you tell them apart?"

"Juliana has a little mole on her left thigh and Nesta has one on her right thigh," Bryan explained. "Nesta's left ear is a little lower than her right ear, and Juliana's cheekbones are more prominent. I heard she was sick last week, so she lost a pound or two," he added in concern.

"What color are my eyes?" Meghan whispered sharply.

"Blue," he answered absently, before the edge in her voice sank in. "No, wait. Um, black?"

"Lucky guess. Are my ears pierced?"

"Sure, you wear earrings all of the time," Bryan bluffed.

The ferocity with which she dragged him away from their vantage point by the side of the stage informed him that he had guessed wrong. He hated to miss the final scene of the first half in which he heard the kidnapped twin was forced to perform her seductive elf dance for the evil sorcerer. But it was one of the troupe's most popular plays, so he was sure he would have plenty of opportunities to see it in the future.

Twenty paces away from the stage, Meghan pushed her potential dragon behind the props wagon. "How can I wear earrings all the time when I'm supposed to be a boy?" she demanded. "And don't tell me that men on Dark Earth wear earrings, I'm not having any of your lame excuses anymore. I know you look at me when we're talking, but you don't see me, do you? Not the way you see Rowan's daughters."

"Is this about the whole Elstan thing?" Bryan asked. "I thought you agreed that it was a great way to hide out."

"It is not about Elstan!" Meghan had to restrain herself from kicking him in the shins to make her point. "It's about us being in this together and everybody else believing that we're married. I do my part, but you wander around staring at pretty women like some sort of..."

"Guy?" Bryan interrupted. "Everybody in the audience was staring at them, and half of the troupe too. Didn't you see those outfits? It's like they weren't wearing anything at all."

"That's not the point. You're supposed to be loyal to me. I saved your life and in return you ruined mine," Meghan added, stifling a sudden sob. She really didn't know why she was getting so upset, since everything Bryan said was absolutely true.

The restrained emotion in the girl's voice accomplished what her arguments couldn't, and Bryan suddenly gathered her in his long arms.

"I'm sorry. I didn't realize I was hurting you. I'll, uh, stop looking."

Meghan was so surprised by Bryan's reaction that for a moment she let herself relax against his body, turning her head up to see if she could read anything from his face. She felt somebody's heart pounding and saw green fire dancing in his eyes as his neck bent and his mouth approached hers.

"None of that," she stuttered, shoving against his chest to put distance between them. He refused to release her and moved one of his hands to the back of her head to hold it in place. The heat from his body felt unnatural, and she wondered for a moment if she had discovered the secret to releasing his inner dragon.

"Hey, save it for after the show," Laitz said, tapping Bryan on the shoulder. "It's almost intermission and we've got to get ready. I was beginning to worry that the two of you came down with a sudden case of stage fright and ran off."

Bryan growled rather than replying, but the distraction was enough for Meghan to gain breathing room and get her mind working again. "Chill," she muttered, gambling on the fever-reduction technique Hadrixia had taught her. The older woman had once joked that it could also be useful in cooling unwanted amorous advances.

"Did you just put the whammy on me?" the young man asked incredulously. He felt like he'd been doused with a bucket of cold water, or maybe dropped in an icy lake.

"It's time for our show," Meghan said, trying to sound like nothing important had happened between them. She turned and followed Laitz back towards the stage.

"You just wait and see what happens next time you're feeling friendly," Bryan called after her. Then he remembered he was doing the lighting for the dragon duel and broke into an evil smile.

The audience oohed as a blue dragon, created by Meghan, materialized from the swirling dust. The illusion grew increasingly solid as Bryan amped up the intensity of the focused fireball he was maintaining in the hooded section behind the slit at the back of the three-sided enclosure.

"It's flying," a child in the crowd cried out as the blue dragon began to beat its wings, moving in a small circle within the space sheltered from the breeze. Then a larger, yellow dragon entered from the side as the blue flew past. The younger and more excitable members of the audience screamed warnings to the smaller dragon.

The head of Meghan's dust dragon turned on its long neck and looked back at the yellow, just as Laitz's creation opened its maw and let out a stream of red dust. Bryan further increased the intensity of his light orb, causing all of the colors to glow brighter. The stream of illusory fire missed the blue dragon as it folded its wings and dove. The yellow dragon stayed on its tail, and for several laps around the open booth, the dragons exchanged jets of flame, always with the large yellow in pursuit of the blue.

Then Laitz caused his dragon to shift its strategy and occupy the center of the airspace, where it hovered with strong wing beats while waiting for a chance to corner Meghan's tiring blue. Audience members who weren't queued up at the kegs for beer during the intermission offered expert combat advice to their blue favorite, which was especially useful as none of them had ever seen a dragon duel before. The red flames spouting from Meghan's dragon were growing weaker as she ran out of dust to release, and Laitz's yellow opened its mouth wide and darted forward.

At that instant, a giant green dragon, twice as large again as Meghan's blue, dove into the scene. It obliterated Laitz's yellow with a gout of real fire that incinerated the very dust of which it was formed. Then the newcomer flew directly at the blue and hovered above it, wings beating in unison as it tried to entwine its neck with that of the smaller dragon.

"It's a mating flight," somebody called out from the audience, and parents covered the eyes of their smaller children. Then the light source went out, dousing the illusion. The children begged their parents for coins to throw onto the stage.

As the men assigned as stagehands for the night quickly pulled down the sides of the booth to prepare the stage for the second half of *The Stolen Twin*, Laitz helped a somewhat dazed Meghan find her bearings.

"Pretty exciting for a first performance," he told her. "I'm not crazy about your husband going off script like that, but it worked. I couldn't have maintained the lighting, a dragon, and thrown real fire like that myself. He's got a lot of talent."

"Where'd he go?" Meghan asked, coming back to her senses and realizing that Bryan was nowhere to be seen.

"He's probably out in the audience trying to get a good spot to watch the second act," Laitz told her. "There's a scene at the end that always brings down the house when the free twin offers herself as a prize to the warrior who rescues her sister."

Meghan thought for a moment about finding and berating Bryan over his quickly broken promise. Then she remembered his hot breath on her neck as she turned her head to avoid his kiss, and the strange feeling she had when his green dragon had enveloped hers on the stage. Instead, she remained in the wings to watch the second act.

"A toast," Rowan shouted, pounding the table with his giant fist.

A dozen conversations came to a sudden halt, and members of the troupe rapidly refilled their tankards with whatever they were drinking. Bryan noticed that five of the men, including Hardol and Jomar, were standing at carefully spaced intervals around the area of tables that had been set out under the night sky. A sort of light yellow haze extended between the sentries to form a perimeter wall.

"To Juliana and Nesta," cried one of the few bachelors with the troupe, and a laugh went up as the revelers took a quick drink. Rowan glowered at the player, but the twins took the compliment in stride, inclining their identical blonde heads towards the young gallant.

"I was going to say, to the return of the prodigal son and the romantic young couple he brought with him," Rowan finally made the toast, and then drained his tankard dry.

"Speech, speech," several of the troupe shouted out jokingly, but Laitz wasn't one to let an opportunity for attention go to waste.

"Since you insist," he declared, hopping up on his chair and striking a pose. His harlequin suit would have made him the center of attention in any other crowd, but the players were used to both his costume and his manner. Laitz raised his voice and continued as if they were all eagerly awaiting his words.

"First, I'd like to thank Rowan for being smart enough to take me back," he declared, drawing a series of hoots and catcalls. "Second, I'd like to thank Meghan and Bryan for making tonight's illusion a great success. They've only been at it for two weeks now, and I'll be surprised if they don't surpass me by the end of the season."

Meghan blushed as people turned to look at her and Bryan. She knew that when Laitz said "they," he was really referring to the stranger she had brought from Dark Earth, who once again had become a mystery to her. Was he serious about his feelings, or was he just inflamed by watching the twins and willing to turn to the most convenient woman, the one with whom she shared a tent.

"On the subject of our new members, I'm sure you've all heard the rumors," Rowan announced suddenly. His voice cut through the laughs and renewed conversations of the players who were ignoring the rest of Laitz's ad-libbed speech. "I don't have to tell any of you that troupe business is none of the king's business, but I want to remind you that a denial is as good as an admission in the ears of a Seeker. If anybody suspicious asks you about new members in the troupe, don't deny it or they'll know we're hiding something. Something else, I mean," Rowan corrected himself, drawing a big laugh from the troupe. "Either answer without lying or don't say anything at all. The Seekers know that they have no friends among traveling players."

"Stand down," Chester shouted, drawing his sword as he moved between Meghan and the soldiers sent to arrest her. "I intend to make Elstan my wife."

Despite the fact that everybody over the age of eight knew the story of the boy who had disguised himself as a girl in an attempt to slip through the lines and bring help, the audience let out a collective sigh of empathy.

"We can't do that, Captain," one of the men replied. "The baron will have our heads."

"I'll have your heads if you try to stop us."

"Let them take me," Meghan cried, attempting to make her voice as low as possible. It was just about right for an adolescent boy. "I've failed my family and everybody who depends on me. I deserve to die."

"Stand down," Chester repeated, pointing his sword at the men who were beginning to spread out to encircle the pair. "You've followed me through eight years of war, yet you would circle now to stab me in the back?"

"He's mad," declared the soldier who had spoken earlier to the others. "Ulric, we'll keep him engaged while you grab the witch who has stolen our captain's heart."

With that, all six men drew their weapons and advanced on the captain in a widening arc, while he backed away, keeping Meghan behind him. Realizing that the uneven odds could only result in one conclusion, Chester drew a dirk with his free hand, and with a cry of anguish, he threw himself at his men. In a matter of seconds, he parried several blows, ran the leader through with his sword, and stabbed his dirk in another man's chest. But he received a wound on the leg and limped heavily, struggling to retain his balance. The remaining four men surrounded the captain, who kept turning like a caged animal, his sword extended in front of him. Then Meghan leaped towards one of the soldiers and stabbed him in the side.

"Elstan!" the captain shouted as the wounded soldier turned on the girl. He ignored the three remaining swordsmen and

charged the man attacking Meghan, thrusting his sword through him. As he struggled to free the gory blade, two of the remaining soldiers fell on Chester and the third grabbed Meghan.

"Captain!" Meghan cried, and with a burst of superhuman strength, the captain left his dirk in one man's heart, slashed the other, and then brought the pommel of his sword down on the head of the man holding the girl. Fake blood released from hidden bladders covered them all at this point, and Chester dropped heavily to his knees, putting his head against Meghan's stomach.

"I would have slain every man in the army to protect you," Chester declared, letting his sword fall to the stage. "They've killed me, but let me taste your lips just once and I'll go to the afterlife in peace."

As the musicians launched into opening notes of "The Ballad of Elstan," Meghan turned her head toward the audience and made her tragic confession, "But I'm a boy." The music swelled, and the players all remained frozen in their positions until the coins began to rain down on the stage. Then they shrugged off their fatal wounds and stood up for a collective bow, after which they began gathering the coins, which included a number of silvers.

"Don't go away!" Jomar shouted, his magically amplified voice cutting through the applause. "We'll be playing *The Duke's Uprising* against Brom's troupe on this very stage after the break, followed by Laitz's *Dueling Dragons* and a second showing of *The Stolen Twin* this evening."

Meghan stumbled from the stage exhausted, clutching at the pendant under her boy's doublet for strength. She couldn't believe how much acting in front of an audience took out of her, and she hoped that she would have enough energy left for Laitz's show. More than anything, she wondered why Bryan wasn't there to support her. Then she spotted him out on the stage, picking up coins with both hands.

"You should eat more," Bryan informed Meghan on the last night of the festival. He licked his spoon clean after polishing off the kitchen wagon leftovers she had procured for him. "You wouldn't need to squander the magical reserves from your pendant all the time if you had more fuel in your stomach."

"If I ate like you, I'd look like I was carrying a child and then I couldn't play Elstan," she retorted. "Hey, that's an idea."

"A bad idea. Give me your pendant and I'll put a charge in it for you. I've got so much energy these days that I have to fight myself not to throw a fireball at the moon."

Meghan was so tired that she handed over her pendant without thinking about what she was doing. Before she could snatch it back, the bones in Bryan's hand suddenly became visible as the glow from the intense magical energy generated in his grasp penetrated his flesh. There was a loud crack, and the light went out like a candle doused by a tub of water.

"Oops," Bryan said, examining the pendant in the dim light from their campfire. "I think it broke."

"You broke it?" Meghan howled in disbelief, grabbing for the chain. "That pendant is the only thing I have from before I lost my memory. It can't break."

Bryan mumbled an apology as the girl examined the piece that remained attached to the chain.

"It still holds my magic." She breathed a sigh of relief and kindled a small light to examine the pendant closely. "It's lighter somehow, but the dragon emblem that was almost worn away looks new. How did you do that?"

"Uh, it's lighter because of this," Bryan said, showing her the piece of pendant that remained in his hand. It looked like a master craftsman had carefully sawed through the heirloom, producing a duplicate that was half as thick as the original. "It sort of split in two."

"Let me see that," Meghan demanded, snatching the piece from Bryan's hand and holding it next to her pendant. "It's not broken. It was originally made as two pieces and held together by binding magic. There's something inscribed on the hidden surface of both halves," she added excitedly. Then came a long pause before she admitted in disappointment, "I can't read it. The inscription must be in a secret mage language I haven't learned."

Bryan leaned in close and casually created a small illumination orb that cast a bright light on the engravings. "It's English," he said in surprise.

Meghan shook her head in irritation at the untranslatable word.

"The language I spoke on Dark Earth."

"That's impossible. What does it say?"

In Dragon's Lair, beneath the tower stair, your path is laid bare, the dragon's tooth is there.

"It's a riddle," Meghan proclaimed unnecessarily. "Dragon's Lair must be a castle if it has a tower, but I've never heard of it. Surely there's more to all that text than four short lines."

"The rest of it isn't English," Bryan admitted. "It reminds me of something, though. Wait, I've got it. I needed to tie a tie once for a funeral, and my dad told me to look in his old Boy Scout manual because he didn't remember how to do it either."

"How can you tie a tie? That doesn't make any sense."

"It's like a scarf for men. Nobody wears them anymore, except for job hunters and salesmen. Anyway, I think all of those little hieroglyphics are showing the steps for making a really complicated knot."

"How could I have missed that," Meghan exclaimed, staring at the two inscribed halves of the pendant. "It's instructions for untying a magical knot of concealment and protection. I'll bet we'll find it below the tower stairs of the castle."

"So I did good?" Bryan could smell the herbal-infused soap that Meghan had started using on her hair, and he snuck his left arm around her narrow shoulders.

"Don't bother me now. I have to memorize this and start practicing so I'll be able to do it quickly. The tower is at the center of every castle's defenses, and it's manned by soldiers day and night. We may come upon the castle as soon as we start traveling. I just don't know all their names."

Bryan stood up abruptly and stalked off in the direction of the wagons to see if the older men were drinking beer.

"Thank you," Meghan called after his vanishing back when she realized he was going. She didn't understand why he couldn't just sit quietly while she worked, and she missed the warmth that seemed to radiate from his body when they were together.

"Eighteen steps," Meghan complained to herself after counting the hand movements diagramed in the pendant. She crawled into the tent, secured the front flap, and began to practice.

Taking down the stage took a little more time than erecting it, but the troupe was back on the road before lunch on the day after the northern festival concluded. The King's Highway followed the river through a broad valley, and an ancient range of worn-down mountains encroaching on the river from both sides loomed out of the fog ahead. The native shaman walked along with Meghan and Bryan, giving them pointers about creating lifelike illusions.

"I'm still confused about the whole dragon thing," Bryan complained to Storm Bringer. "It seemed like half of the booths at the fair were selling stuff with images of dragons, but Meghan says that they're really just mages who take dragon form."

"Bryan!" Meghan cried hoarsely. A week of performing *Elstan* had taken its toll, especially since the part forced her to lower her vocal register to sound more like a boy pretending to be a girl.

"The young lady is correct," the shaman informed Bryan. "But the dragon forms taken on by those powerful enough to make the transformation are real. A mage who dies while transformed leaves the skeleton of a dragon, not a human. My own people haven't had a dragon in our midst for many generations, though there are several with the nations beyond the great river to the west. Our stories tell us that they were more numerous in the past, but new dragons stopped appearing many years ago, and the remaining dragons often fought to the death."

"Meghan said the scrolls tell the same story about dragons in Old Land," Bryan said, ignoring the girl's disgusted look. "Nobody else seems to talk about it much, though I've heard there are at least two dragons on the coast of New Land. If they're so powerful, why don't they rule as kings?"

"Being a king has its drawbacks," Laitz interjected. "For one thing, it ties you down to a court and all of the politics involved in running the kingdom. For another, it puts a huge target on your back for anybody else who wants to be king. And if you don't have any children, it means that one slip can end your family's rule."

"When a king dies without children, can anybody apply for the job?" Bryan asked.

Laitz and the shaman exchanged a look that was becoming quite common amongst members of the troupe when engaged in conversation with Bryan. One moment he seemed wise beyond his years, the next he asked questions you'd expect from a six-year-old.

"He's joking," Meghan said weakly, though that excuse had worn thin over the last two weeks. When Bryan began asking questions, the only way to stop him from making obvious mistakes was to change the subject. "What are those mountains ahead?"

"The peak to the left, which we'll be passing before the sun goes down, is known to my tribe as the Dragon's Lair," Storm Bringer replied. Meghan coughed loudly to cover Bryan's reaction to the name, and the shaman continued. "But as your people moved inland from the coast, they saw it as the ideal place for a castle to control the pass cut through the range by the river. We fought a war over the mountain and many lives were lost before a dragon became involved and put an end to it. The northern duke's castle, Eagle's Nest, is the result."

"The dragon sided with the newcomers?" Bryan asked.

"Not exactly," the shaman said with a smile. "The dragon took the mountain for himself and lived there for generations. My tribe will not go where a dragon has made its lair, so when he finally vacated, your people built the castle that stands there today."

The four walked along without conversation for a moment, though with the rattling from the wagons and the cries of the children, it was hardly silent. Then Bryan asked, "Am I the only one who's hungry?"

"Why can't we just walk around?" Meghan whispered for the third time. "We could enter through the main gate in the morning, when the carters arrive to remove the night soil."

"This cliff is a piece of cake," Bryan replied. "I could climb it in the dark with one hand tied behind my back."

"It is dark, and I had enough trouble getting up the lower slope, even with you dragging me along." She yanked on the rope that Bryan had fashioned into a harness for her to make her point, but he was too intent on studying the rock face to pay attention to her words or the tug on the coil around his waist.

"It's an easy climb to the bottom of the wall, with plenty of ledges for me to stop and haul you up. Once we get there, you can do that sticky thing to the end of the rope, and then I'll climb it and pull you to the top."

"That 'sticky thing' took months of studying spiders to learn," Meghan whispered at his feet. He'd started climbing before he even finished talking and was already well above her head. She stared nervously into the shadows above, barely able to make out his form against the overcast night sky. After what seemed like forever, she felt a short jerk on the improvised harness, and she grabbed on to the rope up high, to make sure she didn't flip over.

Bryan had found a spot to wedge his heels, and he rapidly pulled in the rope, one knot at a time. He knew he was much stronger than he had been before Meghan brought him to her world, but the ease with which he hauled the girl up the cliff surprised even him. In a quarter of the time it had taken him to climb the first section of the rocky face, he had his arms around her and was pushing her flat against the wall.

"Just wait here. I'll climb to the next ledge and bring you up."

"I can't believe I'm doing this," Meghan muttered. "I'm afraid of heights, you know."

"Don't look down," he advised her seriously, and began climbing again.

"I can't see that far anyway," she muttered. "Why do you think I save all of my castle escapes and cliff-climbing expeditions for dark nights?" Receiving no answer, she tried to make herself as small as possible on the narrow ledge. While waiting for the next undignified stage of her ascent, she concentrated on the rope, whispering encouragement to strengthen the fibers and repair any damage from scraping against the rocks.

After the twelfth portage, Bryan announced that they were almost to the wall and decided to take a quick break. The sky began to clear, and from the position of the Big Dipper and the North Star, she knew it was well past midnight. Then she glanced down and her knees buckled. If Bryan hadn't grabbed her arm, she would have fallen.

"Did you look down?"

She nodded weakly, her eyes clenched shut.

"And you say I don't listen," he chided her. "Anyway, start concentrating on getting the end of the rope ready so we can make it over the wall. It's not that high a throw. I could have done it with a grapnel, though it might have made noise."

"I'm not waiting on some ledge without a rope to hold on to," she whispered. Her fingers sought and found precarious holds on the rock face.

"It's my end of the rope we're going to levitate into position," Bryan said. "Don't be a baby, we're almost there."

He started climbing again, and after a long silence broken only by a small chip of rock plinking down the cliff, there was a jerk on the rope. Not opening her eyes, she let go of her hold on the mountain and grabbed the knot above her head. Forty powerful tugs later, she joined Bryan on a tiny outcrop below the base of the wall.

"Here," he said, offering her the end of the rope. "Tell it to cling or something."

Meghan opened one eye and saw to her relief that clouds had covered the moon again and she could barely see the outlines of the wall above. She grasped her pendant and muttered, "Spider silk."

Bryan nodded in approval, took the rope back, and tossed it up, staring after it. It came back down on their heads, and it took another spell from Meghan to get it unstuck from their hair.

"Why didn't your magic work when it was up there?" Bryan demanded.

"The rope end never touched the wall. You have to get the throw right or levitate it into place."

"I can't throw that high without a weight on the end, and it didn't levitate right for me," he complained. "You're going to have to do it."

"I have to be able to see it to levitate it. Wait, I have an idea."

"Are you nuts?" Bryan demanded when he saw what she was doing. "What if the cord breaks or if somebody sees and steals it?"

"The cord isn't going to break, and if somebody sees, losing my gold ring will be the least of our problems," Meghan replied. "Just do it."

As Bryan levitated the ring with the rope attached up to the top of the wall, she saw that the fire in his eyes wasn't just an illusion. A green glow was visible on the stones where he was looking.

"What do I do when it's in place?"

"Stop levitating it, and see if it stays."

Bryan went one better and pulled himself up a knot. "Good," he whispered over his shoulder. "But if it comes down and we lose our ring, it's your fault."

"*Our* ring?"

"There doesn't seem to be much going on," Meghan said, peering around the dim courtyard. The two invaders remained in the shadows at the base of the wall inside the castle, waiting to time the patrols that never came. "Maybe it's protected by magic."

"How often does a castle like this get attacked?" Bryan asked.

"I don't have a clue," Meghan admitted. "Castle Refuge was besieged once in the last seven years, but our baron was always making enemies. This is the northern duke's castle, and it may go for decades at a time without being attacked. Maybe longer."

Bryan straightened up, shaking free of Meghan's grip on his arm, and began striding towards the tower.

"What are you doing?" she hissed, catching up with him. "You're going to get us killed."

"I've got better vision and hearing than you, and I haven't seen or heard a thing since we got here," he replied quietly. "Maybe the guards are all at the front gate, maybe there are some in the tower, but I can hear hundreds of people snoring and not one conversation."

Meghan opened her mouth to argue, but realized she didn't have anything to say. She had rarely left her room at night after returning from work back home, and then only to visit Hadrixia. There were late feasts from time to time, but obviously, this wasn't one of those nights. Before she knew it, they were at the tower. The massive metal-studded wooden doors were closed.

"You know how to pick locks, right?" Bryan asked in a low tone.

"Did you try opening it yet?"

Bryan pushed on the right-hand door, and it yielded inward with a loud creak that told of insufficient lubrication.

"Who's there?" a voice called from somewhere above.

"Quick," Meghan said, slipping through the crack and pulling Bryan after her. "Make me a light so I can see what I'm doing."

A subdued globe of fire appeared floating above their heads, and Meghan squinted around the circular room at the base of the tower.

"The stairway looks solid at the bottom," Bryan observed. "But that doesn't make any sense, since the rest of the steps are on beams stuck into the walls."

A bell began to ring above their heads, and other bells rang in response. Bryan pushed the door shut, causing another loud creak, and then he slid the heavy bar into place. "I'll watch the stairs," he said, drawing his practice sword. "You work on the knot thing."

Meghan wondered for a moment how he thought they would escape with the door barred, but given that the bells had started sounding around the castle, she realized it was the only sensible thing to do. She approached the blank wall beneath the stairway where a door to another flight would appear in a multi-story dwelling and flew through the intricate hand motions diagramed on her pendant. Nothing happened.

"It didn't work," she shouted at Bryan.

"Try it again, go slower," he called back. Somebody began beating against the tower door with something heavy, probably the butt of a spear, and two arrows suddenly shattered on the floor, one of them leaving a bloody cut on Bryan's shoulder. Without thinking, he cast a fireball up the center of the circular stairwell. There was the sound of a trapdoor being pulled shut, and the arrows stopped.

"I know I did it right this time, but nothing's happening," Meghan said desperately.

"Maybe you have to say something, like, 'Open Sesame.'"

"What?" The reply was so nonsensical that Meghan halted her third attempt to make sure Bryan hadn't been hit in the head. The moment she dropped her hands so they were pointing down, the stone beneath her feet suddenly opened up and she vanished.

"I guess that counts as under the stairs," Bryan muttered as he dove into the passage after her.

"Stay out of the way," she warned him, after he landed with the crash of his drawn sword beside her. "I need to do the untying in reverse and put the stone back into place."

"Huh?" Bryan watched without understanding as Meghan went through another bout of hand waving. Suddenly, the light from the orb he had left floating above was cut off by the return of the rock slab, and they found themselves in pitch darkness.

"And give me back my ring," she added.

"Put it out!" Meghan hissed, as a suspicious glow began to form over their heads. "How many times do I have to explain it to you?"

"They aren't working in the dark up there, and I'm getting tired of listening to all that tapping," he retorted. "If there were any cracks in the rock, we'd see their light from above after sitting here in the dark forever."

"It's hasn't been forever, it's been like a half a short candle. It took a while for the watchmen from the top of the tower to work up the courage to come down and let the guard in after you tossed a fireball up there. But I guess you're right that we would have seen a light leak by now," she admitted. "Don't make it bright or you'll blind us."

Bryan immediately kindled a small orb and used the light to examine the thick slab of rock above their heads. "It looks almost real."

"It *is* real," Meghan replied, frustrated that Bryan needed to hear everything repeated at least three times before it sank in. "If it were an illusion or some other trick, anybody who stepped on it would have fallen through. The untying spell temporarily moves a section of the rock to a magically prepared place somewhere else, probably nearby. It takes a great deal of energy and skill to create this kind of doorway, I think it has to do with the weight involved. There's a balance between the two locations where the rock can exist and it doesn't require much work to move it back and forth, but…"

"Too much information," Bryan cut her off. He stood up and bumped his head on the rough-hewn ceiling. "Either we're in a tunnel or in a crevice that got roofed over. I don't see anything that looks like a dragon's tooth."

"It may be hidden," Meghan said, peering around in the dim light. "Is that the entrance to another chamber, or just a shadow?"

"Follow me," Bryan said, and crouching to avoid hitting his head again, disappeared through the opening. "The stairs are steep, so be careful."

Meghan created her own light and ducked through the opening after Bryan, pausing to look ahead. The walls of the new passage were glassy smooth, as if the tunnel had been melted through the rock, but a set of stairs had been cut into the floor. She counted them as she followed, ninety-four stairs in all, before the journey ended in what appeared to be a large natural cavern.

"There's nothing here but a giant slab, a bunch of bones, and a pile of old rags," Bryan complained from the middle of the space. He kicked at the offending garments, which sent up a cloud of dust and fibers.

"Bones? What kind of bones?" Meghan halted to wait for the answer.

"I don't know, animals I guess. I don't see any human skulls, anyway. Maybe the dragon's tooth is in with all the other bones and we're supposed to find it."

"Either those clothes are pretty old or they were never fixed," Meghan observed. She approached the pile and nudged it with her foot. "Is there something covered up here?"

"Let me in there," Bryan said, using the leg bone from what might have been an ox to prod the disintegrating textiles out of the way. "It looks like a roll of oilcloth—no, there's something sticking out the end. It's a sword!"

A moment later, he had unwrapped the scabbard and drawn the sword. He held it aloft, admiring the narrow blade that made his training sword look like a bludgeon by comparison. Meghan saw a faint green fire rippling in the polished surface that looked like it had just been delivered from the swordsmith.

"Are you doing that, or is the sword enchanted?" she asked. She had to repeat herself twice, nearly shouting the question the third time to get his attention.

"What? I'm not doing anything," he replied, fluidly working through the forms he'd been taught just two weeks earlier. "Is it really enchanted? What does it do?"

"Well, it's glowing, for one thing," Meghan pointed out. "I think its humming too. Can you hear that?"

"I can feel it," Bryan growled, cutting energetically at the air. Then he took an experimental slice at a pile of bones, and the blade slipped through so easily that it seemed as if the skeletal remains had parted of their own accord to make way. "Let's go."

"Go? Go where? We have to find the tooth."

"You keep saying I'm your dragon, so this must be my tooth. Now let's go see what it can do."

"Wait. Stop!" Meghan ran to get ahead and turned to face Bryan at the opening to the passage. "What are you going to do?"

"We're going back up there, and we'll see who's boss." His voice was low and threatening, and the hints of green fire dancing along the blade were increasing in intensity to match the flames in his eyes.

"No!" Meghan said, stretching her arms to fill the space so he couldn't brush past her. "They'll give up searching soon, if they haven't already, and we can sneak out without a fight. They probably think it was some kind of false alarm, with the drunk watchmen seeing things and firing arrows at shadows. Why are you so anxious to kill somebody?"

"Come on, let me past," Bryan pleaded. He was reluctant to force his way for fear he might hurt her in the process. "It's always hiding and sneaking around with you. I could take on the whole castle with this sword."

"Whether that's true or not, it doesn't mean you should," Meghan said. "Why do you think there are so few dragons left? According to the scrolls, fighting and killing became such a habit with some of them that either they destroyed each other or their behavior forced warriors and lesser mages to band together to hunt them. Even if your magic combined with that sword can make you equal to trained fighters, I don't want a dragon who falls in love with death. Besides, you'll just get a spear in the back."

"I'm getting really tired of you stopping me all the time," he grumbled, but the comment about getting stabbed in the back made sense. It was a long way from the tower to the wall, and he didn't have any reason to believe he could stop arrows like an experienced war mage. In truth, Bryan wasn't that anxious to kill somebody—he just wanted to try out the sword.

"Aren't you hungry?" she asked, relaxing her arms and shouldering off her pack. "I brought supplies."

By the time Bryan finished devouring everything in the pack, his mood improved markedly. The girl limited herself to a drink from the waterskin, but she wasn't the one who had climbed a cliff in the dark, not to mention hauling up her dead weight.

"My pendant said that our path would be laid bare," the girl said. "What do you think it meant?"

"The pendant was probably wrong."

"How can a pendant be wrong?" Meghan demanded. "It told us about the secret passage, showed me how to open the stone, and you found your enchanted sword."

"That's three out of four," Bryan responded, peering around the cavern. "There must be half a dozen tunnels leading out of here. We're already at the top of the mountain, so any of the uphill ones should come out somewhere."

"If they came out near the castle, somebody would have found them by now, and the sword wouldn't have been here," Meghan argued. She sifted through the mound of disintegrating clothes. "Are you sure there wasn't anything else?"

"Don't worry, I'll get us out of here. Just stay behind me and don't get freaked out if we run into a lot of bats."

"Bats? Hey, come back here."

"They won't hurt you, and we might not come across any if it's still dark out."

"Bryan!"

The young man came to a halt at her unusually sharp tone.

"What does this look like to you?"

"That's the oilcloth my sword was wrapped in," he replied in irritation. "You're going to pester me about littering in this dump?"

"And the map on it, with the instructions in your language?"

"Oh." Bryan returned reluctantly and looked at the oilcloth that Meghan spread out on the flat slab. He followed her finger to where it tapped on the text next to a drawing of a sword, and read out loud, "You are here."

"That's a good start. How about this path with the arrows?"

"Exit to river," he read, pointing in the opposite direction from the tunnel he had been about to try. "I guess it's over there."

"The rest can wait until we're back home," Meghan said, folding the oilskin and placing it in her now-empty pack. She frowned for a moment when she realized she had referred to their tent with Rowan's troupe as home, but she supposed it was the simple truth.

"Let's go," Bryan said, stalking off towards the tunnel entrance indicated by the map. If he was embarrassed at all by his prior attempt to lead them off in the wrong direction, he showed no sign of it. "Don't forget what I said about the bats."

"Now you're just trying to scare me," Meghan retorted. "If the tunnel is sealed, how can bats get in?"

"It's steep, be careful," he called back over his shoulder.

Meghan saw that he hadn't been kidding when she started down the tunnel, the floor of which consisted of long, slanted steps. She quickly became convinced that the original passage had been a narrow fissure, widened with magical fire, the melted rock pooling below and forming the oddly shaped stairs. The descent went on for what seemed like all night before she stumbled into Bryan's back while she was watching her feet.

"What is it?"

"Dead end," Bryan said, pointing out the obvious. "I guess your map isn't so smart after all."

"Let me see. It's probably just a plug stone, like in the tower."

"Then try your eighteen-step thing."

Meghan went through the motions calmly but nothing happened. "Open Sesame," she muttered, hoping that Bryan wouldn't notice her adoption of his nonsense phrase.

"It wasn't that," Bryan said, trying his best not to laugh at the flustered mage. "The rock disappeared when your hands pointed at the floor. Maybe it's the same thing here."

"But we're already at the bottom," she protested, lowering her arms. A moment later, she was underwater, choking. She panicked and started to flail about, barely aware of a large body hitting the water right beside her. Then she felt Bryan's strong hands around her waist as he lifted the whole upper half of her body above the surface.

"Are you alright?" he asked.

Meghan coughed up some water in response.

"We're just below an outcrop near the bank," Bryan told her. "If you had put your feet down instead of kicking, your head would have been out of the water. Remind me to teach you how to swim."

"Fish swim," she retorted when the coughing subsided. "Just hold me up while I close the stone. You never know if it will come in handy sometime to have a secret passage into a duke's castle."

Bryan lifted her high out of the river and set her on his shoulders. After the tunnel exit was closed, her weight helped him walk along through the water until the steep, rocky bank became climbable. The dawn was just starting to break when they reached the King's Highway, and the two were back with the players before the wagon train set off. Nobody asked about their sodden appearance, but everybody noticed that the young man now had two sword belts slung loosely over his shoulder.

Meghan lurched to the back of the props wagon and threw up over the tailboard. Her spew almost hit the two women who were walking right behind the slow-moving conveyance. She mumbled an apology, but Bethany and Dora, the seamstress, offered their congratulations.

"That will be the morning sickness," Dora informed Meghan. "Sucking on a hard candy can help. I'll ask the children if they have any."

"Congratulations," Bethany added. "I couldn't ride in a wagon at all when I was expecting Davie. You'll have to be more careful now."

"I'm not pregnant," the girl protested weakly. "It's just that I've never ridden in a wagon before. I didn't expect all the swaying."

"Whatever you say, dear," the seamstress replied, winking at Bethany. In her experience, the first child always came as a shock to young women. "I'll get the wagon to halt so you can climb down."

"No, don't," Meghan protested when the implication of the troupe's leading gossiper stopping the wagon train sank in, but it was too late. A minute later, as she climbed down with the help of Bethany, she almost fell on her face as the ground suddenly shifted.

"Get Faye," Dora commanded the other woman after one look at Meghan, who had turned white as a sheet. Bethany ran towards the rear of the wagon train and quickly returned with Simon's wife, the troupe's healer. Faye took Meghan's head in both of her hands and turned it to one side and then the other while looking in the girl's eyes.

"Have you been feeling sick recently?' she asked.

"She's expecting," Dora answered for the girl.

"I am not," Meghan asserted again, though her voice was still weak. She couldn't remember the last time she had felt so scared, unable even to maintain her own balance. "Where's Bryan?" she added without thinking.

"I'll get your husband," Bethany said, running off again.

Faye took one of the Meghan's hands and pressed it against the girl's own stomach while closing her eyes in concentration. A small crowd of women and children gathered around and watched.

"I'm sorry," Faye told Meghan. "You aren't with child yet."

"I know that," Meghan gritted out between clenched teeth. "I'm just wagon sick."

"In part," the folk healer told the girl. "There was also something in your left ear, but I think I moved it enough so your balance will return. Don't sleep on your left side for a while, and avoid submerging your whole head when you wash your hair."

"Oh," Meghan said in embarrassment, thinking about her early-morning dip in the cold river. She took an experimental step back, turned slowly, and breathed a sigh of relief. "I think I'm better now. I should have checked my ears first thing, but I guess I was too scared to think straight."

"You know something of healing?" Faye asked.

"I assisted the healer in our castle growing up. She was a sort of foster mother for me."

"I learned a few things from my mother, but she wasn't trained as a healer. I hope you can make some time to share your knowledge with me."

"Of course," Meghan said, relieved to see that everybody else had lost interest as soon as she recovered.

"Are you alright?" Bryan demanded, pulling her arm half out of its socket as he jerked her around to look at her.

"It's nothing," Meghan said, secretly pleased by the look of worry on his face. "I just have to keep my head out of rivers for a few days."

The wagons halted for the evening at the edge of a field with plenty of wild grazing for the draft horses. Rowan gave Bryan the nod to join him for an evening training session. The two stopped at the props wagon to don mail shirts, hooded garments constructed from light chain links with three-quarter-length sleeves. Most of the men and boys who weren't busy doing something else tagged along to watch as Rowan selected a place.

"I see you found yourself a new sword," Rowan said, glancing at the fancy scabbard Bryan balanced over his shoulder with his right hand on the hilt. "Last-minute purchase at the festival?"

"I sort of found it. I mean, it was left for me. From my wife's family," Bryan hastily amended himself.

"If the blade matches the scabbard, it would be a shame to damage it in practice. Mind if I take a look at it before we begin?"

At first Bryan bristled at the suggestion, but then he remembered that he didn't know the first thing about enchanted swords. The last thing he wanted was to get a notch in the beautiful blade while sparring with the powerful giant whose own sword was obviously of the highest grade. He reluctantly removed the weapon from his shoulder and passed it to Rowan.

The leader of the troupe pulled a short length of the blade out of the scabbard and examined it closely. "Beautiful work. This is from Old Land, the imperial armory. This blade could easily be a thousand years old. Does it sing for you?"

"Sing?" Bryan thought for a moment. "I guess it hummed a little when I first drew it."

The men gathered around them exchanged significant looks, and Jomar gave a low whistle, clapping the young man on the back.

"Looks like you're the one who's going to have to worry about getting dings in your sword," Hardol said to Rowan in a joking tone.

The large man snorted. "Old Slayer will hold her own. Make room for us."

The men and boys backed away, forming a circle around the small patch of sand by the riverbank that Rowan had chosen. Bryan drew his sword and tossed the scabbard to Hardol, then he waited for his opponent to make the first move. He heard his sword humming like a tuning fork, but nobody else showed any sign of hearing it.

Rowan usually opened their duels with a bull's rush, after which Bryan was lucky to launch one offensive blow for every ten he parried. Today, the giant approached slowly, his sword resting on his shoulder as if he were marching with an army. Afraid of some trick, Bryan gripped the hilt of his own sword in both hands, eyes on the big man's blade, waiting for the attack. Suddenly he found himself on his back gasping for breath, a dull ache in the stomach where Rowan had kicked him.

"Now that you have the best sword around, I thought I'd better remind you that there's more to fighting than weapons," Rowan said, pulling Bryan back to his feet. "You were staring up above my shoulder like you were looking down a tunnel."

"I didn't know kicking was allowed," Bryan wheezed, bent over and still fighting to catch his breath.

"Allowed?" Rowan bellowed over the storm of laughter from the observers. "It's fighting, boy. Everything goes. If you ever go out with an army, you can expect fireballs from mages, anything that can be launched by a catapult, arrows and javelins, and attacks from any direction that isn't occupied by a friend."

Bryan took advantage of the long speech to venture an opportunist slash at Rowan's hip, the lowest point the chain mail reached on the giant's body, but the man was expecting it and parried effortlessly. A shower of sparks flew off when their swords made contact, causing both men to leap back and examine their blades.

"I haven't seen that happen in a while," Hardol remarked drily.

"No damage here," Rowan said after a minute inspection of his blade. "How about yours?"

"Looks alright to me," Bryan replied. The sword's humming hadn't changed in pitch. "Does this sort of thing happen a lot with enchanted swords?"

"Not as often as you might expect," Rowan replied. "Come now. Why don't you attack me for a change?"

After ten minutes of exchanging ferocious blows, Bryan was dripping sweat and hungry, though he wasn't panting like he had in their earlier encounters. Somehow he was sure that the sword was influencing his actions, making its own choices about when to cut and parry, and he fought without thinking. But his opponent looked as fresh as ever, and Bryan noticed that the five men he thought of as Rowan's lieutenants were grinning broadly.

"What so funny?" he demanded, backing away and resting his naked blade on his shoulder, the universal sign for taking a break.

"Is one of your legs longer than the other that you keep falling off to the short side?" Hardol asked playfully. "Your blade work has gotten pretty fancy all of a sudden, but you must have moved a hundred times as far as Rowan while he just shifts his feet. Look at the sand. He had you running in circles."

Bryan glanced down and saw that the ex-soldier had spoken the truth. Rowan was standing at the center of a small circle, the sand well flattened by his smooth footwork, while Bryan had practically dug a shallow trench around him, moving in an endless left-to-right circle.

"At least he's staying engaged rather than running away," Theodric observed. "That's more than you can say for most who face Old Slayer."

"Where am I going wrong?" Bryan asked, directing the question at Simon.

The old soldier shook his head. "It would be easier to explain what you're doing right." The remaining observers broke into laughter again, though most of the boys and some of the men had drifted off in ones and twos when the odor of cooking reached them. "That sword has accepted you as its master, and from the stories they tell about the old enchanted weapons, it will be your teacher from now on."

"But Rowan is still toying with me," Bryan complained, pointing at the circular track in the sand. "I mean, sure, he's bigger and stronger and has much more experience, but…"

"But nothing," Simon rebuked him. "You've had less than three weeks training, and you're complaining that you can't beat the biggest and strongest man any of us has ever seen. A man with an enchanted sword of his own, I might point out."

"What is your magic, Rowan?" Bryan asked.

The leader of the players smiled. "It's not for acting, I'll admit that much. Shall we go another round?"

The dinner bell on the kitchen wagon began to ring. Bryan reclaimed his scabbard from Hardol, sheathed his sword, and made a beeline for food.

"I get that these are more instructions for unmaking magical knots, four of them, I think," Meghan said. "But I won't know where to go and do the untying until you translate the rest of this."

"It's late," Bryan protested. "I was up all night. Can't it wait for tomorrow?" He wasn't really that tired, but reading faded English calligraphy from a stained old oilskin wasn't his idea of excitement. Instead he moved next to the girl and snuck an arm around her shoulders. "Are you sure you're feeling better?"

"I'm fine, thank you very much," she said, firmly removing his arm and then passing him the map. "The treasure might be around the next curve in the road, or the last curve, for all we know. Just read it to me now, and then you won't have to come up with excuses not to."

"The clues in games usually came as voice-overs," Bryan grumbled. He increased the brightness of the illumination orb he had conjured up in their tent and focused on the faded script, moving his lips silently.

"Well?" Meghan asked impatiently.

"It doesn't make much sense," he warned her before starting to read.

"Above the green fields, a room full of shields, behind she who wields, see what it yields.

Makers of brew, for men who are blue, heat the wort true, check in the flue.

When night turns to black, a stab in the back, an old traitor's sack, something you lack.

Water that's white, falls at its right, from the first bite, take what you might."

"Why is it all riddles?" Meghan mused out loud. "I mean, they're obvious enough, but why not tell us straight out what to do?"

"What's obvious? All I get out of it is that we're on some sort of treasure hunt, and I could have guessed that from my experience playing games."

"Four riddles, four verses each, four colors. Well, five if you count the first riddle from my pendant, but that had four verses as well."

"So?"

"We found your sword at the Red Duke's castle, now we have four to go. The green is next, then the blue, then the black, and finally the white."

Bryan looked back at the oilcloth. "Oh yeah, I forgot about the dukes and the colors. So first we go to the Green Duke's castle and find a room full of shields where we look behind some lady warrior, maybe a statue or a wall-hanging."

"Just like that," Meghan said, eyeing him with a mixture of surprise and respect. "You're willing to go snooping around all of the greatest castles in the land with me, even though there's a reward for our capture."

"Your capture," Bryan reminded her. "Storm Bringer said I was worth the same money dead or alive. Besides, we just raided a castle on top of a cliff in the middle of the night and came away with the goods. Now I have my sword and I'm getting stronger every day, so the rest should be a piece of cake."

"Don't you wonder about the coincidence that our quest is to visit the five castles, and here we find ourselves with Rowan's players who happen to be traveling the same route?"

"Good things happen to good people," Bryan retorted. "You worry too much."

"That's because I have to do the worrying for both of us."

Bryan leaned over, took her head in both hands, and tried to plant a quick kiss on her lips. She managed to turn her face down just enough that he got her nose instead.

"Stop it," she said, getting her hand between their faces and pushing. "Don't you get it? If we share our magic now we both might end up stuck halfway, never reaching our full potential."

"I think you're just scared," Bryan said, but he released her and crawled out of the tent.

"Where are you going? I thought you were tired." she called after him.

"I'm going for another dip in the river."

"But it's cold."

"That's the whole point," he muttered for his own ears, pulling off his shirt as he headed for the riverbank.

"Dragons! Dragons!" the crowd chanted in unison, some of them flapping their arms in a ridiculous parody of flight.

"Are you sure you don't want see my famous illusion of a man walking against the wind?" Laitz responded playfully. He began moving his arms and legs, leaning forward without making progress. There was a smattering of laughter, then a ripe tomato came out of nowhere, adding a momentary splash of color to his harlequin outfit. The pulp and seeds ran off the magically fixed cloth onto the stage.

"Dragons! Dragons!" the crowd resumed its chant.

Laitz shook his head and ducked back into the three-sided booth that they used for illusions during play intermission. He winked at his two assistants.

"Maybe we overdid it earlier when we were trying to drum up business," Meghan ventured. "They sound kind of hard to please."

"Our job is to give the players a chance to rest, so let's draw it out a little," Laitz reminded them. "That means no burning up my dragon with a gout of flame."

"Got it, boss," Bryan replied. He ducked out the back and prepared to conjure up the illumination orb that made their dusty creations visible. What Laitz had told him on their first day of acquaintance about good lighting men always finding work had proven to be true. Bryan had mastered all of the magical stage lighting tricks in record time, and Brom, the leader of a competing group of players, had already tried to hire him away from Rowan. Light orbs and fireballs just came naturally to him.

After the performance, Bryan and Meghan gathered the coins from the boards while Laitz and a couple of the older boys from the troupe rapidly took down the fabric walls. Then Bryan retreated to his spot at the rear of the stage to handle the lighting for the second act of *The Traitor*. Grey, one of Rowan's lieutenants, had been doing the troupe's lighting for years and was happy to train the young man as a backup. He also enjoyed pointing out the nuances of the nearly continual fight scenes as the play moved from political intrigue to open warfare.

"I'm losing track of who's who as they keep on getting killed," Bryan complained. "I didn't know we had so many ex-soldiers with the troupe."

"Shift right," Grey ordered. "You're getting it now. The speeches are timed to let the casualties from the dark half of the stage clean up and reenter from the other side as fresh troops. We're coming up on the grand finale."

"The King of New Land is winning, right?"

"Looks that way so far. Just wait and see."

A new group of soldiers rushed onto the stage at the end of the speech, only to be cut down by the king's men. Rowan played the role of the warrior king, his sword mowing down opponents like a scythe. Finally the action trailed off, the giant troupe master gave a short victory speech, and Bryan dimmed the lights for a quick scenery change.

"Wait for the assassins to get set before you bring up the overhead," Grey instructed. "I like to do it slowly, like the sun rising over the castle walls, since it's supposed to be dawn."

"Who writes these plays?" Bryan asked, while the actors bumped about in the near blackness finding their spots. "Everybody in the audience seems to know them already, like they've been around forever."

"Some of them are classics from Old Land that came over with the exiles, but *The Traitor* is based on the actual events that gave our current king's family the throne."

"Exiles?"

"Has the shock of married life made you forget everything you learned as a child?" Grey asked good-naturedly. Rowan's players were accustomed to Bryan's strange questions by this point and answered according to their store of patience. "All of us in New Land are descended from exiles, not counting the natives, of course," he added with a glance at Storm Bringer, who had just slipped quietly into place beside them. "Alright, it's time to bring up the main light."

Bryan reined in his curiosity and concentrated on smoothly increasing the output of the illumination orb he created over the stage. He wasn't sure how other lighting men went about their work, but he found that a little levitation combined with a tightly wrapped fireball did the trick nicely. He imagined feeding fuel into the fire, and the brightness steadily increased.

"Are you sure the king's whole family is within?" Chester whispered to the armed guards at the door.

"Aye, and we put ten drops in every wine bottle, just like you instructed," the guard replied.

"You've done well," Chester replied with an evil smile. He untied a small but heavy bag from his belt and handed it to the guard. "Here's your promised reward."

As the guard held the small sack on his palm and fumbled at the tie with his other hand, Chester plunged his dagger into the man's throat. Another assassin killed the other guard with a sword thrust through the back of the neck, and the audience gasped at the copious amounts of fake blood that flowed from the wounds.

"If the fools did as they said, we'll take these upstarts in their sleep," Chester told his men. "The dragon will deal with the royal troops in the castle grounds. Our task is putting an end to this pretender and his noxious brood, including the women and the children. Am I understood?"

"Yes, prince," the men murmured in response, and then they followed their leader single file through the door. A moment later there was a stifled scream supplied by the seamstress, who had a dual specialty in vocal effects. A brief composition of sad, wordless music followed, played on string instruments by unseen musicians.

"Dimmer, dimmer," Grey whispered to Bryan. "Alright, bring up a soft light, just on Bethany."

The young mother was illuminated walking across the front of the stage, dressed in a ragged traveling cloak and carrying a small bundle. Bryan gaped at the realistic snow that fell over her head and shoulders, and he shivered in the blast of arctic wind that howled across the stage. Then Grey gave him a nudge and indicated the shaman with a nod. Storm Bringer was living up to his name.

The bundle in Bethany's arms began to wail, and the audience let out a collective sigh.

"Be easy, my king," Bethany cooed to her baby, who had fallen asleep before his big performance and needed a pinch to encourage his debut crying part. "Traitors have murdered your family, but the queen's life magic provided us a way out of that death trap and bought my undying loyalty. I have your father's sword here beneath my cloak, and one day you'll take vengeance on the Old Land prince who now calls himself king in your place."

The audience exploded with cries of support for the orphaned infant, and Bethany had to pull her shawl over the baby's face to protect Davie from the rain of coins. Then somebody started to sing a patriotic song about the exiles building up a new land, and the whole audience joined in.

"I thought you told me that mages in dragon form wouldn't attack people except in defense of their treasure," Bryan said.

"You're talking about the play now, right?" Meghan broke off practicing another unbinding spell and looked up from the oilskin. "They say that dragon had good reasons, a hundred thousand golden reasons, to be precise."

"So dragons work as mercenaries?"

"It's not exactly that, either. The dragon who attacked the royal guard while the foreign prince and his assassins murdered the royal family was also from across the ocean. Two of the dukes had already secretly pledged their support to the prince, whose father was one of the most powerful kings in Old Land. They caught the loyal Blue Duke between them in a surprise attack, forcing him to give an oath of neutrality. From there the armies were equally matched, but our king, I mean, our original king, outfought them. That's when the prince turned to assassination and made a deal with the dragon. But even today, people don't know why Narl agreed."

"Narl?"

"The Old Land dragon. After the prince and the assassins bribed their way into the castle and killed the king and his whole family, Narl attacked the royal guard, allowing the prince's armies time to come up and take the castle. With the two traitor dukes on his side and the Blue Duke neutral, the new king forced the Red Duke and the White Duke to accept his terms, rather than bathing the kingdom in more blood. Little good it did them, since the new king encouraged the barons to fight at every turn, and that continues on today."

"So the Green Duke and the Black Duke are the bad guys."

"Many people think so, but I guess it depends which side you're on. Besides, the White Duke is the only one left alive from that period. The rest of them have been replaced by their sons." Meghan paused for a moment and frowned. "Didn't I go over all of this with you on the walk to Castle Foregone?"

"I had just discovered how to make fire then," Bryan admitted guiltily. "I may not have been paying attention to every word. How long ago was all this?"

"Well, it's Year Forty-Eight on the new calendar now, so I'd say about forty-eight years."

"You don't have to be sarcastic. What about the baby who the nurse saved from the assassins?"

"That part is just wishful thinking," Meghan replied with a sigh. "People want to have something to believe in so they can have hope for the future."

"And the local dragons didn't fight back? They just let that Old World mage, Narl or whoever, sweep in here and take over?"

"I think there was only one dragon left on the coast by that point, or maybe it was a pair, but Narl was older and more powerful. He must have killed them before attacking the castle. Dragons tend to be very private and act on their own concerns without counsel, so they don't make for interesting characters in plays."

"Did you watch my work? Pretty good, huh?" Bryan bragged.

"If I'm ever attacked by enemies in the dark and in need of a lighting dragon, you're the first one I'll call."

"What are you mad about now?"

"I'm not mad," Meghan said angrily, looking back down at the oilskin and ostentatiously beginning to trace her hands through a magical pattern. "Isn't this about the time you usually go and hang out with your friends and drink beer?"

"If that's what you want," Bryan retorted, crawling out into the night. It struck him that he was probably the only guy in two universes who could live with a girl in a tent and not make any romantic progress.

"Six coppers to tour a castle?" Bryan immediately forgot his orders to remain inconspicuous and thumped the table with his fist. "All you people have around here are castles. Whoever heard of paying to get into one?"

"I gave you a bargain, one adult and one child," the cashier replied curtly. "If I charged your little brother the full price, it would be eight coppers."

"Just pay him," Meghan urged Bryan in the boyish voice she had perfected for playing the part of Elstan.

"I'll give you two coppers, and that's two coppers too much," Bryan counter offered. The cashier shook her head, and the people waiting in line behind the pair began to murmur. "Three coppers, and that's my final offer."

"I'll pay, brother," Meghan said, handing the liveried cashier a small silver.

The woman slipped four coppers change across the table, and then she made a crude X on the backs of their hands with a piece of charcoal. "The guided tour begins in ten minutes. I'll ring the bell in five minutes so everybody can gather at the entrance. Don't forget to stop in the gift shop on your way out."

"We'll just wander around by ourselves, if that's alright," Meghan replied, scooping up the change. "Thank you." She dragged Bryan away from the table before he could try to get the money back.

"We should have just left," Bryan grumbled. "I could have charbroiled a stick and made the marks myself."

"What part of, 'don't draw unnecessary attention,' didn't you understand?" Meghan hissed. "Do you want us to get caught?"

They showed their charcoal marks to a bored-looking guard at the entrance to the old section of the castle. He examined their hands under the light of a strange lantern which caused the black marks to turn purple. The guard nodded to his fellow, who lifted his pike, allowing the tourists into the section which was closed off from the non-paying public.

"Well, maybe that just means they're smart enough to know that anybody who doesn't argue about that price is hiding something," Bryan blustered before Meghan could say a word about the security measures. He pointed derisively at the first display. "Oh, look. An old catapult, just like in a museum. I'll bet there's no difference between this catapult and the ones up on the wall except for this one being broken. What a rip-off."

"We're not here to sightsee," Meghan responded vehemently, her voice rising to its normal register and above. "Can't you keep your head screwed on straight for long enough to infiltrate a castle and recover a hidden treasure?"

A middle-aged woman who had been quietly examining an out-of-fashion wall hanging depicting a hunting scene turned and stared at the couple. Meghan's face went beet red, but Bryan just smiled and said, "My little brother likes role-playing games. After we steal the ducal jewels, we're going to be spies in the council chamber."

"I remember when mine was that age," the woman replied with a smile, before turning back to her wall hanging.

"Now who's being conspicuous?" Bryan teased, but he regretted it immediately when he saw the anger in Meghan's eyes. "Alright. Let's go find this shield room."

They walked on quickly, looking through doorways without finding anything like an armory, and they had almost reached the end of the hall when the faint ringing of a bell was heard. A number of people emerged from the various rooms and headed for the courtyard.

"Good timing," Bryan said. "This room must be it."

Meghan followed him through the arched doorway and saw the shields immediately. They were all so brightly colored that it was obvious they were reproductions rather than battle shields used in long-ago wars. Sightseers in New Land had to make do with what was available, and Green Castle was the local destination for peasants with some extra harvest-money to burn, thanks in part to its location near the beach.

"She who wields, she who wields," the girl repeated out loud. "I don't see anything in here that could match that description. Do you think whatever it was has been removed?"

"If it was a wall hanging, maybe it's out being cleaned," Bryan suggested. "Look for a spot on the wall that's shaded differently."

Meghan stuck her head back into the passage to make sure nobody was near. "Do one of your bright lights. I can't see anything by these lousy torches."

The large room lit up like it was open to the sun, and Bryan and Meghan moved quickly around the perimeter, scanning the walls.

"There's no sign of her." Meghan's shoulders slumped in disappointment, and she found herself looking to Bryan for suggestions. As usual, the young man's attention had wandered, and he was staring at the ceiling, playing with his lighting orb. "Would you please work with me?"

Bryan pointed up and grinned. Smoke had dulled the colors of the fresco on the ceiling, but it undeniably showed an angry woman casting a bolt of lightning at a satyr who was pursuing a young girl.

"Perfect, watch the door," Meghan ordered, moving under the depiction of the goddess. "And turn the light back down. I don't need it for this."

As soon as Bryan was in position, she worked rapidly through a complex weave of hand motions that ended with pointing at the artwork. For a moment nothing happened, and then a white mass dropped from the ceiling and enveloped her.

"Bryan!" she choked out, falling to the floor under the smothering folds of fabric. It was a strange feeling, similar to being inundated by sheets of rain that somehow held together like thin blankets. She struggled to free herself for a moment without making any progress, and then she felt the mound of silk being drawn off of her.

"Are you alright?" Bryan asked, still gathering in the folds of fabric to his chest with both hands. "This can't be a wall hanging because there's no picture on it. Maybe it's a tent or a giant tablecloth."

"Check the hall while I do the spell in reverse," Meghan instructed him. "And figure out how we're going to smuggle this thing out of here."

The guards tried to keep straight faces as Bryan and Meghan struggled towards the exit, but they weren't getting paid enough to keep their comments to themselves.

"Found yourself a real treasure in the gift shop, I see," the guard with the magical lantern said. "I'll bet that came over from Old Land at the time of the Exile."

"Well, I don't claim to be an expert on wood, but that looks an awful lot like chestnut to me," his pike-wielding partner joined in. "I don't think the duke would export so much chestnut to Old Land if it grew there."

"Excellent point, Rolf," the first guard agreed. "And those iron bands do look a bit flimsy. You'd almost think that they were glued on."

"Old horses never die," the pike man declaimed, putting his hand on his chest in a mock sign of respect while lowering his eyes.

"Of course, maybe the young man bought it to give his fiancée for saving up linens," the first guard continued. "As long as you keep it out of the rain, the sun, and the heat, it might serve the purpose."

"My advice is to slather it with peppermint oil," the other guard added with a professional air, lifting his pike to let Bryan and Meghan exit. "It will keep her blankets smelling fresh, and discourage the mice from nibbling through that thin wood."

"Thank you," Meghan said, intentionally stumbling to jam the chest into Bryan's side and prevent him from making some smart-aleck response.

As soon as they turned the corner, Bryan let out, "Jerks. I'll bet that gift shop pays their salaries, yet they have to make fun of people who buy the junk?"

"Focus," Meghan replied with a sigh. "Just be thankful I thought of buying the chest. I don't see how we would have made it out of there otherwise."

"I can think of a few ways," Bryan grumbled. He'd been in a bad mood ever since Meghan made him leave his sword behind for the outing, though when he had seen the other visitors checking their weapons at the guardhouse in the main gate, he had to admit she was right. "Just let me carry it by myself, you're slowing us down. We have to get back in time for our show with Laitz, if you've forgotten."

Meghan gladly gave up her end of the awkward load, which Bryan then heaved onto his shoulder. The thin wood on the bottom of the chest made a cracking sound in protest. They continued in silence under the suspended portcullis and crossed the drawbridge into the run-down area of houses at the foot of the castle.

"This whole place is a dump," Bryan continued his rant about everything related to the Green Duke's castle. "And it stinks. You had better sanitation back at the castle where you lived, and your guy was only a baron."

"I don't know much about kingdom politics, but they do say that the Green Duke is a bit of a miser. Hey, why are we turning in here?"

"There's no point carrying this chest all the way back to the fairgrounds, it will fall apart by then anyway," Bryan said. He set his load down in the narrow alley between two wooden structures, and took off the long peasant's coat he'd borrowed from the props wagon to wear in the cold morning air. Then he laid the coat out on the ground. "I'll wrap the silk up in here and tie it with the sleeves, and then I can just carry it like a pack. It doesn't weigh so much, it's just bulky."

Meghan took a quick look around to make sure they weren't observed, and then watched as Bryan poured the silk out onto the open coat. Together they pulled the coat closed around the fine fabric and made up the buttons.

"Let me," Meghan said, stopping Bryan from knotting the sleeves around the mass to prevent the silk from falling out of its crude packaging. She ran her finger over the bottom edge of the coat, murmuring, "Hold together."

Bryan picked up the load, letting the weight fall on his back and holding a sleeve in each hand in front of his chest.

"Thanks, that's much better," he said. "Hey, this whole quest business is turning out to be a lot easier than I thought it would be. We get to see the kingdom, eat good food, and earn plenty of tips. I could get used to this lifestyle."

Following their performance of *Dueling Dragons*, the two latest additions to Rowan's players took advantage of the empty stage to examine the contents of the improvised backpack while the players were all at dinner.

"I still say this could have waited for another time," Bryan complained, unfolding his end of the silk bundle towards one end of the stage. "We could have done it after the evening performance."

"And then everybody would have seen light coming from the stage and been suspicious," Meghan retorted. "Nobody hangs around here in between shows so it's the perfect time. Don't worry, I already asked at the kitchen wagon for them to save us extra."

"What do you mean extra?"

"I mean, more than the leftovers they always save that I give you before bed," the girl explained. "Hey, there's no way this thing is a tent or a tablecloth. Look at what we've pulled out so far."

"Kind of like a snow angel built backwards," Bryan observed. There was still a pile of silk at the center of the stage, but each of them had pulled out a broad tubular section that got narrower as it went. "We need to find some weights so we can hold these ends down while we untangle the middle."

"Stay," Meghan commanded, smoothing the broad swath of silk onto the stage. Then she carefully walked around to Bryan's side and arranged the fabric he'd stretched out on the stage. "Watch, now," she said, and repeated the simple incantation. "Did you get that?"

"What?" Bryan asked, looking back over his shoulder from where he'd moved to unravel the mess of folds in the center. "Hey, I think I found the bottom."

Meghan shook her head at her own credulity that her dragon could pay attention long enough to learn anything magical he considered to be mundane. A great deal of the girl's adolescence had been spent mastering the broadest possible array of magical manipulations through study of the scrolls and the natural world.

It bothered her that Bryan now seemed to take all of her skills for granted, at the same time relegating them to a body of "women's magic" that was mainly handy for keeping house.

"The body is upside down for a snow angel," Bryan complained, backing towards the front of the stage and spreading the silk as he went. "It's getting narrower rather than wider at the bottom. Check for a head."

"What's this snow angel you keep talking about?"

"You know, when you lie on your back in the snow and work your arms up and down to make wings."

Meghan approached what Bryan was calling the top of whatever they were dealing with and found there was little silk left to spread out.

"This seems to be the end of it," she said. "It's a tube shape that's doubled up for reinforcement, almost like a collar. Wait, there's some sort of label with a word in your language. Stop! Don't walk on it."

Bryan groaned and detoured around one of the wing-shaped extensions. Then he crouched and read out loud, "Long."

"I can see that it's long," Meghan said in exasperation. "Did we need a label to tell us that? Let's get it picked up before somebody returns. If we start from the bottom and fold it up neatly before crossing the wing things, I bet it will take much less space than it did all crumpled together."

"Going by the size, it looks like an undershirt for a dragon," Bryan said. "What I don't get is how anything big enough to wear it could put it on. I mean, maybe I could get my shoulders through the opening at the bottom and crawl inside like a tent, but there's room for ten of me in there."

"Maybe if you crawled in there you'd grow real wings and a long tail, and then it would fit you perfectly," Meghan said thoughtfully. "Why else would the map have sent us looking for it?"

"Some other time." Bryan began rapidly folding the giant silk garment from the bottom. "If we hurry, I'll bet we'll make it back in time for dessert."

The lead wagon rumbled to a halt before reaching a small detachment of soldiers who were blocking the coastal road. Behind an officer on a flashy white charger, the eight soldiers were arrayed four across in two rows. In addition to the short swords at their belts, the troopers carried large shields slung across their backs, and an assortment of pole arms. A tall man wearing a white hood walked beside the horse. The officer was armed with a sword, and he wore a cuirass and helmet with a feathered crest.

"Halt in the king's name," the officer declared self-importantly. The troopers looked almost embarrassed by their leader's performance, but Rowan took it in stride. He separated himself from the group walking at the front of the wagon train, which included Storm Bringer, Hardol, and Jomar, and approached the detachment slowly, with his hands spread in a peaceful gesture.

"Now, why would the king's name want us to halt?" the giant troupe leader replied in a friendly tone, as though he were chatting with the men in a tavern rather than being confronted on the road. "We're on our way to play the Middle Festival and we're on a tight schedule."

"You must be Rowan," the officer said with distaste, ostentatiously placing his right hand on the hilt of his sword. "I've heard that you players are no better than outlaws, but I'll give you a chance all the same. My mission is to arrest a girl who fled Castle Refuge without permission of her baron. She's said to be traveling with a young man she claims to be a cousin or husband."

"You'll arrest no such person with us," the giant replied easily. "You have my word of honor on that."

"He is telling the truth," the man in the white hood responded to the officer's unspoken question. "He also hides something."

"Is that so," the officer drawled, looking down on Rowan from horseback. "I'll give you one chance to do this the easy way, and then we'll put you down like mad dogs."

"Not this again," one of the troopers muttered, shifting uncomfortably and signaling to the other soldiers to be prepared.

"Well, your conversation has gone downhill in a hurry, boy," Rowan replied in a cold voice. "I'm sure you won't be offended if we defend ourselves from both your slander and your troops."

Bryan arrived at a run, remembering Hardol's instruction to stick with Rowan if things heated up, but Storm Bringer grabbed his arm, stopping the young man in his tracks with surprising ease.

"Curtiss!" the officer barked without bothering to turn his head. "Take this man into custody. If he resists, cut him down."

The trooper who had muttered earlier moved up alongside the officer's horse and said, "A word, Captain."

"What is it this time?" the officer almost screamed, a fine spray of spittle accompanying his words. "Have I offended your professional abilities by asking you to deal with strolling players? Are my instructions too complicated for such a straightforward fellow as yourself? If the pay and responsibility of your august position weigh so heavily upon you, I'm sure one of the other men will be willing to step up."

"Over there, in the woods, Captain," Curtiss replied in a tightly controlled voice. "Four men with longbows, the kind that will punch an arrow right through that shiny cuirass of yours at this range."

"Seeker," the captain barked, turning to the man standing at the other side of his horse. "I assume you can stop arrows?"

"This isn't the place to find out," the man replied nervously, his eyes flitting from Rowan, to Storm Bringer, to Bryan. "I sense powerful magic in this group and it's not the kind I understand. Let them pass on my authority as King's Seeker and I'll send for instructions."

"On YOUR authority?" the officer yelled, narrowly escaping being dumped from his horse, which was starting to dance about nervously as its master lost emotional control. "Am I in command of imbeciles?"

"They strike me as reasonable fellows," Rowan offered conversationally.

"Shut up, you big oaf!" the captain screamed.

"If you're going to insult me, I'll be forced to challenge you."

"I am Torone, the second son of Baron Massey, and I don't duel with strolling players or outlaws."

A hawk chose that moment to dive into the scene, coming in for a landing on the shaman's shoulder. Storm Bringer communed silently with the bird before calling out in a cheerful voice, "No other soldiers on the road within an hour's walk in either direction."

The captain turned white at the implication of the shaman's words. "Kill him," he shouted, drawing his sword and pointing it at Rowan.

Curtiss moved forward, bringing his pole-axe around in a wide sweep and smashing the flat of the blade into the side of the captain's helmet. Torone toppled from his horse, unconscious, one foot trapped in the stirrup. The white stallion turned and bolted down the road, scattering the troopers and dragging the unfortunate captain after him.

"Sorry about that, sir," Curtiss addressed Rowan. "Wearing a helmet in the bright sun makes some of the young officers a bit crazy. I'm sure he'll see things from a new perspective if he should ever wake up."

"He won't be waking up," one of the other troopers said darkly. "It's said that falling from their mounts while showing off is the leading cause of death for young officers. My brother died fighting for bloody Baron Massey."

"You'll have no trouble from me," the seeker announced shakily, sensing that Rowan and the other players had shifted their attention in his direction. He found that he couldn't keep his eyes off the small man with the crooked teeth who was toying with a throwing knife. "I haven't even gone through the initiation. I'm just a probationary."

"You know that the players have a history with seekers," Rowan replied, moving towards the man, who began to tremble.

"Not with me, no history," the seeker pleaded, sinking to his knees. "I've only been in the king's service for a month. I haven't even been paid yet."

Rowan drew his sword and cut a vicious arc through the air, stopping the blade just short of the man's neck.

"Swear on the sword. You'll leave the king's service immediately, and you'll bite off your own tongue before you ever tell what happened here today."

"I swear it," the ex-seeker croaked, planting a kiss on the glowing blue blade. The man stiffened as the oath-magic entered his body, and Rowan resheathed his sword.

"You other men might consider a different service," Hardol addressed the troopers. "Brom's players should be just a few hours behind us, and I hear they're hiring intelligent men such as yourselves. A number of new troupes are starting up as well, though I can't say anything positive about their productions."

"We'll do that, sir," Curtiss replied, looking at Rowan rather than Hardol. "I saw your performance of *The Traitor* three nights ago, and so did the men. It's been bloody times for soldiers ever since the old king was overthrown."

"Nothing lasts forever," Rowan replied, motioning the lead wagon to start forward. "Not even kings and dragons."

"I don't get it," Bryan complained to Meghan as they pitched their tent. "I know that those guys were no match for all of the veterans working for Rowan, and I saw Theodric and his men grab longbows and head into the woods when the wagons halted. But why did that soldier knock his own leader off a horse with a pole-axe? If the officer wasn't dead when he hit the ground, I'll bet those troopers put him out of his misery when they caught up with the horse."

"I guess it was that or they all would have died," Meghan replied quietly. "Did men always follow stupid orders and run to their deaths in those games you keep talking about?"

"Sort of," Bryan admitted. "They'd usually climb over the bodies of their comrades to keep attacking until you killed the last one for bonus points. But still, if word gets back to the king, the next time there'll be an army waiting for us."

"I don't know who enchanted Rowan's sword, but I've read about oath magic and that ex-seeker will never talk. The man who swears the oath will use his own magic to enforce the promise as long as he lives. The troopers won't go back to their baron or duke again because they're mutineers. They weren't part of the royal guard or things would have gone differently. Phinneas told me that the household troops only travel with the king."

"But there must be records. I don't know, work permits and travel papers, things like that. People can't just go wherever they want without somebody knowing."

"Have you seen any of the things you're talking about since you arrived here?" Meghan asked. "People are identified by their looks, their accents, who they say they are, and the companions who vouch for them. As long as those men don't return to their castle barracks, nobody will be looking for them."

"So soldiers only fight when they want to?"

"What gave you that idea?" Meghan held the tent pole straight and waited for Bryan to pull the ridge rope taut before continuing. "Soldiers fight for pay, and many of them die for pay, but there are certain things they have a right to expect. They sign up to fight against other soldiers with war mages in support. There must be battlefield healers and some chance of winning. Didn't you say that the seeker spoke of unknown magic on our side? Why would a small group of soldiers attack a larger group of armed men who they obviously recognized as seasoned fighters, not to mention the likelihood that a hidden mage could burn them to a crisp before the bowmen turned them into pincushions? On top of all that, the traveling player troupes are well known to soldiers. Bethany tells me that they make up half of the audience for some of the martial plays, and even if they've taken the king's silver, they're men, not slaves."

"It's different where I came from," Bryan told her. "We have volunteer armies, or at least, most of them are, and the men and women join because they care about their kingdoms. Damn, I didn't mean kingdoms. If we ever see Hadrixia again, I'm going to ask for a refund on her translation magic. Our lands are ruled by the people. We vote for our kings."

"You have women in your armies?" Meghan asked in astonishment, ignoring the young man's nonsensical claims about government.

"Women these days do all sorts of stuff that used to be reserved for men. We even have women kings."

"They're called 'queens' here."

"I know that. I just meant women on Dark Earth have more options in most of the kingdoms."

"Like wearing see-through hose," Meghan reminded him.

"That's just—I really don't get women," Bryan cut himself off.

"Poor Bryan. If you work hard studying magic, maybe I'll give you lessons."

"Don't start something you can't finish," he growled at her. He remembered girls who liked to flirt, but it had never led anywhere, at least not for him. "What's the next castle on the festival circuit?"

"The Blue Duke's."

"Makers of brew, for men who are blue, heat the wart true, check in the flue," he quoted from memory. "I've heard of burning warts off with a red-hot nail, but it doesn't sound very magical. Does it mean that guys with warts get depressed so they drink a lot of beer before burning them off?"

"*Wort*, not *wart*," Meghan corrected him with a giggle.

Bryan looked at her blankly.

"Wort is the liquid the brewers get from mash to make beer," she explained. "I know you had beer on Dark Earth."

"Wait a minute, I don't understand something. Those verses were written in English, but we're talking your language and the rhymes still work. How can word pairs that sound the same but mean different things be paralleled in your language?"

"Hadrixia told me that people who learn a new language through magic usually forget the old one," Meghan informed him apologetically. "I didn't think it mattered since you can't go back, but it is funny you can still read it. Wait, have you tried writing?"

Bryan picked up a stick and scratched a few letters in the dirt. "Cat," he pronounced triumphantly.

"But that's our word," Meghan reminded him. "Try pronouncing just each letter alone."

He complied with her request by sounding out each letter by itself, and the girl nodded her head knowingly.

"You're just using the letters you know how to pronounce to spell words in our language," she explained. "I'll bet that the rhymes on the map aren't written in your language at all. Somebody just used your alphabet to write our language phonetically. It means you only have to teach me how to pronounce twenty-three letters, and then I'll be able to read any of these messages. It will be like a secret code between us."

"Twenty-six letters," Bryan asserted. "Our alphabet is better than yours."

"Grow up."

"Are you two planning on visiting the Blue Duke's castle?" Laitz asked his assistants. They were engaged in setting up the illusion booth on the main drag of the festival associated with the middle dukedom, and the question took both Meghan and Bryan by surprise.

"Why do you ask?" Meghan replied cautiously.

"You know that rumors travel faster than draft horses, and it seems that the castles on the festival route have been visited by strange manifestations."

"Like what?" Bryan demanded pointblank.

"Well, there was an odd incident at the Red Duke's castle where the tower watch claimed they were attacked by a fire mage's ghost which they slew with arrows. When the other guards entered the tower, they found nothing but some broken arrows on the floor, but there was fire damage to the wooden stairs and platform."

"The tower watch must have been drunk," Meghan suggested.

"At first the guard commander thought that as well," Laitz confirmed. "Then the duke's wife came forward and said she was out on her balcony before the incident took place and heard the tower watch call out a challenge. When she looked at the base of the tower, she saw two figures slipping through the door, a tall man and a small companion, perhaps a woman. She continued watching as the alarm bell started ringing and somebody pushed the door closed from the inside. Then the castle guard swarmed the place, and she assumed the intruders had been caught. It wasn't until she woke late in the morning and heard the story that she thought to tell anybody."

"Maybe she was drunk, too," Bryan said. "You know what those people are like."

"Yes, I actually do. But her testimony was enough for the guard commander to stop interrogating the tower watch and bring in a seeker, who confirmed the account given by the men. I'm told the Red Duke's mage is going crazy trying to uncover a secret passage."

"Bryan and I were thinking it might be interesting if we could add riders to the dragons," Meghan announced. "I haven't quite mastered it yet, but he can manage a rider and even have him throw a spear."

"Then there's the story of the ceiling art in the Green Duke's shield room," Laitz continued, ignoring the girl's attempt to change the subject. "It's not his real shield room, of course, just part of a tourist trap they set up to bring in some cash, but the painting—did I say painting? It was a fresco done by a traveling artist from Old Land back when that section of the castle was originally built. In any case, it was famous in some circles for its depiction of the angry storm goddess hurling a thunderbolt at some mythical creature who was bothering her daughter."

"Is there a point to this story?" Bryan asked rudely.

"It seems that the painting was the high point of the tour, with the guide providing magical illumination just before the visitors moved on to the gift shop. Imagine when she lit up the ceiling and the goddess was smiling, watching her daughter dance with a young man."

"I thought you put it back the way it was," Bryan said, missing Meghan's frantic cues to keep his mouth closed. "Oh, Laitz obviously knows it was us or he wouldn't have gone through the whole performance."

"He knows it was us now that you've confirmed it," the girl retorted before turning to their mentor. "We're sort of on a treasure hunt," she told him. "An old family obligation of sorts."

"I guessed it was something like that," Laitz replied. "Your affairs are your own. We're all up to something or another around here, but I wanted to warn you. Some of the dukes may be stupid, it happens when leaders are chosen by order of birth, but their advisers and their mages include some of the best minds in the land. If you see the need to extend your sightseeing to the Blue Duke's castle, I would save it for our last night in the area. And be prepared for a higher level of awareness on the part of the guards."

"Thank you," Meghan said. "And I was serious about showing riders on the dragons."

"I'm sure you were. I've been working on that myself, so we'll give it a try as soon as you're ready. Then we really will have the finest illusions on two continents."

"That Red Duke's museum was just a tourist trap anyway," Bryan said. "Serves them right that their ceiling art got screwed up."

"I'm afraid it didn't play out the way you imagine," Laitz told the young man. "Everybody is calling it a miracle. They've raised the price of admission, and local people who never would have given the displays the time of day are lined up around the moat waiting to get in."

"Why do I have to play the evil baron?" Bryan complained. "I do lighting and the dragon illusion, plus I let Rowan beat on me with his sword every day."

"It's just three lines," Meghan chided him. "Do you know how many lines I had to memorize to play Elstan?"

"But the baron is really a jerk. At the beginning of the first act, I order the death of my loyal war mage. At the end of the first act, I order the death of his son, and in the middle of the second act, I send a soldier to kill the mage's dog. I'm on stage for less than a minute, and all I do is give stupid orders."

"Bethany told me you have a good death scene at the end."

"I don't even have a line then. I'm sitting back in a chair getting a shave, and the barber cuts my throat!" Bryan paused and broke into a smile. "It is kind of cool, though. Simon showed me how to work the jugular kit they use. The barber slices the tip off the nozzle glued to my neck while I'm squeezing the bladder, and the blood will shoot halfway across the stage."

Meghan shook her head in mock disgust. Then she retrieved her slate with the painstakingly transcribed alphabet letters from the oilskin map, along with the phonetic equivalents in mage's script. Getting Bryan to repeat himself just two or three times so she could memorize a new letter was a task in itself, but the thought of spurting blood had him in a good mood.

"So when the 'c' and the 'h' are next to each other, you say them as 'ch' instead of 'kuh-huh.'"

"Check in the flue," he reiterated.

"And the 'u' followed by 'e' turns into 'ooh.'"

"You've got it," he replied, already bored with playing teacher. "I'll bet you read better than I do now. When do I try on the dragon gown?"

"You're willing?" Meghan asked in surprise. "I thought you weren't in any hurry to become a dragon."

"It beats reading. Besides, I guess this business about the king having a warrant out for you is serious, so we'd better do everything we can to prepare. Up until now, all of the sword training and stage fighting didn't feel that different from the games I used to play. Watching and hearing a guy get pole-axed off his horse changes things. It's just lucky that we ended up with Rowan rather than being on our own."

"That's what I tried to say earlier," the girl replied. "Do you think it was really luck?"

"Sure. Phinneas happened to come across the players on his way back from that last battle, and he knew Simon."

"You know I've been spending time with Simon's wife, teaching her some of the healing techniques I learned from Hadrixia. It turns out that Faye and the other folk healers always share what they know, but the methods I learned are on a completely different level. Faye thinks it's all Old Land training."

"What's wrong with Old Land? Even Laitz has been there."

"Traveling across the sea is a rare thing. And so are the magical knots that Hadrixia taught me. What I'm saying is that just like Rowan and his veterans are too good to be players, Hadrixia and

162

Phinneas were too good to be living in a minor baron's castle on the frontier."

"So you think they tricked us?"

"What? No, that's not what I mean," Meghan sputtered. "Why are you so suspicious? I was thinking it's odd that two powerful people lived in the backwater castle where I grew up, and they both befriended me."

"Sounds like somebody is suffering from princess syndrome."

"Kill the mage," Chester prompted in an undertone. Bryan stood frozen, looking out at the audience. The experienced leading man improvised, moving to stand directly in front of the rookie actor, blocking his view of the paying public. "What are your orders, Baron?" he practically shouted in the young man's face.

"Uh, kill him," Bryan stuttered.

"The mage?" Chester hinted.

"Yes, kill the mage," Bryan finally managed to pronounce.

"You can go off now," Chester muttered, adding a small shove to get Bryan moving. The new actor exited to the left, and the action shifted to the right of the stage, where Grey brought up the lights on a scene in the woods.

The painted backdrop included the body, folded wings, and long tail of a dragon, but the head was a wood and paper construction, with moving jaws manned by Jomar. The audience gasped at the effect as the dragon began to speak.

"The truce between dragons and men has been broken. The murdered mage was a friend of mine, an honorable man who wore my pledge ring. Take the head of the baron who committed this crime, or I will leave your kingdom to face its enemies alone."

"Now, now," Rowan replied. "A king's loyalty is owed to more than one party, and the baron and his family have supported my rule for generations. Am I to break that bond and start a civil war over one foul deed?"

The men playing the king's attendants unrolled a blanket on the stage, and then began to make a pile of silver goblets and cutlery, strings of pearls, copper and silver coins. The reptilian head drew back and the actor inside manipulated the mechanism in such a way as to cause a sneer to appear on the dragon's lips.

"I smell no gold here," Jomar roared, his magically amplified voice causing the wooden superstructure of the stage to shake. "You would try to purchase the life of my servant with the plunder of the local gentry? You push me too far, King Bane. The head of the baron, or your kingdom is forfeit!"

"Now, now," Rowan tried again, clearly unruffled by the dragon's display. "I realize that my offering is a bit light, but the locals have grown adept at hiding their gold, which they value above their women and children. Take these trinkets as a down payment on what I owe you, and let's part as friends."

The dragon's head reared back and smoke came from its nostrils, as if it was preparing to loose a blast of flame on the king's party. Members of the audience in the line of fire instinctively tensed to flee. Rowan didn't even flinch, and when the dragon opened its mouth, it struck a conciliatory note.

"You can't expect me to carry this junk to the mountains myself," Jomar said plaintively. "It's hardly worth the energy to move."

The rest of the negotiation was drowned out by the audience's cries of, "Cowardly lizard! Evil king," and similar expressions of disdain. A rain of rotten fruit and vegetables hit the netting that had been erected across the front of the stage for just that purpose. *Of Dragons and Men* was notorious as the messiest play on two continents.

Bryan did a little better when he came on at the end of the first act, ordering the murder of the good mage's son, though he almost lost his temper when an egg slipped through the protective net and spattered his costume. When he came back on stage the third time to order the death of the mage's dog, some young men actually tried to rush the stage to punish him, but they were easily handled by members of the troupe working crowd control.

At the end of the play, Bryan was so excited about having his throat slit that he straightened up in the barber's chair and opened his eyes to watch the spurts of fake blood launched by his rhythmic squeezing of the hidden bladder. The first gout of blood almost reached the audience, which everybody seemed to take as a good omen. They switched from throwing rotten vegetables to tossing coins, which easily penetrated the mesh of the protective screen.

Meghan's eyes went wide when Bryan returned from his daily sword exercise with Rowan.

"You're finally transforming!" she exclaimed. "I read that some dragons have characteristic marks that only show when they reach their full power, like secret tattoos that appear under magical light."

"What are you talking about?" Bryan replied in irritation, rubbing at his forehead. "Do you know any healing tricks to repair a dent in the skull? Rowan caught me good."

"Let me see it," Meghan repeated. "It's a red dragon and the wings are extended, which is a sign of power. Have you looked at your reflection?"

"I don't need to see my reflection," Bryan said sourly. "Rowan pommeled me."

"Pummeled?"

"Pommeled. Since the incident on the road, I asked him to stop going easy and to teach me one serious combat trick each day, since I figure that's all I'm capable of learning."

"What are you talking about?" Meghan echoed back his earlier question. "Don't you understand that you have a dragon on your forehead?"

"It's the dragon from the pommel on Rowan's sword. You wouldn't believe how much that hurt." Bryan set down his own weapon and sank into a cross-legged position. "Is there anything to eat? I think I burned a lot of extra energy shaking it off. Hardol said that blow should have knocked me out and required a healer, but they all saw my sword flash white after the impact, and I got right back up again."

Meghan ran her fingers over the dragon mark, which stood out from a round indent in Bryan's skin. "This is from the hilt of Rowan's sword?"

"The pommel. He baited me into trying an overhead blow and blocked it near the base of his blade. When I pulled my sword back from the impact, he suddenly came forward and caught me on the forehead with that metal ball at the end of his hilt. I guess it's an old trick, but I was watching the tip of his blade, and I never saw it coming."

"So the red is just blood under the skin," she said in disappointment. "Oh, I didn't mean it that way. Does it still hurt?"

"Not really, though it itches a little. I bet some food will make it better."

Meghan shook her head and brought out the pot of kitchen wagon leftovers that she kept on hand. She didn't mind that feeding Bryan outside of mealtimes had somehow become her responsibility, but the cooks tormented her with sly innuendos about how her husband was burning up all that extra food. Now that they were at the coast, one of the women always made a show of adding oysters to whatever she put in the pot for Bryan, much to the amusement of whoever else was present.

"Why do you think Rowan has a dragon on his pommel?" she asked, once Bryan was happily spooning in the stew.

"I thought the pommel was for extra grip," he replied between swallows. "Simon said it's more for a counterweight, to move the balance of the sword closer to the hands. Maybe that's how they fine-tune the balance, by gouging a little out."

"What's on your pommel?" she asked, suddenly curious.

"Mmph," he said, busily chewing, but he pushed the weapon in her direction.

Meghan lifted the hilt end of the sword and examined the base of the pommel. The engraving showed the profile of a woman's head with flowing hair. She gave Bryan a dark look and went back into the tent, leaving him to eat alone.

"How long have you and your husband been with the players?" Meghan asked Bethany. The two young women were relaxing together after stowing away the props, the first step in breaking down the show to return to the road. The boys were just starting work, knocking the pegs out of the stage boards from the bottom, a job that came with the bonus of any coins that had slipped between the cracks.

"I grew up in the troupe," Bethany replied. "My parents only stopped coming on the road last year, they stay at the camp now. My husband saw me on the stage and convinced Rowan to hire him on so he could court me."

"I keep hearing people talking about the camp, but I feel silly asking."

"You shouldn't hesitate to ask us anything," the young mother told her. "How else can you learn? You know that we go on the road after the spring planting and the fall harvest for festivals, but the summer and winter we spend in the mountains, just a few days inland from here. Several of the player troupes keep permanent settlements up there."

"We make enough money during the festivals to pay for the summer and winter off?"

Bethany laughed merrily, causing the baby to smile along with her. "You're so funny, Meghan. We work harder at home than we do on the road. During the summer, we put on plays and musical performances for people who can afford to come for a vacation, and of course, we have to feed them, house them, and help watch their children. It's mainly the wealthy farmers and merchants, especially from around the big castles, but we also get the families of barons who aren't too good to stay in a cabin or a tent. My parents and the others who live there all the time work year-round getting the place fixed up for the summer season. Plus, there are some orchards, hunting, and fishing."

"Who is your baron?"

"We don't have one. The mountains are dragon country, going back before the exiles came to New Land. It was all Gwyneth's territory, and even though she's gone now, her magic still protects the mountains. Men have tried to dig through the rubble to her lair in search of treasure, but more rock just slides down from the mountaintop."

"I've heard stories about her," Meghan said, remembering not to admit that she had read the stories. "She's very old, and she moved here from Old Land a long time ago. Some say she could even visit Dark Earth, like the original dragons."

"Gwyneth always had a soft spot for players, and the pact she made with the kings of New Land put us all under her protection. The Old World dragon who took over the coast claimed all of her rights, so now we're actually his subjects. Rowan pays something to him every year, but it's all done through agents."

"Has Rowan always been with the troupe?"

"He grew up as a player, but he left when he was sixteen to become a soldier for the White Duke. He was a famous fighter, no man could stand against him in a duel, and he rose to become the head of the duke's guard. Then an Old Land troupe of players came through on a tour, the first time in over a hundred years, and he fell in love with one of their actresses." Bethany motioned for Meghan to lean closer and whispered, "She's supposedly a highborn lady who ran away with players to avoid an arranged marriage, and from the looks of her daughters, I believe it."

"So why did Rowan leave the White Duke and return to the players?"

"It was right after they married," Bethany continued in a whisper. "I think he quit the duke because her family and the prince she jilted have powerful friends, and Rowan didn't want to cause the duke trouble."

"But that must have been almost thirty years ago. Surely they would have gotten over it by now."

Bethany shrugged. "Maybe he'd had enough of being a soldier as well. All I know is that we're always welcome in the White Duke's castle, and we play our shows there within the walls rather than on the festival grounds."

Getting into the Blue Duke's castle and finding the brewery was easy. Empty wooden kegs with arrows painted on them were positioned at every turn in the labyrinthine passages and galleries that were formed from the arches supporting the upper levels of the castle. If that hadn't been enough, the occasional group of men rolling a full keg in the opposite direction would have gotten them there eventually.

"It looks pretty popular," Meghan ventured. "I don't know how we're going to find what we came for if there's a crowd."

"There better not be a charge to get in," Bryan responded, looking daggers at an unfortunate man in the Blue Duke's livery who happened to be passing by.

"More likely there's a charge for sampling the wares. I asked around before we came, and supposedly this is the best beer in the kingdom."

"Really?" The young man's attitude did an about-face, and he stole a glimpse at Meghan. "Did you, uh, bring any money? I meant to, but…"

"I'll buy you a beer if you behave. Ugh, it doesn't smell very good."

Bryan shrugged and began shouldering his way through a crowd of men who blocked their way, Meghan in tow. She was horribly embarrassed by his rudeness and was muttering, "Sorry," left and right, when she realized that the men weren't lined up to get into the brewery. They were waiting for their turn at a stone trough that must have run into the castle's drainage system. She grabbed on to the back of Bryan's coat, closed her eyes, and stopped apologizing.

"This looks just like a brew pub," Bryan declared as they entered the cavernous gallery. There were lines of barrels along one wall, half a dozen giant copper kettles, and pipes running everywhere. The crowd inside was nowhere near as bad as the mob in the hall, and as if to provide an explanation, a bell above the bar began to toll. Most of the remaining customers pushed away from the bar reluctantly.

"I guess we just missed the lunch crowd," Meghan said.

"Lunch? I wonder if they serve food." Bryan bellied up to the bar and called for two tankards.

"He old enough to be in here?" the barman asked, gesturing at Meghan with his chin. "We've had complaints about kids falling off walls and slipping under wagon wheels. This isn't the small beer you get back on the farm," he added gruffly.

"I'll keep an eye on him," Bryan replied, his eyes searching behind the bar. "You got any food here?"

"Does it look like a cook shop to you?" The barman slid two full tankards in front of them. "Two coppers."

Meghan fumbled in her change purse, removed three coppers, and pushed them across the bar.

"A proper young gentleman, you," the barman said, scooping up the money and the tip. "Sorry I took you for a kid. I see you're just delicate, like an Old World prince." He laughed at his own joke as he retreated, but quickly returned with a basket full of some kind of little dried fish that had been heavily salted. "On the house."

"Thanks," Bryan said, picking up one of the hard little snacks and munching on it. "Hey, these are pretty good. Almost too salty." He took a long swallow of beer to chase it down.

"That's why they're free," Meghan told him in a low voice. "To get you to drink more."

"I don't need little fish for that. So a flue is like a chimney, right?"

Meghan blanched white and stared at him. "What's wrong with you? Has one sip of beer gone to your head?"

"You have a problem with brewery talk?" Bryan countered, twisting on his stool and looking around the well-lit space. "Those copper kettles are cool. I take back what I said about charging to get in. I wish this place did have a tour."

"Interested in brewing?" A short man wearing grimy coveralls and a sooty cap materialized at Bryan's side. "Most people drink village brew, the stuff every widow mixes up in her kitchen cauldron, but we have the most modern facility in New Land. Those copper kettles you were admiring are imported, you know, and that whole wall is honeycombed with air passages for the fires below."

"I wondered where the heat came from," Bryan said, winking at Meghan. He motioned to the barman to bring the newcomer a beer, and the short man nodded his thanks.

"Use my tankard, Phil," the kettle fireman said, settling onto the stool next to Bryan. "Thirsty work, banking the coals, but the manager has a strict rule about drinking on the job, and absolutely no freebies." He sighed out loud after a long pull at his over-sized tankard, and then stuck out his hand towards Bryan.

"I'm Shep."

"Pleased to meet you, Shep. I'm Bryan, and this is my little brother."

"Does the kid have a name?"

"Elstan," Meghan mumbled.

"Just like the play. Name suits, if you don't mind my saying. You look a bit girlish," Shep added.

"How do you heat the kettles?" Bryan asked. "My little brother said it must be magic."

The fireman laughed outright at Meghan, who lifted her tankard and gulped some beer to cover her irritation over having such dumb words put in her mouth. "Kids think everything is magic, they don't realize how hard their parents work. If you look around the courtyard when you go back up, you'll see a little wooden roof on the ground, not far from the main gate. It tips back so the carters can dump in a full load of charcoal, and it all runs down a chute to the fire room below the floor here. We go through enough charcoal to keep a village of burners employed, I tell you."

"It must get hot down there," Bryan prompted.

"It's not that bad," Shep replied, after draining half of his beer. "When they first built the place, men kept dropping dead for no apparent reason, but a healer came in and said it was something about unseen smoke from burning charcoal to boil the wort. So they hung the guy who designed the place and called in the mages, who worked out how to keep the chimneys drawing and the fresh air moving through. You can actually feel a breeze down there."

The fireman lifted his over-sized tankard again, finished the contents in a series of giant gulps, and smacked his hand on the bar.

"So there must be a chimney in the courtyard," Bryan ventured. "I didn't notice it when we came in."

"There's a flue for each coal bed running up the back wall, but we're almost under the castle's outer wall here, and the flues all combine in a single chimney that comes out of the ground outside. It almost looks like the architect didn't know what he was doing and had to add a buttress to the wall. The mouth of the chimney reaches up past the wall-walk."

"Thanks," Bryan said. "We'll have to check that out."

"Good to see young people interested in something other than magic for a change," the fireman said, sliding off his stool. "Well, I'd stay for another, but I'm dead on my feet. Took my family to the last night of the festival, and the kids couldn't fall asleep afterwards."

As soon as the man was gone, Meghan pushed her tankard away. "The riddle must mean the mouth of the chimney. That's the place all the flues come together."

"Or the buttress outside."

"Come on. The wagons have started rolling by now, and you don't want them to get so far ahead that we miss dinner."

"We can walk twice as fast as the wagons, and I'm finishing my beer."

Meghan fumed while Bryan took his time, looking around at the bar fixtures in between sips. Finally he pushed his tankard away, and she hopped off the stool.

"What are you doing now?" she asked in dismay.

"Finishing your beer," he replied complacently. "Just because it was a bargain doesn't mean you should waste it. It cost a copper after all."

The look on Meghan's face caused him to drain the tankard in one long chug, after which he rose, feeling inordinately pleased with himself.

"Stop at the trough on the way out," Meghan said with a scowl. "We can't have you looking around for a tree in the middle of our escape."

There were six separate flues in the chimney that could have been mistaken for a buttress, except for the fact that it rose over the crenellated battlements by the height of two old-fashioned jousting lances. Meghan looked around nervously for guards, but the only people visible on the wall-walk after lunch were a few stray tourists and some carpenters installing a new pulley system in one of the corner towers.

"They aren't exactly on war footing around here," Bryan commented, looking out over the neighborhood surrounding the castle. It was heavily built up with wooden houses, though some multi-story brick buildings were rising along the main streets. "There must be twenty times as many people living outside the walls as in the castle grounds."

"Stand between me and the men working on the pulley," Meghan instructed Bryan, intent on the coming task. "We'll be in trouble if somebody figures out what we're doing."

"Don't worry so much. If anybody asks why you're moving your hands around like that, I'll just tell them you have a nervous condition." Despite his words, he moved to shield her from the work crew, and with a last look around, she began the intricate motions needed to untie the magical knot.

"Done," she said, just as Bryan finished counting the ropes to figure out that the pulley's mechanical advantage was ten-to-one. He was surprised it didn't fall apart at that level of complexity, but then it occurred to him that may have been why they were replacing it.

"What'd we get?" he asked out of the side of his mouth, playing up the part of burglar.

"Lucky," Meghan replied. "It's a scroll canister, and I've already slipped it inside my jacket and resealed the flue. This could be our easiest task yet."

"Let's get going then. If I don't miss my workout with Rowan, our friends probably won't ask any questions."

The two took the nearest stairs down the inside of the wall and headed for the main gate, which was divided by a railing to separate the incoming traffic from the outgoing.

"They should do this at all the castles," Meghan said as they entered the outgoing stream of people and carts. "I can't tell you how many times I saw the gate jam up back home when a couple of carters going opposite directions wouldn't give way."

"Maybe it's not such a good idea after all," Bryan muttered, his eyes on a tall man wearing a green hood. The man stood in the gateway and seemed to be paying close attention to the people leaving the castle. "What's a green hood mean?"

"Mage," the girl replied, her voice going cold. Meghan had seen mages, of course—every baron had at least one in service, and a duke was bound to have several. But she'd been careful never to draw attention to herself before Bryan's arrival, so there had never been occasion for a mage to scrutinize her up close. She had practiced clearing her mind and pushing her magical energy into a small spot, an evasion method described in the scrolls, but it was different with an inquisitive mage just a few paces away.

"A private word," the mage said, stepping into the flow of foot traffic and blocking the way. "I am Sawith, the duke's war mage. Please come with me."

"Don't," Meghan mouthed at Bryan, adding such a pleading look that the young man managed to stop his initial urge to react violently. They followed the mage into the empty gatehouse guardroom, and at a small finger motion from Sawith, the door swung shut after them. The three stood in silence for a moment, then a yellow aura crackled into existence around the mage, and the smell of ozone filled the small room.

"A girl disguised as a boy whose presence in front of me I can barely detect, and a young man, if that's what you are, who practically oozes raw magical potential. No, don't try it," he added, raising a hand as Bryan began to summon up a fireball. "It's clear that neither of you are war mages, so be warned that the shield I have erected will return any magical attack you launch with twice the potency you give it."

"What do you want from us?" Meghan asked, putting a restraining arm across Bryan's chest.

"Isn't that obvious? I'll start with the king's reward for your capture, young lady, as you are obviously the girl described in the circular. Whatever magic you've been practicing in secrecy, however many poorly built towers you've collapsed, you're no match for me."

"I never collapsed a tower, I just caught my boyfriend when he fell off," Meghan rebutted the mage. "It's all I can do, catch things that fall. Whatever potential you sense in him, he couldn't even save himself."

"Is that so?" Sawith said, raising an eyebrow. "That won't diminish the king's bounty by one gold piece. Now, there are some questions you need to answer for me before I put you to sleep for transport. I know you are traveling with one of the player troupes and have visited the castles of the Red Duke and the Green Duke, and now I'll have the reason why."

As he spoke these words, the war mage's voice rose in a commanding tone, and Meghan felt his magical force and intense gaze compelling her to answer. At that moment, Bryan's left fist caught the tall mage in the pit of the stomach, doubling the man over. Bryan followed the punch with a right uppercut to the jaw, which was accompanied by the unmistakable sound of bone breaking. Sawith collapsed in a heap.

"You punched out a war mage?" Meghan half-screamed. "You can't do that."

"I just did," Bryan replied, rubbing his hand. "Hard jaw, I think I might have broken a knuckle. Should I finish him?"

"Finish him? As in kill him? Are you crazy?"

"I'm not kill-crazy if that's what you mean, but we can't have him coming after us," he replied, looking around the empty guardroom. "I'll just grab one of those axes and take off his head. The guys say it's the surest way to kill a war mage."

"No, wait," Meghan said, interposing her body between Bryan and the weapons rack. "He's completely out and his jaw is broken. Let me just spell him to sleep for a few days and we'll be long gone."

"You don't think somebody will come along and wake him up?" Bryan shook his head impatiently and reached around her for the axe.

"It doesn't work that way," she pleaded, trying to hold the axe in place in the weapons rack. "Listen, if you were a war mage, would you admit that somebody broke your jaw with a punch?"

Bryan paused. "That would be kind of embarrassing, wouldn't it?"

"He'd lose his job for sure, and nobody would ever hire him as a war mage again," Meghan said in relief. "I'm just money to him. When he realizes that we're gone, he won't tell anybody. I'll untie his bootlace and we'll close it in the door when we leave. It will look like he tripped and slammed his chin on the table. It can happen to anybody."

Bryan looked skeptical, but he wasn't really that enthusiastic about the idea of chopping the head off an unconscious man, so he helped Meghan move the body and undo one of the mage's long leather bootlaces. In a burst of inspiration, he tied a knot in the end of the lace and wedged it into a crack in the flagstones, just inside the door.

Meghan worked over the downed mage for a minute, her hands on his face, whispering to herself. Then they opened the door just wide enough to slip out into the stream of people leaving the busy castle.

Rowan parried Bryan's attack casually with the sword in his right hand, while simultaneously throwing some sand in the young man's face with his left. Bryan's blink reflex almost saved him, but the smaller particles that traveled a little slower than the larger grains of sand got into his eyes when the lids popped back open. He stumbled backwards with his sword held above his head like a shield, waiting for the inevitable follow-up blow, but none came. Bryan blinked several times as tears worked to clean his eyes, and looked up to see the big man standing at ease.

"What did I do wrong?" Rowan asked.

"You? You threw sand in my eyes."

"What did I do wrong?"

Bryan realized the repeated inquiry was a test rather than an ethical question, and thought for a moment. "You didn't take advantage of the opportunity you created," he admitted. "You should have pressed the attack."

"And you should have killed the war mage when you had the chance," Rowan said matter-of-factly.

Bryan let his sword fall as he tried to come up with a plausible evasion, but in the end he just asked, "How did you know?"

"Storm Bringer sent his hawk to keep an eye on the two of you this morning. You've been taking some serious risks."

"But we all went inside the gatehouse," Bryan protested. "I could have killed him in there and the bird wouldn't have seen it."

"I've been around enough fighting and death to be able to see if a young man has killed for the first time just by looking at him," Rowan replied. "But I can also tell you have the soul of a warrior, so I wouldn't be surprised if you told me your wife talked you out of it."

"She did!" Bryan seized on the excuse. "Meghan said that the war mage would be too embarrassed to admit that somebody punched him in the stomach and broke his jaw. She's always stopping me from killing guys."

"And she's probably right about the mage staying quiet this time. But the Blue Duke is a puppet of the false king, and when the time comes to fight, that mage will be lined up on the other side of the battlefield."

It took Bryan a while to digest what Rowan was telling him, but the big man waited patiently. "So the whole acting troupe, our festival tour, it's all a cover for planning a revolt?"

"No, it's how we all make our living, but we do seem to be performing more tragedies than comedies this year."

"And the natives who are always coming out of the woods and talking with Storm Bringer? The farmers who bring a little produce from their fields and walk along for a while with your group leaders? The local men who gather around for beer after every show?"

"You could say they're sympathetic to the cause."

"I don't know anything about war, but it's hard to believe that the veterans in the troupe and some local militia will be a match for an army, no matter how good you are," Bryan objected. "There just aren't enough of us, even if you add a few hundred sympathizers."

"We aren't the only troupe of strolling players, and the soldiers serving the barons and dukes aren't doing it out of loyalty. It's just a job, a bloody job at that, and men have been known to quit or change sides."

"Why now? Why didn't you tell us when we joined you?"

"Old friends vouched for Meghan, but you and your mythical Castle Trollsdatter were complete unknowns. I wanted time to see if your heart was in the same place as your words."

"I should have punched out a war mage earlier."

Rowan laughed. "With your swordplay, it's the only way you're ever going to beat one, but it was a smart move in any case. Mages are accustomed to instilling fear into everybody around them, and their hoods are a warning to beware. If you'd tried to launch a magical attack or draw a weapon it would have ended very differently, but he wasn't on guard against a street brawl."

"Have you ever fought against a mage?"

"I've fought against just about everything that walks and holds a weapon at one point or another," Rowan answered quietly. "I suppose you could say I have a gift for fighting and leading men in battle. Between you and me, I'd rather have Chester's talent for acting, but we don't always get what we ask for."

The first words out of Bryan's mouth when he met Meghan back at their tent after his training session were, "Rowan knows."

Meghan set aside the scroll she'd been trying to decipher and asked, "About you being a dragon?"

Bryan grimaced and shook his head. "About our outing to the Blue Duke's castle and the war mage. The shaman's stupid bird was watching us."

"I'd say that makes it a smart bird. What did Rowan say?"

"He said you shouldn't have stopped me from chopping Sawith's head off, but I already knew that."

"He was lying on the floor unconscious, and I still believe he'll keep it to himself."

"That wasn't Rowan's point. He finally let me in on what's going on around here, and it turns out that the players are part of some sort of rebellion. That war mage is loyal to the king, so we could end up fighting him again someday."

"I've been hearing rebellion talk ever since I can remember, but nothing ever comes of it," Meghan said, picking up the scroll again. "The baron would even make jokes about leading a revolution on his Naming Day feast. Nobody likes the king, but he keeps the best soldiers around him, including mercenaries from overseas. And in the end, who the king is just doesn't make a big difference in the everyday lives of most people. Somebody will always collect the mill and barrel taxes, and most of that money goes to pay soldiers and bribe dragons in any case."

"Of all the people, you, who needed to summon a dragon for protection against your own baron and king, think it doesn't matter who's in charge?" Bryan had to fight back the urge to shake her by the shoulders. "Life isn't all about magic and dragons. Even if the only choice between leaders is bad and worse, only an idiot would say it makes no difference."

Meghan looked up from the scroll in surprise. He was showing her a thoughtful side she hadn't suspected he possessed, even if she didn't agree. The women in the castle had always dismissed royal politics as something men talked about over their beer, and it hadn't ever occurred to her that things could substantially change in the kingdom. Her only goal had been to find a way to insulate herself from it.

"So you've chosen sides?" she asked.

"I think we both did that already when we fled your baron and started breaking into castles to steal stuff."

"It's not stealing. The items were left there for me, they belong to us. I just wish this scroll was written in my language for a change. All the gifts seem to be for you!"

"Let me see it," Bryan requested in a resigned voice. He cleared his throat and read, "Instructions for reverting to human form."

"I got that far," Meghan said in irritation. "What's the next letter sound like?"

"J, as in, I don't know, J," he said unhelpfully. "Join minds with one who wants you back. Seek your core and concentrate on its essential humanity and solidity while—it's just a bunch of New Age crap," he concluded, discarding the scroll. "This business about a revolt is serious."

"Do you want to get stuck being a dragon forever when you finally change?" Meghan demanded. She picked up the scroll and began studying it again. "It's funny, though. I did make out most of it with the letters you already taught me, and there weren't any instructions for becoming a dragon in the first place. It's all about returning to human form. I wonder if you'll be willing to give up being a dragon."

"Are you serious? Dragons eat raw meat, bones and all, and they probably don't have any beer," Bryan pointed out. "I get that they live a long time, but what's the point if you have to spend it all hanging around a cave to keep watch on your treasure? I have my own solution to that, by the way."

"What are you talking about now?"

"You know all the coppers and small silvers we've been saving up from tips? I traded them in for this." He pulled a cord out from around his neck and proudly displayed the small gold ring suspended there. "It's gold," he added unnecessarily.

"I can see that it's gold, but how are we going to buy anything on the road or at the next fair if you've turned all of our earnings into one little ring?"

"I figure you must have some savings left."

Meghan buried her head in her hands and moaned theatrically.

Juliana ran up to Bryan and Meghan, flushed and breathing hard from the exertion. "My father says the two of you need to hide, right now. Storm Bringer says there's a dragon coming."

"A dragon? I want to see it," Bryan said, trying to shake off Meghan's hands as she pulled him towards the ravine at the edge of the evening campsite.

"You promised on your word of honor that you'd follow Rowan's orders as long as we eat his bread," Meghan argued, holding on to his arm with a death grip. "We'll get into those rocks and watch from there."

"Please," Juliana added, bringing to bear her formidable talents of persuasion. A goofy grin spread across the young man's face and he yielded to Meghan's tugging, all the while looking back over his shoulder at the beautiful twin.

"Stop it," Meghan said, swatting him on the back of the head. "It's not like you don't see Nesta every day."

"That was Juliana," he replied, rubbing his hair where the pretend-wedding ring on her finger had bounced off his skull.

"And I wasn't staring. I just wanted to make sure she didn't have further instructions from her father."

"Stop lying and climb down there to check for snakes," she ordered, adding a shove for good measure. Between the constant eating and his daily sword exercise with Rowan, Bryan was filling out rapidly, and pushing against him was like trying to move a boulder. But he followed her instructions without complaint in the hope that she would forgive his latest transgression.

There was a recently fallen pine, brought down by a combination of storm winds and soil erosion around the roots, bridging the narrow gorge. The broken branches on the underside held the trunk up off the ground, and the green nettles formed a nearly impenetrable curtain. By working their way under the toppled giant where the unbroken branches jutted down into the ravine, the two young people were completely hidden from view, yet still able to see most of the campsite.

After a short wait, a giant shape glided over the wagons and then rose again, as if the dragon was taking a precautionary pass to check for hazards. It wheeled about in the air, its leathery wings flexing and twisting, and then it went into a shallow dive, landing about fifty paces in front of the waiting reception committee. The dragon needed a few hopping steps to bring itself to a halt, its wings spread to their fullest extent and tilted up like a drag parachute.

Rowan stood at the front of the group facing the dragon, his wife on his right and Storm Bringer on his left. Although the big man wore the sword that he was never without, the others were unarmed. Meghan muttered something to herself that sounded like "louder" to Bryan, which he took as a cue to focus his own unnatural hearing on the far-away conversation. The sounds of the birds, squirrels, and insects around them seemed to fade into the distance as the dragon's first words were spoken.

"Colder than I thought," the giant reptile said in a deep bass voice. "Not too windy, though."

"Sun is nice," Rowan responded conversationally. "What brings you to New Land, Shorinth?"

183

"Always straight to the point, Rowan," the dragon responded. "You're as beautiful as ever, Isabella. Surely that's enough reason for me to make the long flight."

"And you remain ever the flatterer," Rowan's wife replied. "Have you angered your elders enough to be driven into exile?"

"This is more of a fact-finding expedition." Shorinth blinked rapidly a few times and settled on his belly. He reached for his face with one of his forelimbs, which forced him to bring his head in close to his body. After a desultory scratch or two at his right eyelid, he extended his neck all the way out, with his lower jaw coming to rest on the ground just in front of Rowan's wife. "Would you mind?"

Isabella sighed and leaned forward to rub the itchy eye ridge for the dragon. Then she turned to Nesta and said, "Go and get some axle grease from the wagon master. Somebody has been scratching to the point where the scales are flaking."

Shorinth let out a rumble of pleasure and closed the eye that the woman was tending, but the other eye, as large as a child's head, remained wide open. "Some interesting rumors have reached Old Land in recent weeks. Castles being torn down by magic, revolution in the air, the barrier between our world and Dark Earth being breached. It occurred to me that if anybody in New Land knew what was going on, it would be you three," he concluded.

"And if you discovered even a speck of truth in those wild rumors, what would you do with it?" Rowan inquired.

"That would depend on the speck," Shorinth replied. "Information wants to be expensive, and I happen to be in need of funds to woo Ethelinda. She's finally left that insufferable flying whale of a dragon, Magnor."

"Isn't she a bit old for you?" Isabella asked.

"Beggars can't be choosers, and she's practically the only dragoness left in Old Land who isn't a sister, an aunt or a cousin. I tried going east for companionship, and I have the scars to show for it."

"So you wish information from us that you can trade for gold when you return," Rowan surmised.

"Even if I could obtain a sufficient hoard here, it would be a tedious operation to get it home," Shorinth said. "Renting a ship, escorting it all the way across the ocean, never knowing if the sailors below deck were dipping their grubby hands in my treasure. Information weighs nothing."

Nesta returned with a tub of axle grease and held it for her mother. Isabella stuck her bare hand in the thick mess without hesitation and began slathering it over the dragon's eye ridge, working it into folds in the hide where the scales chafed. Her daughters watched with interest, as if rubbing down dragons was a useful skill to be acquired.

Back under the pine, Bryan complained to Meghan, "You never do anything like that for me, and we're supposed to be married." Meghan shushed him frantically, but Shorinth had already shifted his gaze towards the ravine. He blinked slowly, and then turned his open eye to Storm Bringer.

"I don't suppose you know any young dragonesses on this backwards coast who would be interested in meeting a sophisticated drake such as myself?"

The shaman snorted and shook his head. "I'm afraid the only dragons on this coast are male, and I doubt they would be pleased by your prospecting on their grounds."

"Narl is an outlaw, and his brother, Barth, is mentally defective," Shorinth said. "Besides, they're both up north at the moment. Back when it happened, there was a rumor that a young dragoness was at stake, which was the only thing that could explain Narl's behavior. But five decades is a long time to remain in hiding, so maybe he broke the pact for a pile of gold after all."

"You're more generous with information than the last time we met, Shorinth," Rowan observed. Isabella moved in front of her husband to work on the eye ridge on the other side of the dragon's head, her daughters following in tow. "Could it be that you're choosing sides already?"

"Oh, I've always been on your side," Shorinth insisted. "But if, for example, a mage in New Land did figure out how to reopen the passage to Dark Earth, I'm sure it would come to your attention. I only ask that you remember your humble servant to said mage as an eligible bachelor."

"And you flew all the way from Old Land just to make that request?" Rowan asked skeptically.

"I believe I've learned what I came for," the dragon answered cryptically. "Thank you for your hospitality, but I should think about hunting something up for dinner and heading back. Ladies, always a pleasure," Shorinth added, nodding at Isabella and the girls. "Wisest thing I ever did was rescuing your great-grandmother from that pack of idiotic wolves. She was such a little thing that they would have been hungry again an hour later in any case."

The dragon turned and took a few steps into the gentle breeze, flapping his wings lackadaisically. His long neck curled back around his body and he addressed Storm Bringer. "A little help? I usually prefer to land near cliffs to make it easier to get airborne, but your campsite was chosen without me in mind."

The shaman shrugged and made a winding-up motion with one arm, creating a vortex of dust between the humans and the dragon. Then Storm Bringer cast his arm forward, and the miniature tornado seemed to flatten out and spring up under the dragon's wings. Shorinth soared into the air, pivoted, and swept back across the campsite, flying directly above Bryan and Meghan's position as he headed for the nearby hills to hunt.

"Laziest dragon I ever met," the shaman commented. "No wonder he never found a mate."

"He did fly all the way here just to warn us," Isabella said reprovingly. "If rumors have reached the dragons in Old Land, they've certainly come to the ears of the false king."

"Just try putting it on and flapping a little," Meghan pleaded. "I've got the reversion-to-human-form instructions memorized, even if you couldn't be bothered to read them. I'm sure I can walk you through it."

"The twins did seem pretty interested in that dragon," Bryan mused. "If I was him, I would have changed back on the spot."

"Maybe he can't, or maybe he's saving the human time he has left," Meghan said. "Dragons can live for thousands of years, even longer if nothing kills them, but they can only spend a human lifetime in human form. And once that time is past, they can no longer breed."

"You mean that dragons all start as humans, and they don't breed as dragons at all?"

"Did you think they laid eggs?" Meghan laughed out loud. "That's why there are so few dragons around. That and the fact that the males fight over the females, and the females fight over hoards. All of the original dragons date back to when your world gave up its magic. A group of the most powerful mages who wouldn't give up their powers left Dark Earth and came here. To prevent those who remained behind from profiting on the treasure they couldn't bring with them, they caused the magical land they inhabited to sink into the sea. There's a play about it that gets performed in Old Land, but the staging is too complicated for the traveling troupes."

"So the mages from Dark Earth came here and created dragons?"

"They came here and became dragons. Didn't you see Shorinth? As large as his wings are and as strong as I'm sure he is, a creature like him could never fly without magic. If dragons were wholly dependent on their wings to stay in the air, they'd be flapping like bumblebees."

"I guess that makes sense," Bryan allowed. "So you're saying that all the dragons around today are descended from Dark Earth mages?"

"A few of the oldest actually are Dark Earth mages, but they tend to lose interest in human matters after such a long time in dragon form. What I didn't know until Shorinth let it slip is that they've lost the ability to bring new dragons from Dark Earth. I shouldn't be surprised, since dragons are so private, and whatever scrolls they might have recorded while in human form didn't end up in my baron's collection."

"But you figured out how to reach Dark Earth and pull me through."

"I explained how I figured it out, and I don't know for sure if I could repeat it with anybody else," Meghan said. "It took a lot of energy, and if you hadn't grabbed my hand, I don't know what would have happened. Maybe a dragon has to be in human form to open the passage to Dark Earth. There are few dragons young enough to have any human time left, and maybe that's not how they want to spend it."

"So now you want me to crawl into this mound of silk and flap my arms like an idiot." Bryan rolled his tongue around the inside of his cheek, considering the idea, and then asked, "What are you going to do for me?"

"I bring you extra food all the time, and I've let you keep my share of our tips, which ended up on a string around your neck," Meghan pointed out. "What else do you want?"

"I've been thinking about what you said about us being with each other like husband and wife, and it doesn't make sense," Bryan replied, stepping closer to the girl. "If our magical energy is going to average out, it means that one of us will become stronger. You keep telling me that you've never heard of anybody learning to channel their magic as fast as I have, and I'm better than you at most of the things you've taught me. If I'm stronger than you, it means you'll be taking from me, and I'm cool with that. And if I'm wrong and it's the other way around, maybe that extra boost you can give me is just what I need to become a real dragon."

Meghan backed away. She recognized the green flames dancing in his eyes as a sign that he wasn't entirely in control of himself. Sneaking away from the camp to a field of clover to lay out the silk dragon suit for Bryan to crawl into suddenly seemed like a bad idea. "Maybe we should just go back," Meghan suggested uncertainly.

"For all your talk about our future together, you don't care as much about me as I do about you. Maybe you'd be happy if we spent the rest of our lives as best friends sharing a tent, but I'm going crazy here, and it's your fault."

"Hadrixia warned me that all boys say that," Meghan retorted, but her voice sounded weak to her, and she felt her pulse racing at more than twice its usual pace.

"I'm not a boy, I'm a man," Bryan grated out in a low voice. "I'd be a man who's killed other men if you didn't keep stopping me. I'll put on the dragon nightgown and dance around like a clown if that's what you really want, but first I need to hear you say that when this quest is over, you'll be mine for real. No more acting."

Meghan swallowed dryly and suddenly found herself falling backwards, thanks to placing a foot in the burrow of some small mammal. Bryan grabbed her shoulders and pulled her upright before her own reactions could even kick in to brace her for the fall. He held her so tightly that she thought he would crush her, and if she had moved her head forward just a hair, their noses would have been touching.

"Deal," he demanded rather than asked.

"Deal," she whispered back, closing her eyes against the brilliant green flames dancing in his pupils. Her heart pounded in her chest and the blood rushed in her ears, drowning out the night sounds of the meadow. Then she suddenly realized that she was standing on her own feet again and that Bryan had released her. She touched her lips and wondered if she had imagined the kiss.

When Meghan finally opened her eyes, a monstrous white shape was moving to engulf her, and she instinctively reached for her pendant to call upon her magical reserves. Then she heard Bryan's muffled voice from within the mass of swirling silk and came back to her senses.

"Get me out of this thing. I can't find the right opening and this stuff keeps wrapping itself tighter."

"Stop struggling," she called back. "It must be magically form-fitting and it's trying to shrink down to your size."

Bryan stood still for a moment, but the wind was picking up and the silk wings of the garment streamed out behind him. It was enough to pull him off balance, and he fell with a thud.

"Get it off of me or I'm going to start burning holes," he shouted.

"Don't! You'll burn yourself if the silk catches fire. Just lie still and I'll get you out of there."

Meghan snatched at handfuls of the heavy silk wrapped around Bryan, searching for the hole intended for the dragon's head and neck. The silk had thickened as the garment resized itself to human form, and she supposed the wings might have done the same if he had ever gotten his arms through those slits. Finally her hand worked its way into an opening in the silk, allowing her to root around inside until she found his face.

"Hey, stop poking me," he complained in a muffled voice. Meghan began to use her other hand to roll the silk down her arm, effectively bringing the opening towards his head. "And hurry up, I'm sweating buckets in this thing."

"Stretch," Meghan muttered under her breath, hoping that the same magic that controlled her native-produced moccasins was in play here. The silk seemed to resist her at first, but then the hole began to grow, and Bryan quickly squirmed out.

"I had just found the wing holes and was beginning to flap my arms when the extra silk I was standing on pulled my feet out from under me and began tightening around my legs," he complained. "I pulled my arms out of the wing openings to try to get my legs free, but instead the stupid silk bound them against my sides. I think it's some kind of weird dragon restraint device," he added, kicking the now quiescent mound of silk. "Where were you all that time I was struggling?"

"I was right here, watching," Meghan said, too embarrassed to admit that she thought they'd been kissing the whole time. "I thought you were, like, making progress."

Bryan jogged up to the front of the wagon train and asked Theodric, "Why are we stopping?"

"Hill is too steep for the horses to haul up the wagon carrying the stage timbers without risking that they hurt themselves. We'll unhook the team from the kitchen wagon and double up, though it means a late supper."

"They need the horses to cook?"

Rowan erupted in laughter, and he thumped Bryan on the back hard enough to make the young man stagger. "You should be on stage," he said. "I'm getting an idea for a new sort of play, without a script. We'll just put you up there and you can ask the audience members questions about how they live. Do they need the horses to cook—I've never heard anything so funny."

Bryan laughed along with the others this time, hoping to pass his question off as an intentional joke. He hadn't really thought that the horses contributed to the food preparation, but the question had come reflexively. It seemed to him that Hadrixia's translation magic had interfered with his internal filter that prevented every thought from being spoken, but as Meghan pointed out, the healer hadn't charged for her services.

"Doubling the teams to haul the wagons uphill more than triples the travel time. The horses have to return to haul the next wagon, and there's plenty of harness fiddling involved," Theodric explained. "Give me a hand with the changeover and you'll learn something."

"Is it just the wagon with the stage that's too heavy?" Bryan asked. "Couldn't a bunch of us just help push it along from behind? Maybe Storm Bringer could add a tail wind."

"Now there's an original idea," Rowan said. "It would save a lot of time if it works, and I do like keeping a schedule on the road. How about it, Theodric? The three of us should be able to take the strain off the horses."

Theodric gave Rowan a close look, shrugged, and took his place at the back corner of the wagon. Bryan took the middle spot for himself to prove that he was no shirker, and the giant leader of the players took the other corner. Somebody signaled the teamster to start the horses, and the men leaned into the wagon. It lurched into motion, and thanks to the extra manpower combined with the fact that the road was just starting to become steeper, the wagon soon reached the regular walking speed of the draft horses.

"This isn't so bad," Bryan huffed, straining every muscle in his body. He tried to remember what Meghan had taught him about magical strengthening techniques and realized that he hadn't been paying attention. "You guys alright?"

"Oh, we're just fine," Rowan assured him. "I've been pushing wagons out of mud holes and snowdrifts since I was ten, though it never occurred to me to try this before. Good workout for the legs."

The hill seemed to stretch on forever, and Bryan's mind went blank as he concentrated on putting one foot in front of the next. He closed his eyes as he pushed, and he thought he heard Meghan starting to say something, but Rowan broke out in an old work song, and the others joined in, drowning her out.

Finally the pushing got much easier and he heard the teamster shouting, so he opened his eyes to see that they were starting down the other side of the hill. Rowan and Theodric were sitting on the tailboard of the wagon, sipping beer and watching him in amusement.

"When did you guys stop pushing?" Bryan demanded.

"Before they started singing," Meghan told him angrily. She looked all red and flustered, and Bryan realized that the other women had been holding her back as they all walked along to watch him push a wagon up the hill. "Even the horses were slacking off and taking a break."

"Best example of strengthening magic I've seen in a while," Laitz commented. "If you don't want to do the one-man comedy play, you should consider a strongman act."

"I never learned any strengthening magic," Bryan admitted, out of breath and hungry, but otherwise no worse for the wear.

The nearby players who overheard the conversation stopped walking and stared.

"You called on that power without trying to?" Meghan asked. "No man could have kept that wagon moving without magic. The horses really did stop pulling near the end."

"I guess I just have a lot of excess energy lately," Bryan said.

"You're so lucky," one of the older women told Meghan. "Enjoy it while you can."

"It's said that if newlyweds put a copper in a purse each time they lay together, and then take one out for each time after their first year of marriage, the purse will never be empty," Faye observed to the general amusement of all.

Meghan turned bright red and fled back towards the props wagon.

Bryan shook his head in disgust and muttered, "What a rip-off."

At the communal supper, Rowan announced, "We're here a day early, thanks in no small part to the efforts of our young friend." He indicated Bryan with one beefy hand.

"Way to push a wagon, boy," Simon called out.

"You made the poor horses nervous about their job security," Jomar added. "They practically trotted the rest of the way."

"The horses have seen him eat and they were worried about the grain running out," somebody else contributed.

Bryan scowled and reached for a turkey drumstick on the latest tray deposited by the boy working as the kitchen wagon runner. His twist-and-yank method failed to separate the joint, and the whole bird slid across the table, bringing a new wave of laughter and comments from the players.

"Don't make fun of him," Hardol remonstrated the others. "A growing boy has to eat."

"We'll set the stage in the morning, but the performances won't start until the day after, so everybody is welcome to take the afternoon off and visit the attractions," Rowan continued with his announcement. "I understand that some of the vendors who keep booths on the fairgrounds actually raise their prices once the festivities start, so this may be our year to find some bargains."

"What's so special about the shopping here?" Meghan asked Faye. Simon's wife often sat next to the girl at meals in order to pepper her with questions about the healing techniques she had seen.

"The merchants around the port here specialize in importing the latest fashions from Old Land. They get a whole shipload of new styles every year, and there are thousands of local women who earn a good living making copies. I don't know of anywhere else in New Land where the production of clothing is so advanced."

Bryan leaned around Meghan and asked, "They have factories? I thought mass production wasn't possible here."

"Mass production, that's an interesting way to describe it," Faye replied. "The way it was explained to me, a merchant will purchase enough cloth to make a large number of garments and then buy examples of the new fashions. An expert seamstress carefully cuts all of the stitching out of the new garment and makes a drawing of how the pieces fit together."

"So a woman can borrow the pieces as a pattern to make a new dress and use the drawing to put them together," Meghan concluded. "What a great idea."

"It's more advanced than that," Faye said. "There are some large sheds down near the wharf with hundreds of women and girls working in each one. They sit at long tables, each of them doing a single task, like cutting the same piece or stitching a particular seam, and then they pass it on to the next person. Within a day of the ship arriving, the markets are flooded with the latest fashions."

"But then they're copies," Bryan objected.

"What's the difference?" Meghan asked.

"Well, if you could buy the original or a copy, wouldn't you pay more for the original?"

"But the original has been taken apart and handled by all of the seamstresses. I'd pay more for a new one."

"You don't get it. I mean, if you could have an original, wouldn't you prefer that over a copy?"

"How could there be copies if the original wasn't taken apart?"

"A different original. There can't be a whole shipload of unique new dresses."

"Well, if the new fashions are already copies, what difference does it make?"

"But the clothes from Old Land are original copies," Bryan insisted. "Get it? Like, people would see you and think that you're really sophisticated because you're wearing new Old Land clothes."

"Either something is original or it's a copy," Meghan replied, unable to follow Bryan's line of reasoning. "What difference does it make if it's copied here or copied on the other side of the ocean?"

"One is original and the other is pirated!"

"You think that pirates are interested in fashion?" Meghan asked. "I've always heard that they wear whatever they can steal. That's how you can tell them from regular sailors."

"Never mind," Bryan muttered, turning his attention back to the food.

"Step right up, the next contest begins in ten minutes. Win a cup of coppers or a stuffed dragon for your sweetheart back home. How about you, sir? With those long legs, the prize is as good as yours."

"What's the deal?" Bryan asked the barker, ignoring Meghan's attempts to pull him away.

"Just two coppers to participate. First place winner takes all the money in the goblet, second place gets the stuffed dragon, third place gets free entry into the next contest."

"How much is in the goblet?"

"Well, that's anybody's guess, but you can see for yourself that it's full."

"And how many men are running?"

"I see we have a regular money counter on our hands here," the barker replied, using a magic assist to raise his voice even further to try to create interest with passersby. "There aren't nearly as many men today as we'll get starting tomorrow, when the fair is in full swing."

"But how many?" Bryan insisted, eyeing the goblet.

"You only have to look at the starting line. Early birds get the best position."

"There must be a hundred men there already," Meghan whispered to Bryan doubtfully. "They all look like runners, do you see how skinny they are? And I doubt there are even a hundred coppers in that narrow goblet. It's like he's taking half of the money for the privilege of letting the men run around a horse track."

"It'll be a piece of cake. You saw me push the wagon."

"There's strength and there's speed. You've proven that you're strong, but for all we know that's making you slower. All of those men will be using magic to make themselves faster."

"It's just two coppers to try," Bryan cajoled.

"My two coppers, because you turned all of our earnings into that little gold ring!"

"Come on. I won't ask you for anything else the rest of the day."

"Horse manure," Meghan grumbled, but she dug in her purse and gave him two coppers, which were immediately transferred to the barker.

"In through the gate you go, contestants only. Your little brother can watch from the rail."

After twenty additional contestants entered the gate, and a long delay, followed by a great deal of shouting, Bryan emerged from the mob at the finish line and found Meghan sitting on the rail.

"They must have all been cheating," he blustered, brushing the dust off of his clothes. "I should go and demand my two coppers back."

"*Your* two coppers? And all of them were cheating?"

"Just the ones that finished ahead of me," he said, managing a grin.

"That would be all of them," the girl replied, unable to suppress a smile of her own. "I hope you learned something, anyway."

"I did, so you don't have to rub it in."

As they left the race area and headed into the market, the barker began calling for contestants to compete in a strongman competition. Bryan snuck a sideways glance at Meghan, but she was pretending not to hear.

"Where do they get all this stuff?" Bryan asked, devouring the display of edged weapons with his eyes. "Back home I could sell these to historical reenactors for a fortune."

"Weapons? They're made by smiths. What did you think?"

"I don't know, magic maybe."

"You've been here almost two months and you haven't noticed that people make everything by hand? From what you told me about Dark Earth, most of the stuff you bought came from the Far East in giant ships. The only things we get from there are silk and jade, occasionally tea. The luxury items that are worth transporting."

"Doesn't seem very efficient," he objected.

"Efficient? You've seen how much the horses eat, so if you're going to fill a wagon with goods, it had better be worth it. Other than weapons like this and other high value objects, there isn't even that much trade between the dukedoms."

"But what about the clothes from Old Land we were talking about last night?"

"The latest fashions are high value, as are spices and precious metals. The kind of things that dragons like," she added, hoping it would sink in that way.

"Is there anything you want?"

"Really? You'd let me spend what's left of my savings on something for myself?"

"Don't be sarcastic," Bryan replied mildly. "It makes you sound like an adolescent boy."

Meghan elbowed him hard, catching her funny bone on one of his ribs and nearly collapsing from the resulting shock that traveled up her arm and left her momentarily paralyzed. The fact that she had inflicted the injury on herself only made her madder, and she stalked off in the direction of the clothing stalls, doing her best to ignore her companion.

"What did I do?"

The girl set her lips in a thin line and ostentatiously looked in the other direction.

"I shouldn't have said you sound like a boy," Bryan apologized, remembering too late that she was a bit touchy on the subject. "I know you're tired of walking around pretending all the time, but Simon told me that after the tour, we'll go back to their winter site and you can dress any way you want. Besides, I like your *Elstan* voice."

This last unexpected compliment brought Meghan up short. "You're weird," she said, but she stopped looking away from him and slowed her steps. "Will you look at dresses with me? We can tell them that I need something to wear on stage."

"Sure, I love shopping for women's clothes," Bryan lied, figuring he owed her that much for losing her money in the race. Besides, it was getting near lunch and there were some food stands he hoped to talk her into visiting.

"I thought this was a day off," Bryan complained as he followed Rowan to the practice area behind the wagons.

"I never take a day off from sword practice, even if I'm too sore to move properly. Fighting is as much about mental preparation as it is about physical conditioning. Your enemies will never ask if you're taking the day off."

"I don't have any enemies," Bryan countered. He ducked under the rope that was tied to the tops of a number of wooden stakes, forming a square reminiscent of a boxing ring, except the rope didn't go all the way around. "Was the rope too short?"

"No, that's today's lesson," Rowan responded. "You may never have to fight in a prize ring, but this is how the noblemen settle scores. It should be eight sword lengths to each side for a proper duel."

"I don't see how it makes a difference. You always stand in one spot and barely move when I attack."

"That's because you don't force me to move. But you've been improving rapidly and I don't want you to get into the habit of thinking that your adversaries are immobile. Starting today I'll be bringing the fight to you."

"So you'll be attacking me as a favor," Bryan summarized. "I guess it can't be any worse than—hey!"

Rowan's sword might have cleaved Bryan into two halves if he hadn't gotten his own up in time to block the blow. Both swords emitted a shower of sparks, as they always did when meeting for the first time in a bout. Bryan tried to spare a corner of his concentration to maintain his sword's enchantment with his own magical force.

The attacks were continual and relentless, and for the first time while fighting Rowan, Bryan found he was continually retreating, often until he felt the rope against his back. At that point, he would put all of his efforts into turning the angle of the big man's attack so he could escape to the side and continue backing. Just when he was beginning to wonder how long he could parry the endless blows, Rowan pulled up and rested his sword on his shoulder.

"You calling it quits?" Bryan huffed, pretending a cockiness he didn't feel.

"No, you did," Rowan replied with a smile. He pointed to the opening in the rope, which was now in front of his opponent. Bryan realized that he had backed out of the ring.

"I didn't know," he admitted. "So that's when a duel is over, when one swordsman backs out of the ring?"

"No," his instructor replied. "A duel is over when one of the fighters is dead. Maneuvering your enemy into leaving through a gap in the rope is my own invention."

"What for? Your opponent can escape without having to duck under, which would give you an easy chance to kill him."

"Exactly. But I'm only fighting you."

"I realize I'm not a match for you at swordplay and never will be, but you don't have to rub it in."

"You don't understand," Rowan replied with infuriating patience. "If you're fighting more than a single opponent, your goal must be to kill or disable them as quickly as possible to keep them from encircling you. If you're fighting one man, you only need for him to run away. If you don't provide a way out, every fight will be to the death."

"But if you let your enemy run away, won't he come back and kill you later?"

"It's possible. It's also possible that your sword will break or you'll get a bug in the eye and an inferior swordsman will take advantage. Stopping fights quickly by leaving your enemy a way out may be the most important lesson I teach you. Just don't try it with a war mage because he'll be more dangerous out of sword reach."

"I liked the trick with the pommel better."

"Why do we have to wait for our last night before doing anything?" Bryan asked. "Don't you want to get working on the fourth clue?"

"You heard what Isabella said. If rumors about my opening a passage to Dark Earth and bringing you here have reached the dragons in Old Land, surely the king and his dukes know as much. I've been talking to the women about the Black Duke's castle, and I think I already know where we have to go."

"To the traitor's sack. What's the big deal?"

"And where would you look for a traitor's sack in a castle?" Meghan shot back.

"I don't know, I'd ask somebody I guess. It worked in the last place."

"The last place was a brewery, and you got the one piece of information that man actually had to trade. Where do you suggest we go to ask about a traitor's sack? The dungeons?"

"Sounds like an idea."

Meghan stared at him in disbelief. "The whole point of dungeons is to keep prisoners inside and rescuers outside."

"So nobody will expect us to try it," Bryan persisted. "That's the element of surprise."

"I think those games you keep talking about affected your brain. Do you think you can just slip into a dungeon, interview the prisoners, and then leave through some magical back exit?"

"It worked in the Red Duke's tower, sort of."

"I don't know what to—it doesn't matter," Meghan cut herself off. "The point is, there's a bronze statue in the courtyard of the Black Duke's castle commemorating the alliance between the two traitor dukes and the prince from Old Land who assassinated the king."

"Who would want a statue like that?"

"The Black Duke's father, apparently, since he was one of the traitor dukes. Anyway, it's the usual sort of thing for a big bronze, the duke sitting on a rearing mount with his sword drawn for battle. But people say that if you look at the rock the horse is standing on, you'll see that it's actually a sack bulging with coins."

"The traitor's sack. But why would the traitor duke pay for a statue like that?"

"Apparently the sculptor made the duke look better in bronze than he did in real life, and there's a trick to balancing statues that made a rework too expensive. If anybody had noticed at the unveiling the sculptor would have spent his life in the dungeon, but who pays attention to the rock?"

"So you admit that checking the dungeon was basically a good idea."

Meghan shook her head and continued. "I'm practicing the untying spell every day so I can do it as fast as possible, but the statue is right in the middle of the courtyard. I don't know if we can count on the area emptying out at night and they may be on the alert for us. We could end up sneaking into a trap."

"What we need is a diversion," Bryan said decisively. "When everybody is looking in the other direction, they won't notice you opening the sack and taking whatever it is."

"I don't want you running around with your sword killing people."

"I guess that would work too, but I was thinking of something less bloody."

"Like what?"

"An illusion."

Something about his broad smile made Meghan nervous, and she wondered if taking their chances with sneaking in at night wouldn't be the better option after all.

The troupe's final performance of the festival was *The Traitor*, and the audience seemed more restless than usual. Some of the parents with small children disappeared during the intermission, and the empty spaces on the amphitheatre grass were quickly filled with hard-looking men who were clearly the worse for drink. A few of them tried jeering at the actors, but the players assigned to crowd control removed them quickly and efficiently.

When Bryan brought the light up on Bethany, struggling across the front of the stage with her baby in the shaman's made-to-order snowstorm, a fight broke out in the crowd. While some people began singing a patriotic New Land song, others were clearly trying to start a riot. Most of the audience was sensible enough to flee, and Rowan and the rest of his veterans quickly waded into the scrum. By the time Bryan got there, the fighting was mainly over, and a few dozen men were sleeping it off in the grass.

"We'll break down the stage tonight and get on the road first thing in the morning," Rowan announced. "Whoever got these men drunk and sent them to disrupt the play must know we've been expecting a move, and they're hoping we'll think this was it. I won't be surprised if they try an attack in force tomorrow."

None of the players seemed particularly surprised by the change of plans, and with the help of lighting globes supplied by Theodric and Bryan, they set about dismantling the stage and packing the wagons.

Isabella sought out Meghan where the girl was helping to pack the props wagon for the road, though there wasn't really all that much to do since the players were experts at keeping ready to move on short notice.

"Rowan sent me to tell you that if you and Bryan need to go somewhere, you shouldn't let packing up stop you."

"Where would we go?" Meghan asked, reflexively trying to maintain the secrecy of the quest, but Isabella just smiled. "Well, we may be planning on a quick visit to the castle, but we were going to wait until the wagons got moving, since we pass it on the way out of here."

"My husband is expecting trouble tomorrow, so it would be better for you not to fall behind. Just be careful, and if something goes wrong, send a signal. We'll have people keeping an eye on the castle tonight in any case."

Bryan found Meghan right after Isabella left. "Rowan came and replaced me on the stage break-down saying that you were looking for me."

"I guess I am now," the girl admitted. "Isabella basically told me that if we're going to make an expedition to the Black Duke's castle, we'd better get going."

"That's fine by me. It's been a long day, though. Do you have enough energy saved up to stay sharp?"

"I'll be fine as long as I remember not to fall asleep in a wagon when we get back. How about you?"

"I had a big dinner," Bryan replied by way of explanation. "If we're going to be sneaking in, I'm bringing my sword."

"Just don't pull it out unless you really have to." She paused and kindled a small light to peer into his face. "You look pretty angry about something already. Did somebody hit you in the fighting after the show?"

"I didn't get there in time," he complained, clearly regretting the fact that he had missed his chance.

"And you're mad about that?"

"I'm mad that those thugs scared off the crowd, so we didn't get any tips!"

"Never mind that and listen. If they're looking for us, they'll expect a tall young man and a girl dressed as a boy, so I'm wearing my *Elstan* dress tonight."

"As long as you don't expect me to wear a dress too, I'm fine with it," Bryan replied.

"It must be some kind of party," Meghan whispered, crouching next to Bryan on the wall-walk. He had scaled the wall without the use of any magical aides and then hauled her up with a rope. She peered down into the courtyard where hundreds of men and women were mingling, some of them obviously very familiar with one another.

"There are guards patrolling the wall in pairs, but they passed just as I was getting to the top, so we have a little time. I guess they aren't trained to look down." Bryan finished coiling the rope around his midsection, covered it with his jacket, and then took his sword belt from his shoulder and buckled it around his hips.

"They probably aren't expecting trouble. Either that or it's a trap."

"You worry way too much. I've already seen two couples head into the shadows in the corner, and a little further up the wall-walk are stairs that must come out in that area. We can head right into the courtyard and everybody will assume that we're just another couple who've been rolling around in the dirt."

"Why would people want to roll around in the dirt?" Meghan whispered back before the meaning of the phrase came to her. She felt her face get hot when he gave her one of his superior looks. "Let's just go, then. I don't think anybody down there will see us moving as long as you keep your head below the level of the battlement openings. The moon is up on that side, so it might catch somebody's eye if you pass in front."

He smiled rather than replying, letting her know that he was still thinking about her last question. Bryan enjoyed not being the naïve one for a change, and he would have liked to take the time to tease her about it, but the patrol was already heading back in their direction. He led the girl stealthily to the stairs.

"Quiet," the girl muttered, and Bryan correctly guessed that she was calling on some magical stealth technique as opposed to giving him instructions. His feet seemed to tingle unnaturally, but he couldn't hear even the slightest scrape as they descended the stairs. He made a mental note to ask her how she learned that trick, then he flashed forward to some long, boring explanation and decided not to bother.

The silence was broken by a woman's soft moaning and a man saying something in a strained voice. Meghan gripped Bryan's arm as he wound his way through amorous couples with his superior vision. As they moved out of the shadows, they encountered a final couple who seemed to be engaged in a wrestling match, and then she had to draw Bryan forward because he paused to watch.

"Whoever is in charge of the lighting here sucks," the freshly minted stage illumination expert commented. He looked up at the magically suspended orb with disdain. "I would have gone with a grid of globes closer to the ground, but this clown is trying to do it with one big fireball that's more yellow than white."

"All the better for us," Meghan reminded him. "If you were doing the lighting, we wouldn't have made it in unseen."

"I have my professional pride," he retorted, which struck the girl as so irrelevant that she didn't see the need to respond.

They joined the general flow of couples meandering around the square, and despite being inside of the castle, most of the men wore swords on their hips. The conversations were surprisingly subdued, and it reminded Meghan of the leave-taking parties back at her own castle before the soldiers headed off to war.

The statue stood at the center of the courtyard, where it was largely ignored as an ever-present outdoor monument that provided no places to sit. Bryan strolled right up to the horse's rear quarters and observed, "It's a sack, alright. The duke must have been blind not to see it."

"Nobody looks at the rock the statue stands on, it's like an afterthought," Meghan said in defense of the long-deceased traitor without understanding why. "There's too much light. When I start moving my arms around, everybody in the courtyard will see."

"Maybe they'll think you're doing maintenance, cleaning it or something."

"Oh right. I'm wiping a bronze horse's butt in the middle of the night. That makes sense."

"Well, if I stand behind you, the statue will shield you from the other side."

"Except that I count four sides."

"Two of them are really small. Do you want me to try my diversion instead?"

Meghan slapped down his hand as he prepared to form a giant dust dragon or something similarly insane, then she took a deep breath and did the fastest magical untying spell on record. Her hands blurred through the air and the side of the bronze sack disappeared, allowing her to reach in and pull out what appeared to be a copy of her own pendant. Nobody raised the alarm about thieves in the castle, and she was about to retie the knot when she noticed that the top of the sack seemed to be moving closer.

"The statue is falling!" Bryan yelled, at the same time grabbing her elbow and pulling her out of the way.

Looking back at the toppling monument, all Meghan could think was that at least she would escape the indignity of being executed while dressed as a boy.

"Just keep on circling and try to look as confused as everybody else," Bryan murmured into her hair. He had kept a tight grip on her arm ever since pulling her back as the towering monument toppled over with a tremendous crash on the courtyard flagstones. "The trick is to blend in. I used to see scenes like this all the time in moving pictures. Oh, you know what I mean. Did you get what we came for?"

"Here," she said, handing over the pendant. "If I hang them both around my neck they'll just clank together."

Bryan casually accepted the pendant and slipped the chain over his head, as if he was receiving a good-luck charm as a farewell gift from his sweetheart.

"Everybody make room," shouted a self-important man in a nightshirt. He mounted the fallen statue and the crowd drew back a few steps, at the same time becoming more closely packed together as people on the fringes pushed for a better view.

"It's the duke's son," a woman walking past Meghan said in reply to her escort's question. "The mean one."

A few uniformed guardsmen pushed through the crowd and began examining the statue while the duke's son began questioning the witnesses.

"Now, did anybody actually see the statue fall?"

"Somebody shouted a warning, and then I turned and saw it coming down," a man called out.

"Was there anybody suspicious nearby?"

"All I saw was the old bronze duke coming at me with his sword drawn," the man replied, approaching the inquisitor. "I pushed Ann out of the way and jumped after her. If not for the warning, we both would have been crushed like those broken flagstones," he added, pointing at the damage.

"He's making it up," Bryan muttered to Meghan. "There was nobody else near."

"Who shouted the warning?" the duke's son demanded. After a long stretch of silence, he added, "Did anybody see who shouted the warning?"

"I think I saw a tall guy near the statue wrestling with a woman, and the voice seemed to come from that direction," somebody finally ventured.

"A tall man wrestling with a woman. Thank you for describing half of the people present," the duke's son said sarcastically. "Anybody else?"

"There's something here," one of the guardsmen examining the statue called out to the duke's son. "The money sack the horse was standing on is folded over, as if it couldn't take the weight anymore. It must have cracked as the duke fell because it's hollow at the crease."

"All statues are hollow, you fool," the duke's son rebuked the man. "Did you think it was solid bronze?"

Some of the crowd laughed in a mechanical way, as if they were accustomed to playing chorus to the young nobleman. As quickly as he had suspected foul play, the duke's son shifted to accepting the statue's collapse as structural failure and lost interest in the investigation.

"Tell the guard to stay on alert," he ordered for the sake of sounding like he was in command. "Tomorrow we ride for the mountains."

Now that it was lying on its side with many of the pointy parts broken off, the statue began to attract attention from tired legs looking for a place to sit. The duke's son shook his head in disgust, and then stalked back towards the palace section of the castle.

"Let's go," Bryan said, guiding Meghan towards the lover's lane along the dark base of the castle wall. Strangely enough, the commotion with the statue had done nothing to interrupt the jousting couples, and they had to take a serpentine route to reach the stairs to the wall-walk.

"Hold on," Meghan whispered, her eyes on the top of the wall. "The guards just started toward the stairs."

"It seems like a shame to just waste the shadows," he murmured back, throwing in an exploratory nibble on her ear.

Her slight body went rigid against him, and he would have sworn he could see black fire sparking in her eyes.

"Oh, please not now!" he heard in his head, as clearly as if the girl had spoken out loud.

"Meghan?"

Her hand flew to cover his mouth, and his superior night vision showed the look of shock on her face. He realized that she thought he had spoken out loud.

"I didn't say anything out loud. I just thought it."

Her eyes grew so large that he worried for a moment that he was shrinking.

"You can hear my thoughts?" she asked in his mind.

"I think it's just the things you say to yourself, if you know what I mean."

"It must be the pendants. I've heard about magical pairing of objects, but I thought it only worked with crystals."

"So tell me something," he said in his thoughts. "How is it that all of these couples we can hear having fun in the dark are so willing to share their magic?"

"Maybe they're all married?" Meghan thought back.

Bryan was sure he detected a shade of concealment in the girl's answer that he never would have caught if she had been speaking out loud.

"Maybe they aren't all married and you haven't been entirely truthful with me?"

"The guards are past the stairs so let's get going." She whispered her sound-muffling spell and sped upwards before Bryan could convince her to join the lovers in the shadow of the wall cast by the full moon.

"Then the duke's son said that tomorrow they ride for the mountains," Bryan concluded his report to Rowan on their outing to the Black Duke's castle. Isabella, Storm Bringer, and Laitz were also part of the group walking out in front of the wagon train, which had taken on the feel of an armed troop moving through enemy territory.

Rowan nodded to the shaman, who exchanged a significant look with his hawk, and then cast the bird into the air. It winged off in the direction of the mountains.

"Better safe than sorry," Laitz commented.

"Maybe in the daylight somebody will examine the statue more closely and realize that a chunk of metal is missing," Bryan speculated. "Nobody seemed to be particularly upset by it, so maybe they've all been waiting for the thing to topple over."

"Traitors are rarely loved, even if they act in the best interests of the community," Isabella observed. "The old duke, the current duke's father, was a man of honor in his way. Given how it worked out, I'm sure that the family would prefer that everybody forget about those times. The duke's men were probably behind the trouble we had at our last performance."

"If the exiles fled Old Land because their uprising against the old kingdoms failed, why did they set up the same system when they got here?" Bryan asked.

"Excellent question," Storm Bringer chimed in. "I've been asking your people the same thing as long as I've known them and I've never gotten a sensible answer."

"Why do you think it happened?" Bryan asked the shaman. His question elicited a groan from Rowan, who had obviously heard Storm Bringer's opinions on the subject more than once.

"It's the castle economy," the native replied. "Building large castles requires funds raised through taxation, a division of labor, and a ruling class to occupy them. Once your barons, dukes, and kings have their castles, constantly attacking one another is the only way to justify the expense. If your people all lived on farms, you wouldn't need the centralized governments and armies."

"Makes sense to me," Bryan said. "But why did the exiles build castles?"

"Why do fish swim?" Storm Bringer responded.

"I don't know."

"Because it's the only way they know how to live."

"Makes sense to me," Bryan repeated, bringing another groan from the leader of the players. "Hey, can I ask you guys something about magic?"

Laitz raised an eyebrow, and Rowan gave the shaman a "See what you've gotten us into," look, but Isabella smiled encouragingly and nodded her head in assent.

"When we were in the castle, there were a bunch of people pairing off in the dark who didn't strike me as married, and I wondered how they could avoid losing their magic to each other."

Isabella turned pink and choked back her mirth. "You men explain it to him. I'll go check on the girls." She walked quickly away, her back shaking with silent laughter.

"Didn't they have the oldest profession where you came from?" Laitz asked.

"Sure," Bryan said. "But what difference does that make?"

"The mage-certified inability to share magic is the main qualification for those who wish to join the guild."

Thanks to the pain-killing magic worked by Simon's wife, the boy had stopped shrieking by the time Meghan got there. But when Jomar's son had tripped and sprawled while running around the wagon, his foot had gone under the wheel sideways and been crushed to a pulp.

"Better put him to sleep for this," Simon told his wife.

She nodded grimly and stroked the boy's forehead while crooning a lullaby. Jomar and his wife arrived just as their child's breathing became regular and he slipped off into unconsciousness.

"I can't save the foot," Faye told the parents. "We'll have to take it off."

The boy's mother gave a sobbing cry and sank to the ground next to him, cradling his head on her lap. Jomar's face took on a set expression that was horrible in its lack of emotion, and he stepped forward and drew his large belt knife.

"I've done battlefield amputations, and the knife is best if you take the limb off at the joint," he said hollowly. "Let's get this over with so he can start healing."

"Wait," Meghan pleaded, pushing her way in between the father and son. "I don't know if I can fix this, but you have to let me try. I've only watched the healing for injuries this bad, but I'm sure I can't make it worse."

Jomar pushed her away impatiently, his mind too focused on the task at hand to even understand her. Rowan had arrived with Isabella by this point, and the large man restrained the boy's father by the simple expedient of clamping Jomar's arms to his sides. Faye happily made room for Meghan to sit by the child and do what she could.

Calling on her memory of aiding Hadrixia with the crush injuries so common among the local quarry workers, she took the mangled foot in both hands and tried to imagine the bone structure before a loaded wagon and a hard oak wheel had turned it into a pulp. The toes were still intact, which reminded her of a trick she had seen the healer use when a drill-holder's hand had been shattered by an errant sledgehammer swing.

"Let me see his other foot," she demanded, pulling the boy's leg out straight so the feet were side by side. Then she started at the little toe on each foot, using both of her hands simultaneously. She traced the path from the toe to the ankle with her index fingers, while muttering every bone-setting incantation she could muster under her breath.

Faye gasped as the mangled foot began to reshape itself under the girl's ministrations. It was as if the bones had suddenly been transformed to snakes that were writhing about under the torn skin.

By the time Meghan reached the big toe, the sweat that formed on her scalp was dripping down her face. The girl had never felt her magic so strongly before, and she started over again at the pinkie toes. By the third pass, the little foot looked almost normal, though it was swollen by the blood from all of the crushed tissue.

"Do you need to take a break?" Isabella asked, crouching next to the girl. "I once saw a court healer lose her ability after overexerting herself with a child."

"I'm fine," Meghan replied, realizing with surprise that it was actually true. She shifted both of her hands to the injured foot and cupped it between her palms. "Some of the soft tissues need help before they can start to heal, but this part is easier."

A glow formed between her hands, more green than blue, and she wondered at the subtle color change in her healing aura. Still, Meghan could sense the boy's muscles and tendons drinking in the energy and repairing themselves, and she held on to the foot until she felt him stir. Her healing energy had infused his entire body and brought him out of his magic-induced slumber.

"What happened?" the boy asked in a sleepy tone, causing his mother to burst out anew in tears and clutch him to her bosom. Her son looked embarrassed and tried to push her away. "I'm hungry. Why is Elstan holding on to my foot?"

"I'm not Elstan," Meghan retorted automatically, but she couldn't help smiling as she rose to her feet. Jomar grabbed her hand and pressed it to his heart, a gesture normally reserved for soldiers pledging loyalty to noble households. The girl blushed red and mumbled something about anybody doing the same thing. She was relieved when Bryan arrived and led her out of the group of players, who were looking at her like she was some kind of goddess.

"Don't I get any thanks?" he demanded as soon as they were clear.

"Thank you for getting me out of there," Meghan replied. "I don't like it when people treat me like I'm somehow better than them."

"I mean thanks for helping you heal the kid," Bryan said. "You were drawing so much magic from me that my pendant started heating up."

"I was?" Meghan fingered the pendant hanging around her own neck. "I'd never felt so strong, but I didn't know why. I thought it was just because the need was so great. Thank you."

"Yeah, well you're just lucky that everybody was so busy standing around watching you that I was able to slip into the kitchen wagon and grab a pie to replace my energy. Mincemeat, pretty tasty."

"I know it's a bit of a rush, but my sister and I think that you should play the lead for *The Good Harvest*. We always put it on for the last day of the festival in the White Duke's castle, so you have eleven days to learn the lines."

"Does she dress like a boy?" Meghan asked.

"Oh, no. She's very girly. And we're both getting too old for the role in any case," the other twin said.

"Thank you, Juliana. That must be the nicest thing anybody has said about my looks."

"She's Nesta," Bryan interjected. "And I'm always telling you how cute you are when you get mad." Meghan cast him a withering glance as they all walked along behind the props wagon. "No, you have to get really angry or you just look disagreeable."

"We'll take turns teaching you, Meghan," Juliana said. "I bet you have the whole part memorized before we even get near the castle. You're so smart."

"Father wants to see you," Nesta added, giving Bryan a little push to get moving.

"You're so lucky," the other twin said as soon as Bryan was out of earshot. "He's so tall and handsome, and father says he has the makings of a great man. I wish I was married to someone so nice."

The pink blush that had begun mounting Meghan's cheeks under the constant stream of compliments now bloomed to rival a rose, and she self-consciously pulled some of her dark hair forward to hide her face.

"But you get proposals all the time," Meghan protested. "Bethany told me that you turned down a duke's son, Nesta, er, Juliana, and that you could have married into the king's family, Nesta."

"Our parents didn't approve of those men, and to tell the truth, neither did we," Juliana replied with a sigh. "Besides, we've both been betrothed to men from Old Land since we were babies. We've never even met them."

"But you must be, uh..." the girl trailed off, not willing to ask their ages outright.

"Oh, we're not quite that old," Nesta replied. "I'm twenty-three and a fraction."

"And I'm twenty-three and a slightly smaller fraction," Juliana added. They both looked at Meghan expectantly.

"I'll be eighteen in a few days," she said. "Please don't tell anybody. I hate making a fuss."

"Well, you have a husband to celebrate with," Juliana replied, winking at her sister. "Are you ready to start on your lines?"

"I guess. How come I've never heard of the play? I know our castle was a bit off the beaten path, but we did get visits from some of the smaller traveling companies."

"We only put it on during the summer or at the White Duke's castle," Nesta explained. "Even though it's for kids, it's kind of political and it causes too many fights at the festivals."

"I would have thought you'd stop performing *The Traitor* if that was an issue."

"The difference is, the good guys actually win in this one."

"What's with you today?" Bryan asked Meghan on his return to the campsite following an exhausting session with Rowan.

"Nothing," Meghan said, giving him a false smile. "I've got my new lines down, and I think I've figured out what the final clue for our quest means."

"Don't try to fool me, I'm not that dense," he said, stepping closer and examining her small face. "What is it?"

"Nothing," she replied. "I just don't like making a fuss is all."

"A fuss about what?"

"Nothing."

"A fuss about what," he repeated, this time without speaking out loud.

"Hey, we said no mind-talking unless it was important," Meghan protested. She tried to back away and found herself up against the tent.

"It's something important to you, I can tell that much," he insisted, reaching under her chin and tilting her head up so he could look into her eyes. "Come on, you know you're going to tell me."

"I am not," she flared, but it was hard not to laugh at Bryan's clumsy attempt to provide emotional support. He looked just like an intelligent dog that had been Hadrixia's companion for many years.

"Those magicians back on Dark Earth I told you about used to do mind-reading acts," he continued, trying to make his gaze hypnotic. Then he went back to speaking without words. "I bet you can't stop yourself from thinking about whatever it is."

Too late Meghan reached up to remove her pendant. She had already said to herself, "Don't think about your birthday," and the thought had been shared.

"Oh, is that all?" Bryan said, releasing her. "I was worried it was something serious. My birthday was a couple weeks ago, I think. I lost track with your screwy calendar. Hey, wait a second. I got you something."

As Bryan ran off towards the wagons, Meghan tried to keep herself from getting excited about the prospect of a present. After all, he had probably made it up on the spot and would return with a cold chicken that he would devour himself when she declined. The girl went into the tent and began practicing the untying spell for the final hiding place of the quest. She was genuinely surprised when Bryan returned with a bundle wrapped up in a thin blanket.

"Happy Birthday. Nobody seems to have wrapping paper in this world."

Meghan took the parcel with low expectations and unfolded the blanket. When she saw what he had brought her, she actually choked up and couldn't stop the tears from coming out.

"You don't like it?" Bryan asked in concern. "When I went back to the shop to buy it, I thought you wanted the blue one with the long sleeves, but the woman insisted that it was this dress."

"She was right," Meghan said, looking up through glistening eyes. "Thank you. How could you afford it after changing all of our money into gold?"

"I saved all of our tips from the festival and went on the last day when everything was on sale. Aren't you going to try it on?"

"I'm not going to risk damaging my new dress by squirming into it on my hands and knees in the tent." She went outside, held the dress up in front of her body, and stood as tall as she could. "How do I look?"

"Like dessert," Bryan rumbled in a low voice that she felt in her toes. "Close your eyes."

"Stay over there," she warned him.

"I will, just close them."

Meghan closed one eye first, and then cautiously lowered the other lid, squinting at him through the lashes until the light was finally shut out. She began preparing an outraged response should Bryan step forward and embrace her, but an image of a young woman holding a dress in front of herself slowly began forming in her mind.

"Is that me?"

"What kind of question is that?" Bryan replied in irritation. "Do you really think there's another girl out here who happens to look just like you and is holding up the same dress?"

"Don't be so literal, I was just asking." She gazed at herself through Bryan's eyes, marveling at her own appearance, which somehow looked much more like a woman than the girl she was used to seeing in her copper hand-mirror. Then she noticed her expression and frowned, but her lips in the mental image remained puckered for a kiss. She got as far as a weak, "No fair," before his arms encircled her and he practically crushed her mouth with his own.

"Water that's white, falls at its right, from the first bite, take what you might."

"If I never hear another bad riddle it will be too soon," Bryan complained.

"Rhymes help people to remember lines," Meghan explained. "Some of the classic plays are all in verse. I was going to suggest you try one of those parts."

"What difference does it make? I could play any part now."

"What do you mean?"

"I have you to be my memory," Bryan said. "You can learn my parts and prompt me through our pendants."

"What?"

"Sure, that's how lots of people who are too busy to learn their lines work on Dark Earth, especially political leaders, though they use gadgets for prompting rather than magic." He moved over beside her and brushed the hair back from the side of her face. "So, you want to fool around?"

"I do not want to fool around," Meghan asserted, though it was hard not to giggle. "I also do not want to learn your lines for you because you're too lazy to learn them yourself. What I want is to solve this riddle so we can find the final piece of the puzzle and turn you into a dragon, assuming you still have the potential."

Bryan ignored her protest and tried nuzzling her neck, and this time she did giggle, but she also moved away.

"At least help with the riddle first."

"What's so complicated about that? We need to find a waterfall, look on its right—no, its left, since the water falls on the right, and then you do your magic thing."

"What about the 'first bite' line?"

"That reminds me, I'm hungry," Bryan said, turning around to crawl out of the tent. "Do you want anything?"

"You want me to memorize your part, and you can't sit still long enough to help solve a riddle?"

"I'd do it for you."

"No, you would not do it for me. You wouldn't even do it for yourself, which is why you're asking me in the first place."

"You know what I mean. Anyway, we'll see it when we get there. All of these clues have turned out to be obvious, which only makes sense since whoever wrote them wanted us to find the stuff."

"Wait, I'll come with you. Maybe they have some of that apple crumble left over from dinner."

When she scrambled out of the tent after him, Bryan lifted her to her feet and stole a kiss. Meghan waited longer than usual before pushing him away. She didn't even protest when he pulled her against his side as they slowly walked to the kitchen wagon, even though his scabbard kept digging into her ribs.

The rain fell in slanting sheets on either side of King's Road, and the players trudged forward through the mud. Storm Bringer was able to extend his protection as far as he could see ahead, so the worst of the water had drained off the road before the draft horses and heavy wagons passed over.

To the vast amusement of the players, Bryan tried to dry the road with gouts of fire, creating a wall of steam that reminded him of his dishwashing days. Other than the occasional boot sucked off in the mud, the magically fixed travel clothing and footwear worn by the troupe remained clean and dry.

"Why isn't the road paved with stones?" Bryan complained, kicking derisively at a puddle. "The Romans were building good roads two thousand years ago."

"The who?" Laitz asked.

"The—I forgot. Don't they have stone roads in Old Land?"

"They do, actually, at least between the major cities. Most of them are turnpikes, though, so it's not cheap to get around."

"Don't forget the dragon roads," Isabella admonished him, looking back over her shoulder from where she was walking in front of the wagon train with her husband.

"You'd like those," Laitz said, laughing at the memory. "Some of the dragons create roads by flying in a straight line and blasting the same ground over and over again with fire until it becomes molten. The locals all form a fire brigade to throw buckets of sand or pea stone on top before it cools. Otherwise, the surface is so slippery that it's impossible to stand on when it's wet."

"Why would the dragons help build roads?"

"Most of the powerful dragons are on retainer with one kingdom or another. In addition to protection from other dragons, they help out with things like construction projects, fighting forest fires, rescuing lost princesses. The funny thing about dragon hoards is that the bigger they get, the more the dragon has to add to see a difference."

"So it's a lot of work to be a dragon," Bryan commented.

"Were you considering it as a career?" Rowan asked without bothering to turn around.

"It's Meghan who's always pushing me," the young man replied without thinking. Then he realized what he had implied. "I mean, she's ambitious for me."

"Young women are like that," Isabella said, shaking off Rowan and dropping back a step to walk next to Bryan. "The two of you look different the last few days, like you've finally settled into the marriage."

"I think it took her a while to get used to me." He paused and looked at his wedding ring. "I guess we really are married now."

"It took a while for my own marriage to sink in as well," Isabella said sympathetically. "Do you know the story?"

Rowan groaned and began to walk faster. Storm Bringer and Laitz joined him.

Isabella laughed out loud and turned to Bryan with a twinkle in her eye. "I just wanted to have a private word and the marriage story works every time."

"Am I in trouble?"

"No. You really are the strangest young man I have ever met. I just wanted to make sure that you knew about Meghan's birthday. She asked the twins not to tell anybody, but we don't have secrets from each other. I worried Meghan might try to hide it from you as well. Some girls are funny that way."

"Oh, sure," Bryan said with relief. "I gave her a dress and it worked out better than I could have imagined. She never even put it on."

"I see," Isabella said, struggling to keep a straight face.

"The funny thing is I always thought she was cute playing Elstan, but I guess she hated it."

"What gave you that idea?" Rowan's wife asked dryly.

"For one thing, she kept on saying that she really hated it," Bryan answered innocently. "But I didn't know what she was actually thinking until, uh, recently."

"Where is Meghan?"

"She's back with Nesta and Juliana learning our lines. I mean, her lines."

"I think I know what you mean."

"You want me to fight with my feet tied together? I'll fall flat on my face."

"You do that anyway," Rowan said, throwing Bryan the leather cord. "Just tie an end around each ankle and leave about a half a sword length in slack."

"Why are so many of the guys here watching today?" Bryan grumbled suspiciously, as he followed the older man's instructions. "Hey, is this another trick like the wagon-pushing thing?"

"You run around too much when you fight," Rowan explained for the third time. "I tell you that every day, but after the first few exchanges you forget, and then it's back to going in circles."

"I have lots of energy," Bryan retorted, moving experimentally from side to side. He had a hard time keeping his balance when the cord jerked his foot to a stop. "You have to give me a chance to get used to this first."

"Behind you!" shouted one of the boys who came to watch the fun. Bryan tried to spin around, got his legs tangled up, and sprawled on the ground.

"None of that, now," Rowan admonished the watchers. He offered his hand to help the embarrassed young man to his feet. "You need to take smaller steps, find a rhythm to your movement. Haven't you ever danced?"

"Sure I've danced, just not very well."

"Show me."

"Without music?"

Chester launched into a popular ballad from one of the plays and all of the other men and boys watching joined in. Bryan began bobbing his head to the chorus and alternated lifting each foot off the ground, throwing in some shoulder rolls for good measure. Rowan stared in disbelief.

"How did you ever get Meghan to marry you?" he demanded as the ballad was replaced by general laughter. "Does that really pass as dancing where you grew up?"

"I'm better than some," Bryan said defensively. "At least I try."

"Cord," Rowan called, without looking at anybody in particular, and a short leather strap came flying through the air at him. The giant caught it, bent over, and tied his ankles together with about the same amount of slack that Bryan had allowed himself. "Again," he instructed Chester.

The men restarted the ballad, and Rowan began to move about with a glide-step-step, glide-step-step. He held one arm around an invisible partner, the other extended to hold her hand, and he moved about with a grace that was all the more surprising in a man his size. Then he drew his sword and glide-step-stepped towards his opponent.

Bryan reflexively set his feet to draw his sword, but the cord was too short for his normal stance, and he went to one knee, extending his sword at a crazy angle in an attempt to maintain his balance.

Rather than delivering a blow with the flat of his sword as a corrective measure, Rowan moved blindingly fast, sheathing his own blade and grabbing his opponent's extended wrist. As Bryan struggled back to his feet, Rowan grabbed him around the waist and pulled him close.

"Glide, step-step. Glide, step-step," he instructed. Some of the men watching laughed so hard that they fell on the ground, and even Chester, the consummate professional, was unable to sing and smile at the same time. "Glide, step-step. You're getting it. Glide, step-step."

Bryan felt like an idiot, and he kept tripping up at the limits of the ankle tether or stepping on Rowan's toes. His instructor continued with the relentless chant, which was taken up by the observers as they recovered their breath.

"Glide, step-step. Glide, step-step." The men and the boys paired off, some of them approaching each other with formal bows, and then they crowded into the practice area, all of them showing appreciably more talent for dancing than Bryan.

"Imagine if the king could see us now," Hardol called to Rowan as he glided past with Jomar, the two men moving like they had formerly been employed as dance instructors.

"Maybe he can," Rowan replied, casting his eyes up to indicate a large raptor circling high overhead.

"If I was the king and I was watching, I'd be scared," Bryan muttered, wincing as he lost the rhythm and the cord brought his ankle to an abrupt stop. "Glide, step-step."

"What a beautiful castle!" Meghan exclaimed.

"They say that the White Duke's family was in the construction business back in Old Land," Bethany replied. "There's a fancy water park behind the castle, with fountains and a waterfall."

"Told you so," Bryan said, ducking away as the girl attempted to thump his shoulder with the side of her fist. "So we're all friends in this place?"

"Rowan lived here for years and the duke treats him like family," Bethany affirmed. "They also have a permanent stage in the courtyard so we don't have to set up. It's wonderful for putting on performances where there's a wall, and they even built a fake balcony, since so many of the classics have a scene with one."

"Will I be in the balcony for the entire second act?" Meghan asked in dismay. "I thought my character was supposed to be held captive in a tower."

"No, the men will build a bit of round wall on the stage, just enough to give the impression of a tower. Children have very good imaginations, and they all know the story in any case."

"How come we only do plays that everybody already knows?" Bryan asked.

"That's the mark of a good story, when everybody knows it," Faye said, coming up to the three young people and returning Davie to his mother. "He just woke up, but he's already hungry."

"What about new plays?" Bryan demanded, as Bethany dropped back to nurse her baby.

"We practice them over the winter, and then we try them out during the summer," Faye explained. "We only do proven crowd-pleasers at festivals. Some of the audience will only see one play a year, so it's not fair to experiment on them. The people who come to the mountains during the summer may attend two plays a day."

"Playing the lead for *The Good Harvest* actually makes me a little nervous," Meghan admitted to Faye. "I mean, I was on the stage a lot as Elstan, but that was mainly running around and looking scared. Half of the time I'll be out there alone speaking directly to the audience in this part, though I'm supposed to look like I'm talking to myself."

"You'll be fine," Faye assured her. "I'm still amazed that a girl your age could heal a crushed foot without keeling over from the sight of it. You're a lot tougher than you look."

"I guess I didn't realize until that moment that Hadrixia had trained me as a healer. I thought she just wanted an assistant, but I look back on it now and it's clear that she never needed my help."

"Hadrixia?" Faye asked, her face turning pale. "You studied with Hadrixia?"

"I told you I was brought up by a healer from the age of ten," Meghan replied.

"A healer. Not THE healer. Hadrixia is a legend, some say she's immortal, but she disappeared when I was a child. What castle did you say you were from?"

"Refuge. But everybody knew her. Well, I guess they all called her 'Healer,' except for Phinneas when we were alone, and she did warn me not to use her name in public." Meghan stopped suddenly and then added in a small voice, "Could you forget I said that?"

"Don't worry," Faye replied. "Your secret is safe with me, and it explains quite a few things. Frankly, I think there are too many secrets in this world, but I get the feeling that we'll all have the opportunity to share them soon enough."

"What?" Bryan asked, not bothering to look up from the striped bass he was carefully dissecting.

"Rowan is telling our hosts about you, and I think the duke may ask you a question," Meghan replied. "You have to pay attention."

"I am paying attention," Bryan retorted. "Do want me to choke on a bone?"

"They're looking in this direction. At least pretend you weren't raised in a barn."

Bryan set down his knife and looked towards the head of the table, just in time to see the old duke laughing and pounding the table with his fist. Rowan looked rather pleased with himself and made a little circle with his forefinger when he saw Bryan looking in their direction, the troupe's hand-sign for "Be alert."

"I don't believe it," the White Duke exclaimed when he finally recovered his breath. "Is he some new kind of jester or bard?"

"The duke is very interested in your ideas about governing," Rowan called down the table to Bryan. His raised voice caused the other conversations to taper off, and the young man realized that everybody was waiting for his reply. Meghan gave a little head shake and an expression that he interpreted as meaning he should offer a polite retraction. Instead, he resigned himself to eating cold fish and rose to the bait.

"I'm just saying that everybody should have a vote. This whole business of kingdoms, with dukes and barons who get the job from their fathers, it's not fair."

"Not fair to who?" the duke enquired.

"To everybody who isn't a king, a duke, or a baron. I mean, I'm sure you're a great guy and everything, but why should all these people have to do something just because you say so?"

228

"I hope I put more thought into governing than just saying things, but somebody has to be in charge," the duke replied. "Do you have an alternative system we should try?"

Meghan tried to make herself as small as possible as her ears turned bright red from embarrassment, but Bryan wasn't the least bit daunted.

"Elections, to start with. Let everybody in the kingdom vote for a new king every four years. We could select new dukes and barons at the same time."

The players were used to Bryan's odd notions and didn't let the discussion keep them from eating, but the duke's household retainers dissolved in laughter. The duke struggled to keep a straight face as he tried to restore order, and eventually he was able to resume the conversation without shouting.

"Is everybody in the kingdom allowed to stand for this election?"

"Yes, I mean, not all at once," Bryan replied. "You need to have, uh pre-election votes to choose the, uh, candidates for king and the other jobs. I guess you could have local people choose representatives, and then those people would vote for the king, maybe."

"And where would the new king, the new dukes, and the new barons get their castles?" the White Duke asked.

"The way it worked where I come from, the castle goes with the job," Bryan told him, watching sadly out of the corner of his eye as the last piece of honey cake was devoured by Theodric. "Besides, Storm Bringer says that if everybody lived on farms and in villages, we wouldn't need castles and the taxes to pay for them."

The shaman leaned around Rowan and said something to the White Duke, who again fell into a fit of laughter.

"Quit while you've a head," Meghan muttered to Bryan.

"What's that supposed to mean?"

"I meant exactly what I said. Laitz spent three months in a dungeon for making fun of a duke. You just suggested taking away our host's family inheritance."

"Why are we sneaking around if the White Duke is on our side?" Bryan asked.

"He's on Rowan's side and we're on Rowan's side, but that doesn't mean the White Duke is on our side," Meghan explained. Once the words were out, she realized it wasn't likely to satisfy Bryan and she tried again. "The castle and the water park belong to the duke. He might think that anything hidden here belongs to him as well, and we can't take that chance."

"It's not that I mind doing it this way, I always liked fooling around in the dark. I've been thinking about the whole 'water falls on its right' thing," he added to Meghan's surprise. "It could be either side, depending on how they sell wagon parts here."

"Are you kidding?" Meghan asked, halting on the barely visible white pebble path that led to the artificial waterfall. "What do wagons have to do with anything?"

"Well, it's the best example I can come up with in this language, so let's say I needed a new sideboard for a wagon. Is the left sideboard the one to the left when you're sitting in the wagon, or when you're looking at the wagon from the front?"

"Are they even different?"

"Sure, just like fences. The smooth side faces out."

"I'd bring the wagon to the carpenter and show him what I wanted replaced."

"That's not the point. One is a left sideboard and the other is a right sideboard, it just depends on where you're standing. It's the same with this waterfall thing. If water falls on its right, it depends whether the riddle means when we're looking at the waterfall, or when we're looking out from whatever it is."

"And you say that I'm the one who makes everything complicated," Meghan complained. "The waterfall is close enough that we're shouting. I don't know what 'from the first bite' refers to, so look for something you might eat. You should be an expert on this."

The waterfall was actually the overflow from the elevated aqueduct that brought the castle's water supply from the nearby hills. The aqueduct was intentionally oversized, and the water that wasn't diverted into the castle fountains and other uses fell from the high wall into the park just outside. The cascading pools and aquatic plants were considered one of the wonders of New Land, but neither of the trespassers saw anything that reminded them of food.

"Do you think it could be in one of those frogs?" Bryan eventually asked. "There used to be a fairy tale about a frog that had a treasure—no, wait. It was a frog that was a prince. You have to kiss it to break the spell."

"I know you just made that up to try to get me to kiss a frog, but I'm not that gullible. Maybe what we're looking for is actually underwater."

Bryan sat down and began wrestling off his boots. "You may as well do the same," he advised loudly. "I know they're waterproof, but that won't keep them from filling up."

"One of us should keep dry just in case."

"In case of what?"

"An emergency," Meghan yelled back, though she couldn't think of one. "Anyway, you're the expert swimmer."

"These ponds won't come up to our knees," Bryan asserted, stepping over the stone boundary. His foot kept going down, and he fell in and disappeared with a splash that was inaudible over the background noise of the waterfall. A moment later he surfaced, looking annoyed. "It's full of slimy plant stuff," he shouted, treading water with difficulty.

"Don't tear it all up," Meghan hollered back. "Just come out if there's nothing obvious. Maybe we'll need to return in the daylight to look around."

An area of the pool's surface around Bryan began to glow a dull red. "How about that?" he shouted boastfully. "Underwater fire. Do you see anything now?"

"Don't heat the water too much or the plants will boil," she warned, scanning the pool for anything they had missed. "Is there something near the surface in the white water by the side there?"

Bryan half paddled, half waded in the direction she indicated, and then stopped and shouted something she couldn't hear over the roar of the water. "What is it?" she asked in her head, hoping that Bryan hadn't removed his pendant for some reason.

"It's a bronze salmon," he replied the same way. "I guess it's supposed to be leaping into the falls. You'll have to come in to do your untying spell thing."

"I'll try it from here," she replied. "Be ready to catch something if it drops out."

He didn't say anything, but she caught a hint of a surly thought from her pendant. Turning all of her concentration on the dimly lit salmon, she went through the motions detailed in the scroll.

"Did anything happen?" Meghan asked in her head.

"I don't see anything."

"Check it with your fingers. Maybe a hole opened up in the side."

Bryan obligingly ran his fingers over the large fish, shook his head, and then as an afterthought, checked in its mouth. "Got it," he said, slipping a large ring onto his finger. "Fix the salmon and we're out of here."

"I can't believe we've found all five of the objects and none of them were for me." Meghan pulled the signet ring back off her middle and ring fingers, which together, had still made a loose fit.

She tossed it back to Bryan. "I guess it's yours. Let's get some sleep."

"It's too big for me, too. Can't you say something and make it resize to my ring finger?"

"I already tried that when I had it," the girl admitted. "It has some sort of charm on it that I can't figure out. There wasn't much in the baron's library about working out unknown spells, it's sort of a specialty among mages."

"Maybe it just needs a good jolt," Bryan replied, and before she could stop him, the bones in his hand showed through the skin as he let the energy flow into his clenched fist. "Ow!"

"What happened?"

"It got hot. Real hot," Bryan complained, rubbing his palm. The ring lay on the ground where he'd let it fall, glowing dully. "It burned me pretty good."

"Let me see." Meghan took his hand and peered at the palm like she was reading his fortune. "That's funny. I'd swear that's the same dragon glyph that you had on your forehead when Rowan smashed you with the hilt of his sword."

"Pommel. It stings pretty badly. Can you fix it?"

Meghan mumbled some basic burn-healing encouragement under her breath while gently rubbing the red mark with her index finger, and gradually it blended in with the surrounding skin. "All better?"

"Thanks." Bryan bent to pick up the ring again and Meghan flinched, but apparently it had cooled down. "I guess that is the same dragon mark as Rowan's sword. Maybe the two are some kind of set."

"Did you check the ring for an inscription?"

"You're the big reader in the family," he said, flipping the ring back to her.

Meghan steeled herself for the catch, but the metal was barely warm to the touch. She kindled a small glow light that wouldn't draw attention to their campsite in the castle's park grounds and examined the band.

"At least it's in standard mage-script for a change," she said, flipping the ring around so the words wouldn't be upside down. "One ring to rule them all and in—Ha! Got you."

"I never should have told you about that book," Bryan said ruefully, embarrassed by the fact that his eyes had popped out of his head. "What's actually inscribed?"

"Please return to King's Castle. Reward."

"Come on, what's it really say?"

"That is what it really says," Meghan replied, cocking her head and staring at the inscription. "And it wouldn't give an address as simple as 'King's Castle' if it wasn't royal property that everybody should recognize. I wonder how it got here?"

"I wonder what the reward is."

"We're on the side revolting against the king. Remember?"

"Yeah, but maybe we could get the reward first and then be on the other side. You know, like spies."

The girl shook her head. "Not unless you ask Rowan first."

"Alright," Bryan said, looking around in the dark. "I think his tent is over there."

"Not now, you goof," Meghan almost shouted. "In the morning!"

The road which paralleled King's Highway headed down a gentle slope towards a large section of fields covered with the stubble of harvested crops. The expeditionary force sent by the White Duke was deployed in advance of Rowan's players, but they came to a halt when another column of men and horses emerged from the woods across the fields.

"Are we going to fight them?" Bryan asked Rowan, fingering the hilt of his sword. "There are four, no, five mages in hoods riding with them, and we only have the two mages from the White Duke."

"Well, we'd better avoid fighting them in that case," Rowan replied complacently.

"That's it? Don't you have to issue orders or something?"

"My voice is a bit hoarse today, chill from last night. Do you think you can make yourself heard to all of our men if I tell you what to say?"

"I'm ready when you are," the young man responded, cupping his hands around his mouth, as if that would help with magical amplification.

"Don't attack our allies," Rowan said.

"Don't attack our allies!" Bryan shouted, employing the barker technique he had learned from Jomar. His amplified voice rolled through the valley like thunder, and was answered by laughter from hundreds of men on both sides of the field.

"That was really impressive," Laitz said, slapping Bryan on the back. "Lighting and announcing makes you a double threat. If you can learn some weather control from Storm Bringer, you'll be the most valuable man among all the player groups."

"So they're really joining us?"

"It's only chance that we're meeting here," Rowan told the chagrined young man. "All of our people are making their way separately to the shore, and I hope we can convince the Blue Duke to declare his neutrality. There's no advantage to grouping up before we get there, just ruins the roads."

"But this is really it. You're moving against the king."

"The false king," Laitz interjected.

A hawk appeared from the north, descending in a shallow dive, and the shaman materialized at the front of the wagon train to catch the bird.

"That's not the same hawk," Bryan said accusingly, as if Storm Bringer was trying to pull a fast one.

"No, this lovely bird is the companion of a friend of mine who lives on the coast overlooking King's Island." The bird perched on the shaman's shoulder and the two stared into each other's eyes,

Storm Bringer occasionally nodding his head. "It's as we thought. The king's men have been collecting all of the boats on the south shore within a day's sailing of the island. They're trying to defuse the revolt without having to call on the dukes for troops."

"If we were coming from the north it would hardly matter, but the river on the south side must be more than a thousand paces wide," Laitz pointed out.

"I thought you claimed walking on water amongst your many skills," Rowan needled the illusionist.

"Also," the shaman continued after further communion with the bird, "there's a delegation of the royal guard on the way. They must have left several days ago and ridden hard, because they're almost here."

"Go inform the White Duke's men to let them through when they arrive," Rowan instructed Theodric, who immediately began jogging forward.

"That reminds me," Bryan said. "Meghan and I, uh, found this ring in a fish, and it says something about returning it to King's Castle in the inscription." He groped around in his pockets and eventually drew out the large ring and passed it to Rowan.

The leader of the players looked truly surprised for the first time Bryan could remember. "You got this from a fish?"

"A metal fish, in a pool," the young man explained. "Next to a waterfall."

Rowan peered at the inscription and then pulled the hilt of his sword forward to compare the engraving on the pommel with the relief on the ring. "Well, well. This comes at a good time," he said. "I think I'd better talk things over with my wife before the delegation arrives."

"It said something about a reward," Bryan called after him hopefully. Not receiving an answer, he went to find Meghan to complain.

When the royal guard delegation arrived, the players were just finishing up lunch and getting ready to start out again. Rowan signaled for everybody to take an extended break and carefully eyed the six approaching horsemen, who carried no visible weapons other than the sword no self-respecting soldier would be caught dead without.

"What do you think?" he asked his companions.

"If any of them are mages, they're doing a better job hiding it than I've ever encountered," Storm Bringer replied. "The senior fellow there obviously isn't used to long stretches in the saddle."

"I'd say five guards to fulfill court protocol and one of the king's inner cabinet," Isabella said. "I wouldn't be surprised if he was picked for this job because he's the farthest thing from a mage among them. Somebody is trying to put us at ease."

Theodric and Hardol stopped the horses on the road and exchanged a few friendly words with the guardsmen. Jomar appeared with a short wooden stepladder and helped the older man dismount from the large warhorse. The messenger almost fell over when he reached the ground, and spent some time vigorously rubbing the backs of his thighs before slowly straightening. Then he steeled himself and managed to convey a certain degree of limping dignity as he approached the waiting players.

"I am Lyman, the king's minister of ducal affairs," he announced. "I have been appointed special envoy to the, er, you."

"Rowan," the leader of the players said, offering his hand to shake. The signet ring fit snugly on his finger and had been shined to a high gloss so the visitor could hardly miss it. "Do you like my ring? It returned to me just recently."

"I see," Lyman muttered, obviously recognizing the dragon symbol. "If your intention is to claim the throne for yourself, my peacemaking mission has been wasted. I only wish I had known before sitting on that infernal animal for three days and having my bones shaken apart."

"A peacemaker's mission is never wasted," Rowan said agreeably. "Please, join us for a cup of tea. My wife has been saving it for a special occasion, and you look like you could use a little pick-me-up."

"I accept your hospitality," Lyman said, and then began looking around as if he'd misplaced something. "I'll just lean on the wagon there, if you don't mind. I've had enough sitting for the time being."

Rowan's daughters prepared the decorative samovar and served the tea. In deference to the guest, everybody gathered around the wagon bed and took their tea standing.

"Lovely piece," the envoy said, though it wasn't immediately clear whether he was talking about Nesta or the samovar. He seemed to realize the ambiguity of his comment and quickly followed up with, "From your home?"

"The samovar, yes," Isabella answered him. "Where are you from in Old Land?"

"The Korizan Mountains," Lyman replied. "I traveled through your birth land many times before I emigrated. They still talk of the runaway bride there."

"I'm glad I was able to afford the people with such entertainment."

Bryan nudged Meghan to make sure she wouldn't be startled and then spoke to her in his mind. "Rowan's wife was an actress in Old Land? I thought she was some kind of princess."

"Isabella really is some sort of Old Land nobility, and their marriage gives Rowan as good a claim to rule as anybody," she thought back. "The ring must be from the king's collection, so wearing it in front of the envoy is a statement of opposition."

"The tea is quite good," the envoy said. It seemed to Bryan that the man was relaxing, or perhaps, resigning himself to an unpleasant conclusion. "I had hoped to negotiate a nonaggression pact, but I doubt that fits in with your plans."

"Oh, I'd be best pleased if we could get through this without aggression," Rowan replied. "In fact, you could say that if not for the unending cycle of violence in the land, I would have been more than happy to live out my days with my family in the honorable profession of strolling players. But your master is cast in the image of his father, a ruler who sees a kingdom as fields for growing men and fighting them against each other, like boys playing with toy soldiers."

"You're pursuing the throne for the people's sake?" Lyman looked Rowan up and down as if he was a prize specimen in a zoo. "I see you believe it. My sole talent is the detection of willful lies, so if you are deceiving me, you must be deceiving yourself as well." He drained his tea and cleared his throat. "The king has authorized me to offer you one hundred thousand gold pieces and the lands west of the river beyond the frontier if you will give up your revolt."

"Enough to buy sweet dreams for a dragon, perhaps, but I wouldn't be able to sleep at night," Rowan replied with a smile. "My counteroffer is that I will grant the king permission to keep his one hundred thousand gold pieces and return to Old Land, preferably taking Narl and Barth with him."

"I gathered that would be your response from the reports of armed men moving towards King's Island, not to mention the ring. We assume that you'll have the support of the White and Red Dukes, but you know the current Blue Duke owes his position to the king, and the Green and Black are committed."

"The Black Duke sent an expeditionary force into the mountains two weeks ago, and I imagine they will be bogged down in the snows by now. The Green and the Red hold each other in stalemate, so I doubt very much the king can expect support from that quarter."

"You plan to build a fleet of rafts and cross the river in twelfth month?"

"That remains to be seen," Rowan answered. "I have great hope that your king will accept my offer to vacate. I understand that a fleet has recently arrived for that purpose."

"The fleet carries elite troops from the king's supporters in Old Land!"

"So they may have to sleep double on the voyage home. I hope they brought enough mages for a smooth passage in high seas."

Lyman snorted. "Very well, I won't waste any more of your time since you have a long march ahead of you."

"How come the river's down there and we're up here?" Bryan asked. The ten-day march to King's Island had proven entirely uneventful, thanks to the fact that the Black Duke's best troops were off trying to attack the home base that the players maintained in the mountains. Rowan's forces now numbered over ten thousand men, the majority of them veterans who had lived for years as farmers and traders, biding their time.

"Geology," Laitz replied, even though that obviously wasn't the answer the young man was seeking. "Rowan will give the inhabitants of King's Island a few days to think about where they stand, and of course, we have friends there speaking on our behalf. You can see how the royal guard units are deployed blocking access to the castle, as if the so-called king fears the populace of his own island."

"What I'm interested in is what that line of men entering and leaving the castle is all about. If I was just a little higher, I'd have the angle to look into the courtyard."

"Probably drawing weapons or bonus pay," Laitz replied, but Bryan had already unbuckled his sword and started for a giant chestnut tree that grew near the edge of the cliff. Its leaves had fallen weeks earlier, so the young man was clearly visible as he casually shimmied up the trunk and began climbing one of the large boughs that jutted out into space.

"He's nuts," Meghan commented to nobody in particular. "Did you know he climbed our tower back home and got knocked off by the guardian gryphon? I had been pretending to be magicless, and after I caught him, we had to run away."

"And all this time I thought I was harboring a dangerous war mage who could knock down towers like blowing out candles," Rowan said with a smile.

"So you DID know all along. Was it Phinneas or Hadrixia?"

"Dragons coming," Storm Bringer interrupted suddenly. "Not friendly."

Rowan nodded to Jomar, who began to whistle a single note that grew and grew in volume until everybody within eyeshot was looking in their direction. Then he simply pointed at the sky.

The noncombatants among the players quickly gathered up the children to carry or drag back inland. The soldiers formed up in odd hedgehog formations, their shields held over their heads. The war mages who came with the White Duke's forces hurried forward along with several older men dressed in a variety of farmer's garb, but with telltale signs of magic crackling around them.

One of the dragons stayed aloft, turning lazy circles above the river, while the other came in for a landing on the edge of the cliff, braking to a halt with a few short hops. Then, in a brilliant flash of red, the large dragon was replaced by a tall, middle-aged man.

"Narl," Rowan said, keeping his hand on the hilt of his sword. "Taking a bit of a chance, aren't you?"

"You think too highly of yourself and your allies, Rowan," the mage responded coldly. "Yes, you could beat that fool of a king if my brother and I stood aside, but there's only one way that's going to happen."

"If you're looking for another hundred thousand in gold, I'm afraid the king has me beat," Rowan replied, his eyes fixed on the mage.

"Barth is still circling," Storm Bringer interjected tersely.

"My brother alone could put a stop to your revolt," Narl continued. "I'm here to give you a chance, and it's nonnegotiable. Hand over the girl."

"I understand that it was going after a woman who didn't belong to you that got you into this mess in the first place," Rowan said. "Why don't you and your brother return to Old Land and throw yourself on the mercy of your peers? If nothing else, they'll give you a quick death."

Narl shook his head slowly, there was another flash, and he was again a giant dragon. A sweep of his wings knocked the nearby men off their feet, and he made a sudden lunge towards Meghan.

"No!" thundered a voice from out above the river, and an intensely bound fireball struck the dragon on its side.

Narl shook his head in surprise, glanced at the spot where his scales were smoking, and pivoted back towards the cliffs. Rowan managed to slice a bit of leather off one of the wings as it swept by, but then the dragon launched himself into space, dropping towards the river. After a few powerful wing beats, he gained altitude and turned towards Bryan's perch in the tree.

"Come down, Bryan," Meghan cried in her thoughts. "You can't fight a dragon alone."

Whether or not he heard her, now that Bryan didn't have to worry about injuring the players, he was creating and casting fireballs with abandon. Narl dodged them or tucked in his head to shield his eyes when that wasn't possible, but his only other response was to fly straight at the young man.

"Behind you!" Meghan screamed, but by that time it was too late, and Barth emitted a blast of flame that caused the tree to literally explode. Bryan's body fell towards the water, his clothing in flames, and Meghan's legs folded under her. She would have collapsed if Juliana and Nesta hadn't moved close and been ready to catch her.

"Kill those bastards!" Meghan heard in her mind, and she sobbed out loud at Bryan's last instruction. A moment later, a brilliant green dragon rose above the cliff edge and coughed a mouthful of flame at Barth.

"Bryan?" Meghan asked in her mind.

"Busy now," Bryan replied, pivoting and letting loose a torch at Narl. The older dragon fired back, and Barth recovered from his surprise to spray more flames in the new dragon's direction. Bryan twisted and struggled to gain altitude, but the older dragons were stronger and faster than he was.

"Dive! To your left. Your other left!" Meghan wasn't sure whether he was still receiving her thoughts or not since he ignored her instructions. The two brothers were obviously well practiced in aerial maneuvers, and they bracketed Bryan from behind, pouring flames at him. "Pull strength from me," she sobbed, clutching her pendant. "You can't let them kill you."

Bryan feinted towards King's Island, and then cut back sharply towards the cliff, perhaps intending to find a position from which he could die defending Meghan rather than running away. As the three dragons wheeled about, the two brothers were momentarily aligned with the sun and a river of fire engulfed them. It seemed to go on forever, and when the flame was extinguished, what remained of their charred bodies fell into the river.

"Pick up the girl and follow me," a female voice said in Bryan's head. He scanned the airspace and spotted a giant silver dragon, more than three times as large as Narl. Her dive took her low over the river before she gracefully looped back and turned towards the northwest.

"Can you slide back a bit?" Bryan thought at Meghan. "My neck is getting tired."

"If I move back any further, my butt will be hitting your wings and I'll get thrown. Is that what you want?"

"I'd catch you," he thought back reassuringly.

"I doubt that very much," she said. "I'd drop like a rock while you circle around looking sad. Are we still following that big silver dragon?"

"Can't you see her?"

"I haven't opened my eyes since I climbed on your neck," the girl retorted. "Did you forget that I'm afraid of heights?"

"Sorry. Hey, how about if I think about what I'm seeing?" Bryan focused on sending a vision of the dragon he was following, the mountains ahead, and then shifted to a flock of sheep moving down a valley.

"Stop! I'm getting dizzy. I think I'm going to be sick."

"Sorry," Bryan replied, closing his own eyes to stop himself from sending what he was seeing. "Oops, this isn't going to work."

"Just don't think about what you're looking at," Meghan begged him. "Go back to the way it was before."

"I'm trying, but it's like saying not to think about an itch."

"Try focusing on how it will feel when I throw up on your neck."

"Don't you—hey, I think we're landing. The dragon is flying right at that cliff."

"Shut up!"

"I'm serious. What's she doing? Whoa, she just disappeared right through the stone face."

"Stop thinking!"

"It's an illusion," the voice of the silver dragon said. "Land as soon as you get in."

With Meghan screaming so loudly that he actually heard her through the wind, Bryan braced for impact with the cliff and instead found himself in a giant cavern, lit as bright as day. He remembered how the other dragons had landed by holding their wings up like air brakes, tried the same thing, and flipped a neat summersault before landing. Fortunately, Meghan had a death grip on his neck with her arms and legs and didn't fall off.

"Nicely done," the giant silver dragon said. "I assume the acrobatics were unintentional?"

"Sort of. You okay, Meghan?"

"Are we on the ground?"

"Yes."

Meghan opened her eyes for the first time since Bryan had launched them from the cliff overlooking King's Island to the cheers of Rowan's supporters. She blinked repeatedly, trying to clear the flashes and sparkles that interfered with her vision, and then she realized it wasn't her eyes.

"Is that, your, uh, hoard?" Meghan asked the dragon in a small voice.

"You recognize it," the dragon replied with satisfaction. "Your block should have started breaking down as soon as you began flying. Do you remember who I am yet?"

"No, and I didn't recognize the hoard, but what else could a huge mound of gold and jewels be?"

"Could I, uh, take a closer look?" Bryan asked.

"Let me down first," Meghan demanded. "Is the sight of so much treasure causing you to tremble like that? You're making my teeth chatter."

"That's because I'm freezing! You were wearing a winter coat and you probably know a hundred enchantments to keep warm. I'm in my dragon birthday suit and it's cold up in the sky."

"Why aren't you wearing the thermal underwear from the Green Duke's castle?" their host inquired. "I know you untied the magical knot."

"That's what it was," Meghan exclaimed. "We didn't know. I've never heard of a dragon wearing anything."

"That's because there are no other young dragons around," the silver dragon replied. "Your young man hasn't developed scales yet, it takes a few decades. It's lucky he's so good at dodging flames or he might have been burned much worse than the minor toasting he got. You've been healing him through your link, Meghan."

"Who are you?" the girl inquired.

"Wouldn't your young man prefer to slip back into human form before we have a long discussion?"

"Yeah," Bryan said. "How do I do that, exactly?"

"I'm sure there were instructions in the scroll," the silver dragon suggested.

"Meghan's in charge of scrolls. What do I do, Meghan?"

"New Age crap," the girl replied.

Bryan sat on a rock, alternately rubbing his own shoulders and gazing at the mound of treasure.

"Anything yet, dear?" the dragon asked Meghan.

"Just impressions," the girl replied. "I remember a woman with silky, black hair looking at me, but that's about it."

"Your mother," the dragon said. "You can't guess who I am?"

"Well, with all the treasure and the way you burned Narl and Barth out of the sky, I can't help wondering if you're Gwyneth?"

"Oh, I thought that was obvious. I meant, who I am to you?"

"Uh, does my family serve you or something?"

Gwyneth shook her giant head in frustration. "I think I overdid it with your block. I'm your grandmother. Well, your great-great-great grandmother, to be precise. Your father was the youngest of my line."

"But I thought that dragons only married other dragons, and if they had children while in human form, the children would—I'm a dragon?" Meghan concluded, her voice turning shrill.

"Not so funny when the shoe is on the other foot," Bryan interjected.

"Of course you're a dragon, that's why I had to block you," Gwyneth explained. After Narl and Barth killed your father, your mother was so grief stricken that she sent you to me in Hadrixia's charge. Then she returned to Dark Earth where your father had found her."

"I thought I could never return to Dark Earth," Bryan interrupted.

"You can return, but only to die," Gwyneth replied sadly. "She believed it was her fault that Narl came after your father, because she was the prize that he wanted. The other dragons thought that she had taken you with her, at least until the rumors about the two of you began."

"You mean that more of them will come for her now?" Bryan demanded. If Meghan heard the question, she didn't react, because she was struggling with the onset of memories that had been locked deep within her psyche.

"Perhaps. There are few dragons left who are young enough to be able to return to human form for even a brief period, but it's not something you can tell by looking at one. I used up my human time over two thousand years ago, and I left Old Land long before the exiles because I'd had enough of dragon politics."

"So you found all of this gold in New Land?"

"There is plenty of gold to be found south and west of here, but most of my hoard is from Old Land. I doubt there has ever been a treasure fleet as rich as mine," Gwyneth added immodestly. "Are your memories beginning to return now, child?"

"But why did you block me?" Meghan demanded.

"You weren't even ten years old when you threw yourself off this very mountain so you could transform into a dragon and avenge your father. Ten years old! Narl would have taken you and locked you in a tower like a fairytale princess until you were old enough to be his mate. You were extraordinarily strong for a child, even for one of my descendents, but not nearly strong enough to beat the dragon who killed your father."

"And why didn't you do something about those dragons fifty years ago when—wait. How can Narl have killed my father at the time the traitors sold the king to the assassin prince? I just turned eighteen!"

"Dragon children age slower than normal humans. And I had Hadrixia put you in a long sleep after your mother chose death, in part to give the other dragons a chance to forget about your existence. If anybody had seen you that day you transformed, who knows how many dragons would have shown up here trying to claim you."

"But you could have defended me. You burned Narl and his brother out of the air like they were moths!"

"They were distracted with chasing your young man," Gwyneth replied. "Dragons my age who take care of themselves, and there can't be a dozen of us left in the world, are very powerful. But speed is another issue altogether. The only way for me to catch one of Narl's generation is to take him unawares."

"Did you even try?"

"No, child. I chose to shake my mountain instead, bringing down rockslides and pretending to be dead. I thought it was the surest way to keep you safe, and my time for getting involved in the day-to-day affairs of men is long behind me. You may not believe this, but the old king who was assassinated was no prize. His main occupation was leading his people in wars against the natives for the sake of glory. It only took a few hundred years for the exiles to develop the same society that they had rebelled against and fled."

"There's going to be a change," Bryan predicted. "Now that the dragons are out of the way, Rowan will beat the king for sure, and I'm going to help him. Maybe he'll even stop laughing when I explain how governments work where I come from."

"He may hire you as the court jester," Gwyneth chortled. "Rowan will be a king, like his father before him, but after a half a century of life as an orphan, a soldier, and an actor, at least he'll have a better understanding of the common people."

"I'm not jumping," Meghan insisted, turning away from the ledge and returning to the comforting depth of the cavern. "You jump, turn into a dragon, and then you can come back and get me."

"Come on, you're going to make your grandmother embarrassed," Bryan pleaded. "You did this before you were even ten years old."

"That just goes to show how dumb I was. What do you care if Gwyneth is embarrassed?"

"Well, she saved my life, for one thing. And she created these pendants and had her agents hide one for me, not to mention my sword, my flying suit, the dragon instructions, and Rowan's ring."

"Me, me, me. I know why you want to kiss up to Gwyneth. It's her hoard."

Bryan glanced back to where the giant silver dragon was snoring up a storm. "Well, she is your closest relation, and I thought that dragons were pretty old-fashioned, so there could be a dowry and all."

"Keep it up and I'll jump just to get away from you," Meghan warned.

"That's the spirit. She told you that your fear of heights was just part of a safety she added to your block, to keep you from getting into a situation where you might accidentally fall and transform. Don't you want to put that behind you?"

Meghan pursed her lips and took a step towards the disguised opening in the cliff.

"What's the worst thing that can happen?" Bryan continued. "If you don't transform, you'll be dead before you know it."

"Argh, you make me nuts!" Meghan took a step backwards again, but a strong, warm breeze lifted her off her feet and propelled her into space. "Brryyyaaaannnnn!"

"Way to go, Grams," Bryan yelled over his shoulder at the amused dragon, then he dove after Meghan, arms spread wide. He didn't actually remember what it took to become a dragon, and he had a sudden moment of doubt when he recalled that he had fallen from the castle tower without transforming, but of course, Meghan had interfered that time.

"Where are you?" he heard Meghan ask in his mind, just before the air caught his newly formed wings. He sailed off to the side barely in time to avoid colliding with a cute, copper-colored dragon that was climbing awkwardly.

"You look beautiful," he sent to her, swooping alongside for a closer look. "Are you over your fear of—open your eyes, already. You're going to fly into a mountain that doesn't have a hidden opening."

One of the copper dragon's eyes opened to just a slit, then the other. "Hey, I'm flying!"

"You'd be smooshed by now if you weren't," Bryan reminded her. "Shall we go check up on Rowan?"

"It's a long way," Meghan said. "I don't think I could go that far without eating something. I've never been so hungry."

"Now you're getting it. Let's go back and see if Gwyneth keeps anything around."

"I can't believe I just caught myself thinking about those cute sheep we saw earlier," Meghan admitted. A feeling of guilt transmitted clearly with her words. "I don't think I could just eat a living animal."

"I was figuring on killing mine first."

The two young dragons landed a short distance from the player's camp overlooking King's Island and resumed human form. All of the fighting-age men were missing, but the children were playing around the wagons and the women were preparing a picnic, so they obviously weren't expecting trouble.

"What's happening, Bethany?" Meghan asked as soon as she spotted her friend.

"Meghan! We knew that Bryan was supposed to turn into a dragon, but I never would have guessed that you'd be brave enough to climb on his back and fly off. You even got sick riding in the wagon."

"I kept my eyes closed and I still got sick," Meghan admitted. "But never mind about that. What happened with Rowan and the king?"

"After the big silver dragon toasted his allies, the king saw it was over, and he took Rowan up on the offer to flee. The fleet sailed for Old Land this morning, royal guard and all. Was that dragon really Gwyneth, like everybody is saying?"

"Yes, and she's been secretly watching everything from hiding, though I'm sure she slept through plenty."

"Did you say that you knew I was a dragon all along?" Bryan asked.

"That's what Isabella told us before you arrived with Laitz. I guess she was in touch with the people who raised you, Meghan. Everybody around here has been keeping so many secrets that it's giving me a headache."

"Do you have any secrets?" Meghan asked.

"Well, you knew that my grandmother was the one who rescued Rowan when the old king and queen were killed. Right?"

"How would we know that?"

"It's why I always get that part in the play. My mother had it before me."

"And did all the players know that Rowan was the son of the assassinated king?" Bryan asked.

"Uh, let me think," Bethany replied, bouncing Davie in her arms to calm him. "Yeah, I guess."

"So why didn't the king, the one who just fled, I mean, kill Rowan while he had the chance?"

"How would he know who Rowan was?"

"All of the players knew and nobody talked?"

"Why would they talk?" Bethany asked in puzzlement. "Besides, Isabella would have known if they weren't trustworthy. She sees into people."

"So where are all the men?" Bryan continued.

"They're over at King's Island choosing soldiers for a garrison. Rowan said he's not moving into the king's castle this winter. Our cabins in the mountains are warmer."

"So when the king and his retainers fled, the people living there brought all the boats back to this side?"

"No, I think the owners went over the bridge this morning to find their boats and sail them home."

"What bridge?"

"The ice bridge that Storm Bringer and the other shamans made. Didn't you notice it flying in? I think that was the plan all along, to use ice bridges, and the shamans wanted to get credit for showing up and supporting Rowan, even though they weren't needed in the end. Are you guys going to come back to the mountains with us? We've never had a dragon in the players before."

Bryan and Meghan looked at each other. "We haven't really planned that far ahead," the girl admitted. "You don't think we'd make everybody uncomfortable?"

"Why? Oh, you mean the way Bryan eats? Everybody is used to that."

"I sort of flew back on my own," she said, watching Bethany out of the corner of her eye to see how her friend would react to the hint that Meghan herself was a dragon as well.

"We kind of guessed that you might be a dragon yesterday," the young mother told her. "Narl wouldn't have gotten himself killed over a young mage, even if you did turn a castle into a pile of rubble with a single word."

"All I did was catch Bryan!" Meghan protested.

Bethany looked the couple up and down and nodded in agreement. "So now that you've caught him, what are you going to do with him?"

"We're thinking of a magic show for children," Bryan said. "I'm going to be her assistant."

From the Author

My goal for "Meghan's Dragon" was to write a humorous story about young people discovering themselves in a magical world without having the fate of mankind resting on their shoulders. I also wanted to build a world where, unlike the near-omniscient Stryx in my EarthCent Ambassador series, nobody has access to perfect information and characters frequently misinform each other because they don't know any better. If you'd like to try a space opera series that presents the beginnings of a brighter future for humanity, the first book of the EarthCent series is "Date Night on Union Station."

About the Author

E. M. Foner lives in Northampton, MA with an imaginary German Shepherd who's been trained to bite bankers. The author welcomes reader comments at e_foner@yahoo.com.

About the Artist

Keith Draws is an illustrator working mainly in the fields of Science Fiction, Fantasy and horror, and has produced hundreds of covers in the last five years. He loves creating these imaginary worlds and is always open to working with new authors keithdraws.wordpress.com

EarthCent Ambassador Series:

Date Night on Union Station

Alien Night on Union Station

High Priest on Union Station

Spy Night on Union Station

Carnival on Union Station

Wanderers on Union Station

Vacation on Union Station

Guest Night on Union Station

Word Night on Union Station

Party Night on Union Station

Review Night on Union Station

Family Night on Union Station

Book Night on Union Station